FROM INSIDE THE HOUSE

A DI GRAVES THRILLER #BOOK TWO

WD JACKSON-SMART

BLOODHOUND
— BOOKS —

www.bloodhoundbooks.com

Print ISBN 978-1-5040-7261-8

ALSO BY WD JACKSON-SMART

THE DI GRAVES SERIES

The Demons Beneath (Book 1)

CHAPTER ONE

He switched off the kitchen light. The room disappeared. The moon cast tendrils of soft light through gaps in the trees outside to lie across the slate countertops and appliances. The LED display on the oven showing the time was the only source of unnatural light: a tiny beacon in the dark. He turned and padded out into the hallway, the wooden floorboards chilly under his bare feet.

The house was still, apart from the creaks made by a building settling for the night. He could just about hear the wind outside, its invisible fingers searching through the neighbourhood, and felt the welcome feeling of security that came with knowing the elements could not get in, that the house would protect him.

Without turning on the hallway lights, he checked that the chain was in its slot on the front door and that the bottom lock was engaged. The action was habitual, done every night. He barely noticed he had done it. With a yawn he turned and started up the stairs, glad of the change in temperature from wood to carpet, the thick threads that poked up between his toes.

The bathroom light made him squint; his eyes were not prepared for the brightness. The bulb was a daylight type, to allow one to see one's reflection better, but at night it was harsh and unforgiving. He frowned at his tired face in the mirror above the sink, then grabbed his toothbrush, loaded it up and started brushing. The scratching of the bristles against his teeth seemed awfully loud, and he pushed the door shut. He didn't want to wake Anna. That never went well. She was the proverbial sleeping bear that should never be poked, and he didn't have the energy for another argument. There had been enough arguing already that evening.

He had come home late again – not entirely deliberately, although if he were honest with himself he knew he hadn't exactly rushed to get back. They were trying for a baby. The problem was, he didn't want one. At least, he didn't think he did. It didn't feel quite right. He loved his wife – but a child? The thought didn't sit well. Naturally, he had not voiced this to her beyond signs of mild doubt. The fact that he had got home late, too tired for them to have sex, had not gone down well at all. After a tense dinner and a back-and-forth sniping session largely revolving around his lack of commitment to the cause she had stormed off upstairs and he had let her, feeling like a shit.

He jumped when the bathroom window rattled next to him, whipped by the wind outside. It seemed to be getting stronger. A vague recollection of a weather warning on the morning news seeped into his tired brain. Another thing for her to complain about. *Why haven't you fixed the window? I've asked three times!*

Again he felt guilty. It was easy to paint his wife as a nagging, irritating drain, yet he knew that wasn't really true. She was funny, kind, fiercely loyal. Was it enough, though? He wasn't certain any more, and he had no doubt that a baby would not fix that. He felt like a total bastard, not sure what do with his feelings beyond weak attempts to bottle them up.

He spat out the toothpaste, rinsed the sink and checked the window, just to be sure. It was locked. A little loose, but it would hold. The weather wasn't *that* bad.

As he stepped out onto the landing, flicking the bathroom light off behind him, he stopped, his gaze fixed on their bedroom door. Would she still be awake? Lying in bed reading, the heat of her anger vibrating across the room at him? He glanced at the spare bedroom, considered it for a moment before disregarding the thought. That would only make things worse.

From downstairs came a click, clear and distinct.

Still motionless, he pricked his ears, waiting. He couldn't place what it was, but the sound did not come again. He dismissed it. *Probably another bloody window needing repairs. Lucky me.*

Rubbing his eyes, he realised how exhausted he was. He'd delayed coming to bed so he could avoid another argument. He pushed open the bedroom door and let out a hushed sigh of relief when he saw that his wife was fast asleep. As quietly as he could, he undressed and slipped under the covers beside her. She didn't stir. He felt a tension in his shoulders release – he hadn't known it was there to begin with – and let sleep take him.

He woke with a start when something pressed down on his mouth – firm, rough. He felt groggy. As he tried to take a breath, he struggled. A scream caught in his throat as he locked eyes with the masked man standing over him. The whites of his eyes practically glowed in the dark, wind-battered house.

CHAPTER TWO

'Do I even want to see?' Detective Inspector Daniel Graves asked, his eyebrows raised, as he registered the revulsion that was bubbling across the face of the sergeant standing next to the front door. The man shook his head. Daniel wished he had the option to say 'Sod it' and leave. Wet strands of hair stuck to the sergeant's forehead from the recent downpour and he looked utterly miserable, as if he wanted to be literally anywhere else.

Daniel steeled himself as he stepped into the house. The October cold whipped in forcefully behind him, like a boisterous child trying to push past a parent. His trench coat fluttered and he pulled it closer. Someone had once told him that London weather was nicer than up north, that it saw more sun and was usually a few degrees warmer, even in winter. But the borough of Camberwell begged to differ; Daniel could swear he had seen just as much sunshine before he moved down south. Inside the house was just as chilly and grey, as though the violence that had occurred here had bleached out all colour and warmth.

This was the worst part of his job: visiting violent crime

scenes. He dreaded it. He had worked hard over the last year not to let the death he encountered every day in his job get under his skin, but he knew he would always find it difficult. He followed the sound of the commotion upstairs, to be greeted on the landing by Stephanie Mitchum. Severe as ever, her hair pulled in a tight ponytail, the forensic anthropologist gave him a formal smile and nod before starting to update him.

'The victims have already been identified. The homeowners, Jane and Henry Alton.'

Daniel was not a fan of Stephanie Mitchum. He wished she had at least a modicum of warmth about her. Looking at dead bodies was chilling enough without the steely woman exacerbating the experience. When he had first met her, he had felt as though she had been judging him or looking down on him for some reason, as if he was a naughty child and she was the head teacher ready to give him detention. He thought he might have pissed her off somehow, unknowingly earned the cold treatment. It had not taken long to discover, however, that she was always like that. His work partner DI Charlie Palmer had confirmed as much. Daniel often wondered if he should say something about it to Stephanie, to make it easier to work with her, but so far he had chickened out. Now wasn't the right time either. He brushed off the frost she emanated.

'It's definitely them? I heard that they were...' He didn't really want to say the word he was thinking of, as though verbalising it would make the situation worse.

'Disfigured? Don't beat about the bush, Graves; it serves no purpose. Yes, they are, but both bodies have been ID'd by the medical and dental records we have for them. I've no doubt they are the Altons.'

The smell of what lay beyond was starting to seep into Daniel's nostrils. Gagging a little, he stepped forward.

'I hope it's been a while since you ate, Detective,' Stephanie warned before stepping aside, her tone more condescending than caring. With a shiver, Daniel moved cautiously to the bedroom door and crossed the threshold. He didn't want to see what waited in the room but knew it was necessary. Immediately he felt bile rise into the back of his throat, and swallowed to keep down the burning fluid and the two slices of toast he had eaten for breakfast. He pressed a coat sleeve over his mouth and took in the scene.

The bed was soaked with blood: deep shades of red where it was still damp, brown and muddy where the duvet had started to dry. On her back on top of the duvet lay Jane Alton, naked apart from a blood-stained bra and pants. Her throat had been slit, as had her wrists. Her face was a mess of bruises, cuts and torn flesh, to the point where her features were pretty much indistinguishable. It looked as though she had been hit multiple times. Her death had been brutal.

If it was possible, Daniel thought Henry Alton's body was worse. The man had been crudely mounted to the wall above the bed with large metal nails in his hands, wrists and shoulders. His legs dangled over his wife's head. His skin had started to discolour, with the blood collecting in his feet and lower legs. He too wore just underwear and, like his wife, his face had been smashed to a pulp, his features obliterated. Unlike Jane, his throat and wrists were intact. Unlike Jane, his heart had been cut out of his chest: the hole was ragged, lacking precision.

'Jesus...' Daniel muttered, allowing his gaze to fall to the floor, away from the gore in front of him. He had never seen anything like it.

'I warned you,' Stephanie said without any hint of sympathy. 'One of the worst I've ever seen.'

One of? Daniel thought.

Despite her words, Stephanie's expression remained calm.

Daniel couldn't help wondering how bad a murder scene would have to be to extract a more human reaction from her.

Eager to leave the room, Daniel stepped past the anthropologist and headed back downstairs, the smell of decay thankfully lessening slightly as he went. Stephanie followed and joined him in the cramped, but tidy, kitchen at the back of the ground floor. Daniel took a seat at the table and let out an exasperated sigh.

'Are you okay?' Stephanie asked, finally showing a possible shimmer of empathy. Daniel nodded, though he felt a little shaky. Everyone had trouble stomaching murder scenes – everyone apart from Stephanie Mitchum, anyway – but he did wonder if they affected him more than others. He didn't know any other detectives who had had such an early introduction to blood and violence as he had; he had been forced to save his teenage sister from possible rape, still a teenager himself at the time. He knew that taking a life so many years ago would always stay with him, that it had impacted so much of his adult existence, including his career choice. The grim tableau he had just laid eyes on, however? That was something else entirely. He took a few deep breaths.

Thoughts of Jenny Cartwright flooded his brain, unasked. She had been killed – he had failed to save her – only a few months ago. He still had to get over her death. Her smile, her laughter, her bloodied heart cut out and left gift-wrapped in a box on his doorstep... After that, seeing another body lacking its heart was a lot to handle. Could the same person who had killed Jenny Cartwright have killed this couple? He shook off the notion. It was a coincidence, of course. Had to be. Just because her killer was still at large didn't mean there was a connection. Nonetheless, his fingers pulled at his shirt collar, restless. He was sweating and was prepared to take his coat off, despite the cold of the house.

'What can you tell me, then?' he asked once his pulse settled down. Surprisingly, Stephanie seemed to be more patient than normal, and had been waiting quietly for him to say something.

'Not too much, unfortunately. Both victims likely died of massive blood loss and trauma, but I imagine that you had already figured that out. What's more interesting, if that's the right word to use, is what the killers did before and after.'

'Go on,' Daniel said.

She was leaning against the door frame. Next to her, pinned to the fridge with a magnet advertising Thorpe Park, was a photograph of the now deceased Alton couple beaming at the camera, looking as if they didn't have a care in the world. He looked away, keeping his gaze on Stephanie instead.

'Both bodies show clear signs of being tortured first.'

'Okay, I wasn't expecting that. You're sure?'

Stephanie nodded, her tight ponytail bobbing. 'It looks like they were bound to the bed frame initially. We found traces of cheap rope fibres on the pillows and dotted around the room. Both show signs of friction burns around their wrists and ankles, and we found a thread that was likely from a sock in Jane Alton's mouth, suggesting they were gagged. A sock with blood on it was on the floor – probably the same item.'

'Presumably the intruders found that in the house. I wouldn't have thought they would bring socks with them.'

'It's unlikely,' Stephanie continued. 'The victims were also both beaten around the face before death. Our blood spatter analyst was able to separate out patterns on the back wall of the room and bedding from various different injuries. The bigger sprays were caused by a slit throat and a heart being ripped out.'

Daniel grimaced.

'I can't imagine why their faces were beaten so much, though I would hazard a guess that it had nothing to do with concealing identities, since they left the teeth and fingerprints intact. And then, of course, the bodies were posed – quickly and messily, but the killer clearly made some effort. Whoever did this seems to have had…' Stephanie paused.

'Fun.'

Stephanie swallowed. The sheer brutality of the murders seemed to have rattled her.

'Detective, this was a messy affair and extremely violent, but from what we've found so far the killer had no finesse. There was clearly no attempt to keep things tidy, to take time over the victims.'

'I'm inclined to agree. It's almost opportunistic. So what was the motive? Especially displaying the bodies in that way?'

'That's your remit, I'm afraid, Graves.'

They both fell silent, expelling matching sighs. Daniel stood up. 'I'd better call DI Palmer.' Pulling his phone out of his pocket, he made his way down the hall and out the front door, stopping when he reached the street. The fresh air felt good, but didn't rid of him of his unease. He glanced back at the house, looking up towards the bedroom window. The killings were gruesome, extreme and carried out with relish. Whoever had murdered the Altons was not to be messed with … and Daniel had no doubt in his mind that there would be more to come.

CHAPTER THREE

Outside, the weather had taken a horrible turn again. Rain pelted the windows that ran along the side of the office. The weather reflected Daniel's mindset. Gloomy and overcast.

Waiting for his partner DI Charlie Palmer as well as Superintendent Peter Hobbs, Daniel had been sifting through some of his emails when his mind got distracted. Before he knew it he was on Facebook, Jenny Cartwright's memorial page filling his computer screen. Her profile photo showed the smiley redhead – a woman he had barely got to know before she was murdered. A woman whose death he believed he was responsible for.

'You really need to stop doing that,' a voice said into his ear. Daniel jumped before spinning around to see Charlie Palmer perching on the edge of the desk behind him, his arms folded over his broad chest, a gentle smile curling the corners of his mouth. The man looked far too pleased with himself for provoking a reaction in Daniel.

'You really need to stop doing that! You scared the hell out of me!' Daniel gasped, his breathing ragged as he tried to recover, one hand to his heart.

Charlie shrugged before nodding at the screen, his smirk fading. 'I'm serious, mate. It's not healthy.'

Daniel went to defend himself but his partner cut him off. 'I'm not kidding. It wasn't your fault, and you couldn't have known that would happen. You need to move on.' His last words pricked under Daniel's skin.

'Move on?' Daniel said. 'Some bastard killed her just to get at me and you think I can move on?'

'You know what I mean,' Charlie answered, his tone already softer. They both knew what a touchy subject it was.

Daniel swivelled back around in his chair, closed Facebook and sank his head into his hands. He took a slow breath, felt a hand on his shoulder.

'It's okay, Dan, honestly, but just... try to give yourself a break, right? We've not found anything on it. We have no leads. And you know as well as I do, we looked at it from every angle we could think of. For now, we just have to accept it. She's gone and there's nothing we can currently do about it. I know it's shit, but you have to try and get past it. Now, come on. I saw Hobbs come in. We need to go catch up about this new sicko on the block.'

Daniel heard Charlie heading off across the office behind him but did not follow immediately, giving himself a minute to calm down.

He knew Charlie was right, technically. Daniel couldn't have stopped Jenny from being murdered because he could never have anticipated it. It had come out of the blue. She had been cut down by a vindictive, brutal person, apparently treated as collateral damage in the killer's bid for revenge against Daniel for another woman being killed. It didn't seem to matter that the other woman had been a psychotic killer and had murdered at least three people. Daniel had saved Jenny's life, stopped her becoming victim number four, but she had been taken anyway in a cruel act of revenge. Jenny Cartwright had done nothing to deserve such a horrible end to her life. There had been undeniable chemistry between Jenny and Daniel. He thought that perhaps they could have become something. That just added to the sting.

Neither logic nor reason helped to prevent the guilt that Daniel felt, however: the all-too-frequent nightmares, the chilling moments when he glimpsed someone and could swear it was Jenny, until he got a better look. It had only been three months. He also knew that they had been as thorough as they could be on the case, given the available resources. A crack team of detectives, sergeants, CSIs and more had tried to find anything – anything at all – that would point to who had killed Jenny Cartwright, but they had turned up nothing. They hadn't even found the rest of her body. The police knew that the connection had to be to the case Jenny had given them information on, but that knowledge didn't help. Daniel was left with the sickening belief that Jenny was dead simply because someone out there was pissed off at him and wanted to get their own back. And the message that had been sent in the box with the heart – Jenny's heart – had made that pretty clear.

You took something of mine, Graves, so I took something of yours. An eye for an eye, so to speak. And guess what? She was just the start.
Game on.

He had to assume that whoever had killed Jenny had not finished their sick game. His feeling of helplessness was almost as overwhelming as constantly being on edge, expecting every phone call, every email, every ring of his doorbell to be another horrific piece of the puzzle. Daniel had felt like his move to London had been worth it after he'd saved Jenny the first time, solved the case and stopped a killer – but now? He couldn't help feeling that he had made a terrible mistake and had started a chain reaction of misery.

'You coming, sir?' said another voice from somewhere behind him. Daniel took a quick breath in an attempt to compose himself before turning round to see Sergeant Amelia Harding waving at him to follow her.

'You don't need to call me sir, Amelia,' he said. She gave him a warm smile before heading for the incident room, and he let the sight of her warm him back up a little. Her company always made him feel better. He'd opened up more to her than to any other colleague, including Charlie. Amelia knew all about his sister, Amanda, and the death of the bully who had tried to rape her, that Daniel had been the one to take the would-be rapist's life, and she had listened and understood with no judgement. He cherished the friendship that was starting to grow between them.

As he reached the glass-walled incident room, he could hear a lively debate within. He mentally geared himself up before joining the fray.

'It's fucked up, is what it is,' Charlie said with disgust. He was tapping a finger on one of the crime scene photos pinned to the wall. 'No normal person would do that.'

Shutting the door behind him and avoiding looking at the grisly montage of photographs, Daniel nodded a polite hello to the superintendent and to the junior sergeant joining them to keep a record of everything. Daniel could see that Hobbs was on edge – never a good thing. He was fingering his salt-and-pepper stubble, something he did when stressed. He was a fair man but very demanding – rightfully so, really, given their work. If he was feeling the pressure, though, then everyone would be.

'Good, you're here, Graves. What do we know? We need to

shut this down as fast as possible, so tell me everything we have.' The lines around Hobbs' mouth were deep as his jaw tensed.

Daniel filled him in on what they knew of the victims, Jane and Henry Alton. Neither husband nor wife had any criminal record, they weren't particularly well off, and they weren't, as far as research could tell, involved with anything untoward. They seemed to be a typical married couple in their early thirties with no skeletons in their cupboards – and no known reason that anyone would to want to kill them.

'So we don't have a motive?' Hobbs responded. His voice rose at the end of the sentence, but Daniel knew it wasn't a question. He continued to detail the crime scene and everything he had discussed with Stephanie Mitchum. The couple had been killed in the very early hours, they had been tortured, and the killer had shown a lack of precision. The wounds inflicted on the victims were messy, and a sock had been used as a gag. The rest of the house had apparently been left untouched, and nothing obvious had been taken. Other than a lack of a clear point of entry the murders seemed spontaneous – acts committed potentially for sheer amusement.

'And then, of course, there's what the killer did with the bodies,' Daniel said, glancing at the photos – not that he needed a visual reminder. He was fairly certain that he would remember the scene for as long as he lived.

'Do you think–' Amelia started.

'Go on, Sergeant,' Hobbs said. 'Any ideas are worth throwing into the ring at this stage.'

'I was going to say, do you think there's any religious connection? I mean, Henry Alton was kind of... crucified. And a cross was found in the sitting-room window in the Alton house, pretty visible from outside the house. Could they have been targeted because of that? Religion is sometimes a good motivator for violence.'

That got everyone thinking. Daniel could tell that Hobbs and Charlie were mulling over the theory. Junior Sergeant Ross Hayes, sitting at the end of the room typing notes, was also frowning thoughtfully.

'It's possible,' Charlie admitted. 'Some sick bigots, anti-religion, decide to have some fun. They go out looking for someone to mess with, see the cross in the window in passing and bingo.'

'They?' Hayes asked, pausing as he sought clarification. 'There's more than one killer?'

'Well, look at this,' Charlie said, moving to the wall to tap a finger on one of the photos again. 'One person couldn't have done that, not alone. No way.'

'I'm afraid I have to agree,' Daniel admitted reluctantly. 'It would take a lot of effort, and one person acting alone would have struggled. Someone must have held up the male while another pinned the body to the wall. We can't currently prove that two killers were there, though – or in fact, any number. It's disconcerting that we found no traces. No footprints, no foreign fibres or other particulates aside from rope threads, and certainly no fingerprints. The victims may have been random, but the intruders clearly still operated with caution and knew what they were doing.'

'Okay, well, I don't have anything else to add in terms of motive,' Charlie said. 'Amelia, can you start looking into the religion angle? Ask the neighbours what the Altons were like. Were they pushy about their religion? Did they go to church regularly? We also need to canvas the area, see if we have any witnesses to anything, or if the neighbours heard any commotion, like the body being nailed up. Hobbs, can we get someone else to help? I think we need someone to dig more deeply into the Altons – see if we can find anything else that could suggest why they were chosen.'

Hobbs nodded instantly. 'Of course. I'll get you a few. I want this wrapped up quickly. It hasn't broken to the press yet, but it's just a matter of time. One of the Altons' neighbours is bound to have called in the fact that a couple were murdered on their road. If I'm going to make a statement, I want some facts. The bastards from the nationals and main stations are relentless about this sort of thing. It'll be the main headline for every news outlet in the country if the details of the murders get out.'

Daniel could feel his blood pounding, giving him a headache. He thrived on this feeling, though: the need to crack a case, the urgency. He knew he wouldn't stop until he had done everything he could to find the people responsible for the Altons' deaths.

'Time to go to war!' Charlie said as they left the incident room. He sounded fired up, ready to take on the world.

CHAPTER FOUR

K elly Malone had been praying it was something juicy long before she turned her battered dark-blue Astra into Vassall Road, just down from the Oval Tube station. She didn't know the area that well and had been forced to rely on her Citymapper app to get her there, trusting her gut feeling that it would be worth the trip across the city. When she saw the police vehicle halfway down the road, the instantly recognisable yellow *Do Not Cross* tape, and the neighbours watching with morbid curiosity, her heart soared. Nosy locals – always a good sign. Nobody bothered to hang around if they couldn't gawk and gossip.

Knowing that if she expected results she couldn't just waltz up to the house and start asking the police questions, Kelly sat in her car along from the scene, tapping on the steering wheel as she figured out a plan of attack. She had to get it right. It looked like she was ahead of the curve, and she was not about to fuck it up.

'Neighbours first,' she muttered and fumbled in her handbag for her ID, her beloved – if old-school – Dictaphone and her trusty notepad and pen. Not relying on her phone to take notes made her feel like a more legitimate journalist. Her fingers ran along the edge of the pad, fingering the gap where she had ripped out a load of pages – a story that had gone nowhere except into the bin. She had been furious about that, wasting so much of her time only to be told that the paper was no longer interested in the story. The holy grail of both home page and front page had ended up featuring another MP scandal, her oh-so-darling colleague Jennifer Khan winning the race yet again.

'Not this time, you smug bitch,' Kelly said, proud of herself for getting a lead she knew Jennifer was unaware of. Thank God for Steven, the office exec she regularly flirted with to get info on incoming stories first. He had told her about the call he'd received from a resident on Vassall Street that morning, something about a suspicious death, and had chosen to go to her over Jennifer or anyone else. She'd probably have to pay for it with Friday drinks and a late-night snog, but it would be worth it.

She checked her make-up in the mirror, ran her fingers through her hair, then hopped out of the car. She brushed a crease out of her new Jigsaw pencil skirt and marched confidently down the pavement towards the crime scene, but on the opposite side of the road. Two policemen were posted outside the house, one of whom was signalling to a passer-by to move along. On her side stood two women who looked to be in their forties, gossiping over mugs of tea, the steam drifting lazily in the early afternoon breeze. One was wearing a dressing gown, and Kelly could see their breath in the air as they – no doubt – theorised over what had happened. A swift glance around showed no signs of any other journalists. If these women were willing to stand in the cold for the sake of mere gossip, then there was no doubt this was going to be big with other news outlets.

'Perfect,' she whispered with a smile. Pride flowed through her. Kelly aimed directly for the conspiratorial pair.

'Hi – do you know what happened here?' she interrupted them, her voice dripping with curiosity in an effort to engage the women. The woman who had bothered to get dressed threw her a 'who the hell are you and why are you talking to us' frown, but the one in the dressing gown took the bait instantly.

'They were murdered, can you believe it? Someone broke in last night and killed them both.' Her words should have conveyed shock and fear, but her face expressed quite the opposite. It was evident that she was enjoying this unexpected event on her road – an exciting turn of events to break up the daily routine.

Kelly took a step closer. 'Do you know how? Like what happened?'

Dressing-gown-woman shook her head. 'No. I asked one of the policemen this morning but he told me to piss off, pretty much. I did get a glimpse through the upstairs window, though – you know, before they pulled the curtains. I definitely saw blood. All up the wall!' Her voice was laced with excitement.

'Claire!' Her friend shook her head.

'What?'

'I don't think our neighbours being killed should be giving you such a thrill,' she said, her face screwed up with distaste.

Kelly thought that was a bit rich, coming from someone who had been discussing the news excitedly only moments before, but she said nothing. 'Did you know them then?' she asked, trying not to sound too pushy but desperate for more. A bit of blood up a wall was good, but it wouldn't get her the reader clicks she was after.

'I did, a little. Jane and Henry Alton – they were a nice couple. Always said hello when they passed me. I can't say that I know much about them, but–'

Her friend cut her off. 'Sorry, but who are you, if you don't mind me asking? I know you don't live on this street.'

Dammit!

Kelly had hoped to get a bit more information from them before revealing who she was. 'No, no, I don't. I'm actually a journalist. For the *City Post*. Sorry, I forgot to say. My name's Kelly Malone. I'm hoping to write a story on what happened here.'

'Right. Well, I'm afraid we don't know anything else,' the frostier of the friends said, making it clear that she wanted Kelly to get lost.

'Not to worry. But here, let me give you both my details. If you think of anything, give me a call, okay? There may even be some money in it.' She handed them both a business card. Frosty shoved it into her jeans pocket without even looking at it, but dressing-gown-Claire gave it a once over. Maybe she would call Claire when she was alone, Kelly thought.

'Anyway, I shall leave you ladies to it,' she said with a smile. As she headed further up the road, she could hear the women whispering behind her.

The neighbouring house on the block was empty, a to-let sign sticking out of the small front lawn. At the next house, she was considering knocking on the door when the sound of a car pulling up made her turn around. Her pulse raced as she realised who was getting out of the car.

Holy shit, jackpot!

Knowing they wouldn't speak to her but wanting to try anyway, Kelly sped across the road and thrust herself into the path of Detective Inspectors Graves and Palmer.

'Detectives, hi! Kelly Malone from the *City Post*. It must be serious if you two are here!' she squealed, nodding towards the cordoned-off property. Her Dictaphone was already recording, poised to get a snippet of a quote.

'Not now, Malone, okay?' Charlie Palmer snapped. 'How do you even know about this, for Christ's sake?'

'I have my sources,' Kelly said with what she hoped was a coquettish smile, but Palmer was already turning away from her. She sighed. That was to be expected, given their history. She angled the Dictaphone towards Graves.

'DI Graves, it's nice to finally meet you. I've read so much about you. Kudos on the demonologist case. God, I wish I'd had the exclusive on that! Can you tell me anything about the couple who were murdered last night?'

Graves frowned at the Dictaphone, then at her. 'We can't provide any statements at this time, Miss Malone.' With that, Graves followed his partner. Kelly watched them slip under the yellow tape and start up the path to the front door of the murder house.

'Nice to see you again, Charlie!' she called after them, unable to help herself. She'd royally messed things up there and knew he was unlikely to come round, but she couldn't help thinking about him from time to time. And man, was he looking good. As handsome as ever. Charlie turned to scowl at her again before he and Graves entered the house, shutting the front door behind them.

'Kelly, I think you've landed a big one here!' She giggled to herself. She had victim names, a brief anecdote about blood-covered walls, and now she knew the leads on the case. They were not the type to work every run-of-the-mill crime either. With just a little more information she could say hello to a spread in the evening edition – maybe even the front cover and a home page headline after all. She grinned as she walked down the street to question more neighbours, with added pep in her stride.

'Are you going to tell me what that was about, or do I have to beat it out of you?' Daniel asked, his curiosity bubbling over. Charlie stood back from the window, looking out onto the street with caution. Charlie pulled the curtain back a little.

'Charlie!' Daniel shouted.

His partner jumped. 'Sorry, I was just checking to see if she's gone.' Charlie was visibly flustered. It was a side of him Daniel was not sure he'd ever seen. Charlie was never less than well put together, cool and collected. The nervous, sweaty, fidgety man in front of him was a world away from the norm – and he was suddenly that bit more relatable. Daniel quite liked it.

'So I gathered. But what's with this?' Daniel pointed at Charlie, his finger moving up and down. Charlie let the curtain drop back into place. For a while he was silent, and Daniel could hear the CSI team milling about upstairs, still looking for trace evidence and, God willing, a fingerprint or rogue hair. Their footsteps echoed down through the ceiling, emphasising the quiet in the sitting room.

'She... Kelly and I... we used to date. It didn't last long. Nearly two years ago. She played me for a total fucking fool.' Charlie's voice trailed off, despite the anger in his words, but Daniel urged him to continue. There was clearly quite a lot more there. Evidently it hadn't just been a fling, otherwise he suspected that Charlie would have mentioned it before – at least, he wouldn't be so bothered now.

'She used me. To get information. Didn't tell me she was a journalist, and I was stupid enough to tell her things I shouldn't have about a case. Not loads, but enough. Then it got out, her story, complete with things I told her that she wasn't supposed to know and that we didn't want becoming public knowledge. I was almost suspended. I broke up with her and that was that. I've barely spoken to her since, and I've avoided her if I ever saw her trying to canvas a crime scene.' Charlie turned to look at Daniel, his face full of shame. He was clearly embarrassed.

Daniel felt bad for him. Charlie was becoming a close friend. For Daniel, seeing the normally infallible Charlie in such a state was upsetting. It wasn't supposed to be that way. Daniel was used to his 'cool as a cucumber' persona and hadn't really expected to see anything else; had not, in fact, been certain there *was* anything else.

'Shit, Charlie, I'm sorry. Journalists can be such devious people,' Daniel responded, not sure what else to say.

Charlie took a deep breath, straightened up, and flashed a thin smile. 'Too right. Fuck her.'

The moment was over. Just like Kelly Malone, they were there to canvas the area and look for witnesses. It wasn't really the time for heart-to-hearts. Maybe over a beer at some point, but not in a house where a couple had been brutally killed.

A quick check outside showed no sign of Kelly Malone – perhaps she'd already headed back to her computer to work on her story. The duo stepped out into the cold street once more. Daniel suspected that Kelly had affected Charlie more than he cared to admit.

There'll be time to dig later. Not now.

They headed left, Daniel hoping for a witness who could tell them anything about what the hell had happened to Jane and Henry Alton.

CHAPTER FIVE

'Katy? You up?' Lawrence yelled into the house as he stepped through the front door and pushed it closed behind him, shutting out the icy night. He dropped his gym bag on the floor in the hallway and pulled off his coat, hanging it on the rickety banister. Even as he did it he knew that Katy would be annoyed that he hadn't put it in the closet but he left it there anyway, too worn out to care.

Lawrence and Katy Rhodes had moved into the house in West Kensington last summer. It was small and overly expensive. Lawrence had worried about the cost even before they put in an offer. Katy, however, had been adamant that they could make it work, and to be fair she had been right, although only just. Lawrence always played it down if anyone asked about it. His sister had said they were insane. For the same price as their pokey little house, which had two small bedrooms, she had a four-bed semi with a conservatory and a garden in Birmingham. She also didn't have to work thirteen-hour days to pay for it, unlike Lawrence. The long days were beginning to take their toll; yet again, he was only just getting home as the clock ticked past eleven.

His day had been exhausting, seemingly endless, and he hadn't even gone to the gym in the end. He was getting a belly, and it pissed him off, but there never seemed to be the time to get to the gym. Now he felt totally spent, ready to crawl into bed with his wife and pass out.

Hearing no response from Katy, Lawrence kicked off his shoes and padded into the kitchen. His stomach rumbled. Despite his exhaustion, he knew he needed to eat something before he went to bed. He wouldn't sleep properly otherwise. Pulling open the fridge he found a plate of dinner prepped for him, wrapped in cling film.

The third time this week, he thought, feeling guilty that he had not sat down with his wife for dinner since Monday. At least it was the weekend soon. As far as he knew, they didn't have any plans, and if he could get out of having to work on Saturday then maybe they could do something nice.

Plate in hand, Lawrence was digging in a drawer for a fork when he thought he heard something upstairs – a door closing, maybe.

'Katy?' he called again, angling his head towards the ceiling. If she was awake, he didn't need to remain quiet.

The house was quiet. Maybe the sound had come from next door. The walls were thin and they could always hear the neighbours moving about.

His stomach growled again, and he put the chicken breast and new potatoes into the microwave. As he leant down to set the timer he caught sight of his reflection in the glass door. He was not surprised to find that he looked like shit. When he had been younger his dark skin had been flawless and his deep brown eyes had shone with life. The late thirties reflection he saw now was almost greyscale: his colour washed out, lines spiking out from the sides of his eyes. Spots dotted his temples, a sure sign that he was not feeling at his best.

He was the breadwinner. Katy earned okay and had been pushing for overtime but she couldn't match his wages, so the bulk of the mortgage was on him. And if he wanted that promotion at the bank, he had to work as hard as he could and suck up the long hours in the hope of extra money. There was one client he was eager to impress too, a super-wealthy property manager called Carlos Mancini who could have a job opportunity with Lawrence's name on it, but this had not yet come to fruition. Every day he chanted internally 'It's all worth it, it's all worth it' as he marched towards the Tube, often before seven, in a bid to get in early and win over his line manager. She was okay with him, not a bad boss, but he knew he could get her to favour him more if he worked hard enough.

The chicken Katy had made went down well, quickly too, and Lawrence finished it in just a few minutes. He left the plate in the sink – another thing he knew would annoy his wife, but he couldn't be bothered to empty the dishwasher.

A thud came from above him, like something very heavy being dropped onto carpet, and immediately his skin was speckled with goosebumps. Even as his brain told him to shout out again, something deeper down made him bite his tongue. Katy was not a stomper, and she certainly wouldn't be rearranging furniture that late. What had made that noise? He pulled one of the drawers open and grabbed a kitchen knife. It would do the trick if needed. Lawrence felt sick even thinking about using it, but if push came to shove he would, no question.

Terrified of making any noise, thankful he had kicked off his trainers when he got home, Lawrence started into the hallway leading to the front door. The stairs went up to his left. Double-checking that the living room was empty, he twisted to try and look up to the first floor through the banister. The upstairs landing was dark, and he could see nothing but a glint of reflection in the mirror mounted on the wall at the top of the stairs. If Katy hadn't been up there, he would have been out of the house in an instant. He didn't take risks, he never had; he would rather be made to look a fool for unnecessarily calling the police than march into a potential ambush. But he couldn't leave Katy. If something happened to her, it would be the end of him. Swallowing hard, his hand already aching from its tight grip on the knife handle, he began to ascend the stairs.

His heart pounding so hard he was worried someone would hear, Lawrence reached the top step and pressed his back to the wall. All the doors were closed, visible as slightly lighter rectangles in the darkness. He didn't know what to do and stood there feeling helpless, his palms clammy. His mind was telling him that everything was fine, that he would soon be laughing at himself, that Katy would take the piss out of him when she found out he'd been standing sweating in the dark, a knife in his hand. His gut, though, was pretty fucking sure he should be worried. And he trusted his gut. He read the news – break-ins happened all the time. Gangs. Knife crime. Sick opportunists with over-entitled attitudes.

The house was still silent. From somewhere in the night he heard a siren, off to deal with an emergency.

Fucking ironic.

He realised he should have called the police first, then maybe the sirens would be coming to him. He felt his pocket, and realised that his phone was still in his coat. Should he go down and get it? Whatever he decided, it was time to move. He had to. He couldn't just stand there like a dickhead all night. Looking down the stairs, he could see his coat. It would only take a few seconds to get his phone, but then he'd have to make the call. And if there *was* someone there, in his house, they'd hear him.

Shit! Am I crazy? This shouldn't be happening!

Still horribly unsure, he took a step forward. The landing

carpet masked the sound. Another step, and another, and he was standing in front of their bedroom door. Raising the knife, he gripped the door handle with his other hand and slowly twisted it. He pushed the door, holding his breath.

The room was empty, the duvet pushed half off the edge of the bed.

'What?' he whispered. Where was Katy? Maybe she was up after all?

He spotted the strip of light under the door to the en suite and let out his breath in a silent laugh. He felt like an idiot.

'Dickhead is right,' he said to himself. 'Katy, you scared the crap out of me!' he said louder, through the door. There was no response. 'Oi, Katy. Did you fall asleep in there or something? I'm so sorry I'm late again. I didn't mean to wake you when I came in. What was that banging a second ago?'

Lawrence pushed the door open. Light spilled over him – and over Katy's body, which was splayed out in the bathtub. His throat closed and black dots spotted his vision as he took in the details. Blood was smeared up the cream tiles, filling the tub up to Katy's ankles. His wife's skin was pallid and sticky, her eyes replaced by hollowed-out, ragged holes.

A blade plunged into his shoulder, slicing through muscle and flesh. Pain sliced through him. He screamed and fell forward to his knees. Katy's body was right in front of his face. He struggled to turn around, to get a look at the monster who had destroyed his world. A man stood before him, all in black, his features obscured by a balaclava. Except his eyes and his smile. That smile tore through Lawrence as much as the knife in his attacker's hand had. Lawrence pushed off the edge of the bath and charged forward, colliding with his attacker. The knife clattered off the bottom of the door frame.

Katy's killer fell to the floor and lay there, looking stunned. Lawrence seized the moment, clambering over and past him.

His shoulder throbbing, blood spilling down his back, he stumbled out of the bedroom. He had to get out, had to find help. A flash of guilt for wanting to live without Katy threatened to derail him, but he pushed on. He had reached the top of the stairs when the door to the main bathroom opened. Without hesitation a second figure lunged at him. Lawrence dodged, slamming against the wall. Pain ricocheted through him, and blood from his wound smeared up the light blue wall like tar. As he raced down the stairs he spotted his coat again and thought of his phone. He was close to the bottom, his hand outstretched, when something hit him hard in the back and he fell down the remaining steps, hitting the hall floor with a brutal thud. Before he could move, someone was on him, pinning him down. A fist hit him hard in the back of the head, again and again.

Lawrence blacked out.

CHAPTER SIX

Amelia Harding had pounced on the opportunity to take Junior Sergeant Ross Hayes under her wing, knowing full well that it would make a good impression on her higher-ups. She had been determined to be the one to find a solid-gold motive for the murders of Jane and Henry Alton. So far, she and Ross had failed.

Pulling together a quick report of their findings – from speaking to friends and family of the victims and information found by trawling their social media and online activity – they found with a resounding sense of defeat that the religious motivation theory didn't seem to have legs. The Altons had been mildly religious at best. They occasionally visited St Mark's in Kennington, but never more than once a month. They had been known to speak about their faith every so often, should the topic come up, but they never pushed the subject or deliberately brought it up.

'Does it matter that our research hasn't proved the theory?' Ross asked as they finished flipping through their work for the third time. Amelia raised an eyebrow.

'What I mean is, does it really matter that they weren't that

outwardly religious?' he continued. '_
been targeted because of the cross in the
still be because of that. The killers didn't
personally.'

'I suppose potentially it could still be, but on
feel enough of a reason to be the only motivation.
how she looked at it, the religious motive wasn't sitting .. It
didn't seem enough to make the Altons the targets of a killer.
Their deaths were too extreme, and she now thought that the
husband being nailed to the wall was not so much to echo a
crucifixion but to shock: to be impactful, grisly and unsettling.
The killers obviously wanted attention, and that was one way to
get it. True, Amelia had to admit that she had come across
numerous stories about other cases where the reaction
considerably outweighed the provocation. She also knew that
religion in general was known to be a dangerous catalyst for
violence. It made her feel ill to think that someone could rip out
a person's heart and nail them to a wall just because they
believed in God. Especially in south London.

They agreed to have one last look into crucifixion
specifically, to be sure they could rule out religion. Together
they pulled stories from all over the world that featured
crucifixion in the modern day. Most were acts designed to make
a statement or portray a protest of some sort, like the artist Chris
Burden, who had himself crucified to the bonnet of a car. There
were also the Filipino devotees who, in an act of remembrance,
would each year nail themselves to crosses, mimicking the
suffering of Jesus Christ. Then of course there were the stories
related to radicalism.

Amelia found the research gruesome and shocking but she
still could not relate it to the case, beyond the basic premise.
Crucifixion was historically used to inflict on the victim the
maximum pain and suffering, but the coroner's office had

...cluded that Henry Alton had already died by the ...his body had been nailed to the wall of his bedroom. It was also a sign that the victim had been disgraced somehow, but that didn't fit either. The body had not been publicly displayed, and neither she nor Ross had found anything in the lives of the Alton couple that would qualify as a disgrace.

'So maybe it's just a loosely put together statement? A kind of "fuck you",' Ross said, looking at an illustration portraying Jesus on the cross.

'To who? The Altons, to us? Religion in general?' Amelia asked.

'All of the above? Who knows. It's pretty clear that whoever did this is messed up, so does it need to be that thought-out? Honestly, does there even need to be a reason behind it at all?'

Hayes had raised a valid point. Maybe there was little motivation. They had found nothing so far that suggested there was more to it. The killers could simply have been projecting. Maybe it was just a case of a severely disturbed mind, exorcising something in a visceral, brutal fashion. Maybe the religious connotations were a total coincidence, a red herring. She shivered. The thought terrified her even more than the idea of a religiously motivated killer.

Lucy Hastings was a worrier, no doubt about it. She knew it, her friends knew it, even her Labrador probably knew it, based on the looks he sometimes gave her. Most of the time her worrying was pointless, which only resulted in stressing her out. On occasion, though, she was bang on, as though her worries could sometimes tap into a sixth sense. As she stood outside the front door to her friend's house, she couldn't help feeling that this was one of those times. It made her feel sick. This time, unlike normal, she did not want the vindication.

It was after five, and sunlight had retreated earlier than ever as winter crept on. Lucy pressed her gloved finger to the doorbell for the third time. All her calls and texts had gone unanswered, and that never happened.

They had arranged to meet for brunch – to talk about men, mainly. Lucy had been dating a guy she had met at a book signing. He was geeky and funny and she really liked him, but she needed to talk things over with her friend. She had sat in the coffee shop in Soho where they had arranged to meet for forty minutes before she eventually gave up. Most people would have been angry, but not Lucy. She was instantly concerned and as the hours ticked by without so much as a 'sorry' message, her concern only got worse. Now here she was outside the house, her heart in her throat as her imagination ran wild.

No one came to the door after yet another ring and knock. Lucy stepped off the porch and moved to the sitting-room window, not concerned by the muddy earth beneath her feet. Cupping her hands around her face, she peered in. The room was dark and partially obscured by the closed curtains. Her mind filled with images of her friend in the shower, having slipped and banged her head, or having fallen down the stairs and broken her neck.

Lucy decided to take matters into her own hands. She knew there was a spare key hidden somewhere in the front garden. She had seen it a few months ago after a boozy evening had resulted in her friend losing her house keys when they had decided to go home for more wine and a Chinese takeaway. Five minutes and some digging later, her friend had the key in her grasp, having retrieved it from inside one of the plant pots that lined the wall by the front door.

The silence inside was disconcerting as Lucy pushed the

door closed behind her and stood in the small hallway, relieved not to have found a body at the foot of the stairs.

'Katy? Are you here? It's Lucy,' she called, her voice dissipating into the house. No one responded. Her heartbeat was quicker than normal as she tried to calm herself. Lucy walked through into the kitchen in case her friend was at the back of the house and could have missed the doorbell and knocking. The room was empty.

'Katy!' she called again. She pulled out her phone once more, but there were still no messages or missed calls from either Katy or Lawrence. She had tried Lawrence's mobile but got his voicemail, which had been understandable. He was always busy. She wished she could have phoned their workplaces as well, but she didn't know exactly where Lawrence was based and Katy had the day off – some sort of teacher training day. It was the reason they'd picked today for brunch. Selecting her friend from her contact list, Lucy called again. From upstairs came the unmistakable sound of a mobile phone ringing. Lucy felt herself sway as her skin chilled, the quiet, harmless melody continuing to sound until she ended the call.

Hesitant but knowing she needed to check, her mind filled with worst-case scenarios again, Lucy headed back out into the hall. This time she spotted Lawrence's gym bag and shoes, which was odd. Katy kept their house very tidy. She could practically hear her friend admonishing Lawrence for dumping his stuff when he got in.

She turned and looked upstairs. It was almost dark, with just a hint of light getting in through a window somewhere. Something inside her warned her against going up there. She unlocked her phone again, this time calling Lawrence's mobile. It went to voicemail again. A second later, a beep sounded out above her. Lucy felt like as if she was going to pass out. It didn't make sense. What could have happened that her best friend had not shown up to meet her, and neither she nor her husband had answered their phones? Why were their phones both in the house?

One shaky step at a time, Lucy made her way up to the first floor. As she got closer to the top she spotted the marks up the wall.

'What is that?' she whispered before realising it was blood. 'Oh God...' She thrust a hand out to steady herself and had to force herself to carry on. If they were hurt, couldn't call out, she had to help.

On the landing, she switched on the hallway light. She was faced with two closed doors and one slightly ajar – to a room she recalled was the tiny spare room and home office where Katy sometimes marked homework. On one door was another smear of red.

'Oh God, shit.' It was bad, it had to be. She desperately wanted to turn back, to leave and call the police, but she had to know what she was dealing with. Crossing the landing seemed to take forever but then her hand was on the door, pushing it inwards. Once more she switched on the light. Blood was splashed across the light cream carpet, arcing towards the closed bathroom door. Lucy pulled out her phone, struggling to dial 999, her hands were shaking so much. With the call ringing in her ear she took a deep breath and dared to open the door to the en suite.

She didn't hear the operator answer; her screams drowned out everything else around her.

CHAPTER SEVEN

There was absolute chaos. The normally quiet West Kensington street was lit up like it was Christmas. How the fact that two people had been murdered was already common knowledge, Daniel Graves could not say, but he knew it meant his and Charlie's jobs were about to get an awful lot harder. With the expected attention-seekers calling in fake witness accounts and the inflammatory news stories that would soon be splashed over every outlet, their casework could become very complicated very quickly. The article in the *City Post* had mentioned the murders in Camberwell as the jumping-off point. Now they had two extremely violent crime scenes in three days, and public interest was ramping up. It was a big deal, for them and everyone else.

Daniel had stepped outside the victims' house to speak to one of the sergeants attempting to keep people at bay, and questions had erupted all around him.

'How were they killed?'

'How would you describe the scene?'

'Are you concerned for other residents?'

'Do you have any suspects?'

'Was it a murder-suicide?'

He thought he saw the journalist from the day before, Kelly Malone, but if it had been her she had vanished into the crowd instantly. She had been the only reporter seen around the other case and her article, while full of so-called juicy details and ridiculous hyperbole, had thankfully not caused many waves in the morning news cycle. Only a few other outlets had picked it up. Now, though, with another crime scene and two more deaths so soon, the story was starting to gain traction. Malone would, of course, be aiming to be the woman in the know, as she'd had the initial scoop, but every other journalist in the city would be gunning for the biggest story. From what Charlie had said of Malone, she would not pull her punches and would aim for maximum impact, and Daniel knew that other journalists would do similar. Daniel shuddered at the thought of tomorrow's headlines.

He had come out to check if Lucy Hastings, the woman who had called in the bodies, had been taken back to the station for questioning yet. The sergeant at the police tape barrier had assured Daniel that she had, although she was apparently in shock and incoherent. The employee in the emergency call centre who had spoken to Hastings had struggled to get any details from her, and eventually had just sent a squad car to the address that she had given. No one in the first car had been prepared for what awaited them.

Daniel told the sergeant to keep a beady eye and ear out for any female journalists from the *City Post* before darting back inside the house, glad of the comparative quiet as he shut out the crowd behind him. Not that inside the house could be considered calm or relaxed.

DI Charlie Palmer stood at the top of the stairs talking to a paramedic. When he saw Daniel come back in, he came down to join him. Worry and disgust painted a twisted expression over his features. Daniel knew his partner had a fairly strong stomach, but nevertheless he looked a little green around the gills.

'It has to be the same killers, right? It's even worse than the Alton couple.'

Daniel had already dared to glimpse the horror that was above them. Like a Polaroid going off in his brain, the image was suddenly in front of him, disgustingly vivid. Just as with the Alton murders, he doubted that he would ever forget what he had seen.

The male victim, identified as Lawrence Rhodes, had been stripped down to his underwear and posed, kneeling by the bath in their en suite. The skin on his back had been flayed to reveal sticky fat, muscle, and flashes of spinal discs and ribs. His throat had been slit and he had bled out into the bath. His wrists had also been slit: they stuck out awkwardly, again over the bath, where his blood had mixed with that of his wife. He looked like a man praying, or perhaps offering himself up to a higher entity. The religious element was not lost on Daniel or Charlie, despite the fact that Sergeant Harding had come up blank on that avenue so far.

In comparison to her husband, and in fact the first victims, Katy Rhodes' body remained fairly intact. Stephanie Mitchum had ascertained that she had been killed by a single stab wound to the heart. Katy's eyes had been taken out, seemingly post mortem. They had not yet been found. The rest of her looked untouched, beyond a couple of bruise marks, presumed by Mitchum to have been caused when she struggled with her attacker.

'Another couple, another home invasion, and another body part taken. The bodies may have been arranged differently and there are no real signs of torture this time, but everything else is pretty consistent with the other murders,' Mitchum told Daniel and Charlie in a matter-of-fact tone. Daniel was still sometimes surprised by how desensitised she seemed to be, but in her line of work, he suspected it was essential to keep her sane.

'Obviously we'll perform a full autopsy and examination, but more to look for trace evidence than anything else. It's pretty clear how they were killed. And I don't think it would be much of a stretch to say that this is the work of the same killers. Same over-the-top violence, another couple, body parts taken, and all rather messy and lacking in finesse.' She promised to give them more details when she and her team had them, then went back to supervising the scene. Daniel doubted that anyone else had dealt with crime scenes quite like this but they all seemed to be taking things in their stride, as professional as always. If there was any evidence to be found, he was sure they would find it.

Daniel moved part way up the stairs and pointed to the blood on the wall. 'So one of them made a break for it? The smear angles down. Maybe one of them got free, saw a chance to escape.'

'Seems likely,' Charlie answered. 'It must have been terrifying.'

Daniel descended the stairs, not wanting to go upstairs again if he didn't have to. Charlie joined him on the ground floor. For the second time that week Daniel found himself sitting in a stranger's kitchen and feeling a bit sick.

'This is all so... God, fucked up,' he muttered, twisting in his chair to look at Charlie, who was leaning against the counter, nodding, looking pale. Daniel was glad it wasn't just him. 'Who breaks into houses in the middle of the night and then does that? And doesn't steal anything? Except body parts.' Daniel tilted his head back, looking at the ceiling, as though he could look through the avocado paint and see the horror that was just one floor above him. He half-expected to see blood seeping through, ready to drip on him.

'Since another body part has been taken, do you think that's the killer's calling card? If this happens again, is there going to be a different piece missing?'

'Let's not look ahead to crime scene number three just yet, Charlie. But maybe. Or maybe he's just collecting souvenirs.'

'They,' Charlie corrected. 'I know we're not certain, but after seeing this new... arrangement of bodies, and the fact that one of the victims seems to have been stopped from getting away, I really don't think one person could do this. It's a lot to do, all of... that.' He pointed a finger vaguely upwards.

Daniel sat back in the chair and sighed. 'I think we need to see if we can find some connections between the two couples. Maybe they were friends, worked together, maybe two of them dated the killers. Who knows? There has to be something, though. I don't believe they're random murders – I can't. Because if they are, then...' Daniel didn't finish his sentence. The possibility that no motive existed didn't bear thinking about. Intelligent, twisted killers choosing their targets at random, just for fun? How could the police ever anticipate the next victims if even the perpetrators didn't know who they were yet?

'Yeah, they must have picked the victims somehow. It's extremely rare for something like this to happen with no motive. Maybe they watched them first. Stalked them.' Charlie glanced out of the kitchen window at the night sky that was now covering the garden and fences and anything else hiding out there in shadows. 'And we're sure the religious angle is a dead end? The male victim upstairs, the pose – it could easily be read as a religious reference.'

'Amelia was pretty certain. There's no religious paraphernalia on display in this house either. I'll see if she or Hayes can find anything on the Rhodes family, but I'm not convinced that's why this couple was chosen. It's possible that the posing of the victim is supposed to echo a praying pose, but it could also just be a coincidence or, grim as it sounds, perhaps it was just the best way to get the blood into the bath from his wrists. Whoever is doing this wants to make a show of it. I reckon they're enjoying it. They're psychopathic – have to be. And we both know how crimes involving psychopathic serial killers tend to go...'

'They escalate,' Charlie said, his voice a broken whisper, his eyes wide.

CHAPTER EIGHT

By ten that night the story was finally coming together. The office was much quieter than it had been during the noisy afternoon that had resulted from yet another famous sportsman having an affair. Kelly Malone could feel her skin singing with excitement as she skimmed over what she had typed again. The Senior Stories Editor at the *Post* hadn't been aware of how much interest there was in the murders when she had knocked on his office door, ready to pitch her idea for making them the go-to outlet for news on the case. The second he was up to speed, though, he had told her to run with it, to make her second piece extreme, serious and scary. It needed to be much bigger than the first article. There were four victims now. He wanted a headline that would get everyone in the UK talking, filled with nervous panic, desperately refreshing the *City Post* website and social feeds to get new information as it came.

'Psychotic London killer murders second couple,' came a snarky fake-newscaster voice from over Kelly's shoulder as she checked the intro paragraph for the fifth time.

'Hi, Jen, something I can do for you?' Kelly asked through gritted teeth, recognising the irritating, nasal voice without turning around. Her tone barely avoided crossing the line into 'fuck off' territory.

Clearly deciding that she would prefer to talk face to face rather than to the back of Kelly's head, Jennifer Khan was suddenly leaning against the desk, inches away from Kelly's mouse and notepad, forcing her to stop and pay attention.

'Nope, just came to see what you were doing,' Jennifer answered, flicking her long black hair over her shoulder.

What I'm doing is none of your business, you nosey bitch, Kelly said in her head.

'Just finishing off a story, actually, so...' Her manner was deliberately cold and dismissive, making it clear she wanted to be left alone. *And I don't need your thoughts on it either, so piss off,* she finished silently. She did a lot of that when Jennifer was around: talking in her head rather than out loud. It was her way of avoiding full-blown arguments with the woman, which would be a regular occurrence if Kelly was more outspoken with her colleague.

'So I saw. Quite the headline. A bit on the nose though, no?' Jennifer asked, a thin smile curling the edges of her overly bee-stung lips. Kelly wanted to slap the maroon gloss right off them.

God, can't you take a hint? Read the room, Jen! Kelly turned back to her screen and made sure she had saved the copy. Out of the corner of her eye she could see Jennifer flicking her hair again, clearly trying to keep Kelly's attention on her, or at least distract her. Kelly knew that Jennifer was petty enough to try and get in the way, do anything to halt Kelly's efforts.

Their relationship as arch enemies had arisen, to Kelly at least, totally out of nowhere. Jennifer was, by most accounts, the prettier woman, her naturally darker skin, Pantene advert hair and genetically superior figure making her the official office hottie. Jennifer had been at the *Post* longer than Kelly, and had gained more column inches and front pages. She was clever too

– not a woman who had ever needed to coast on her looks, despite still clearly using them to her advantage. She had won more awards for her stories. She had even helped revamp the *Post* website to increase clicks and online readership. Really, the schoolgirl bitch routine made no sense. It was entirely unwarranted. For some reason, though, Jennifer evidently felt threatened by Kelly. Kelly was certainly more popular – with other women in the company, at least – and while they shared the 'do anything it takes' attitude when it came to getting the best juicy details, she thought there was more than enough room for both of them. Apparently Jennifer thought differently. Kelly was just waiting for the day when Jennifer told her that the town wasn't big enough for the both of them.

Yet another hair flip forced Kelly to respond. 'To be honest, Jen, I need to get this submitted to Brian imminently. I don't really have time to chat it over with you. Thanks, though.'

Kelly wanted to tell Jennifer to back off and leave her be, but it was late and she didn't have the energy to argue. She was also not a fan of work confrontations. They always left a bitter taste in her mouth and she never felt like she came off well. Being on the frontline of petty drama and office politics was not, in Kelly's opinion, the way to get ahead in one's career. Instead she spoke calmly and hoped her words would simply close off conversations she no longer wanted to be a part of. She felt the tension instantly drain from her shoulders when Jennifer stood, making a show of fluffing out her hair.

'Okay, message received. I'll leave you to it. Good luck with the story. I'm sure Brian will love it.'

Kelly knew that her colleague's words were totally insincere, but gave her a quick thanks anyway, glad to be rid of her – and that she had held her tongue. Kelly even chose to ignore Jennifer's passive-aggressive parting shot as she headed off across the office. 'And it's nice to see you in so late, Kel. Makes a change for me not to be one of the only people still working late into the night.'

Kelly read her work one last time, took a deep breath and clicked 'send' on her email to Brian before getting up to go and speak to him in person. She wanted to be there when he read it, and she wanted to know that her article would make the morning cycle. And most of all, she wanted to make sure she would get a nice bold headline to rub in Jennifer Khan's smug, made-up face.

'Can someone explain to me exactly what kind of operation you're running? This article alludes to details about the cases that have not yet been made public! Why are they somehow now in national bloody news stories?' Superintendent Peter Hobbs slammed his newspaper down on the table in the middle of the small kitchen. Charlie and Daniel jumped, Charlie almost spilling his second coffee of the morning. Immediately Daniel felt his body react: his stomach flipped and his heart rate increased. He had been dreading the inevitable bad headlines since the chaotic scene in West Kensington the evening before. But what details was Hobbs talking about? He had no idea, and that unnerved him further. They had been careful to keep anyone away from the scene who was not permitted to be there, and to make no public statements beyond the absolute basics.

'Fuck,' Charlie muttered, despite being in the presence of his superior.

For a moment no one said anything. It was as though the three of them were waiting to see what would happen next. A junior sergeant stepped into the kitchen holding a box of porridge before sensing the atmosphere and ducking back out without a word.

Given the scale of the case, everyone knew there was a possibility that information could get out. Perhaps they could have contained it for another day or two if they had been lucky, but everyone in the department knew that with big stories like this, the task was like stopping a wildfire from spreading.

'What did I tell you? Malone is a real piece of work,' Charlie said, having checked the name on the byline.

'Gentlemen, I don't give a shit who wrote it. I would rather know how the hell she knew so much! We haven't even made a formal statement, yet here's a front-page story with names of the victims and theories about how the murders are connected, with you both namechecked, for Christ's sake! Do you know how much more complicated this will make the case?'

Again there was silence. The question was rhetorical, but still seemed to deserve some sort of response. Daniel looked at his boss. Hobbs was boiling over. Daniel had never seen the superintendent quite so furious, and wasn't sure how to react.

Hobbs was right to be angry. The story would blow up, and public attention would be sky high. He was certain that it wasn't his or Charlie's fault, however. They had refused to talk to Kelly Malone at the first crime scene in Oval and, although Daniel had thought he had spotted her at the scene of the second murders, no one had spoken to any members of the press, especially not Malone, beyond a quick 'no comment' or 'we're not willing to provide further information at this time'.

'I'm sorry, sir. I don't know how this happened, but let me assure you that—'

Hobbs did not let Daniel finish. 'Save the half-arsed excuses and promises, Graves. You two are leading this case, so that makes you responsible. I don't know how this happened, but make damn sure it doesn't happen again. End of discussion. Now, sort yourselves out and get downstairs to the conference room in twenty minutes. We're holding an emergency press conference. I want you both to look slick, professional, competent and, most importantly, to keep your mouths shut!' Hobbs ran a hand over his grey hair, turned on his heel and strode out of the kitchen. His footsteps boomed down the corridor as he left them in a stunned silence.

Charlie took a sip of his coffee but pulled a face, no longer wanting the drink. He tipped it down the sink and plonked the mug down on the counter. On the mug was the slogan *World's Okayest Detective* – likely a result of an office secret Santa. Charlie huffed at it and turned it around to face the other way.

'That was a great way to start the day,' he said, his face twisting into an expression of pained embarrassment.

'I've never seen him like that. How buggered are we on a scale of one to ten?' Daniel asked his partner, hoping that Charlie would make at least a weak attempt to reassure him. After all, Charlie had known Hobbs for longer and knew him better.

'Thirty?'

'Bollocks.'

They stood in silence for another minute before Daniel decided to make a move. 'I'm going to go and get a fresh shirt from my desk. I think I sweated straight through this one from stress,' he joked, trying to relieve the tension in the air. Charlie gave a weak smirk in response. 'See you downstairs?'

He was stepping out of the kitchen doorway when Charlie's words stopped him in his tracks. 'I barely said anything to her.'

Daniel's heart sank. He turned to look at his partner. He looked like a teenager who had just confessed to cheating on an exam or having a secret stash of weed in his bedroom.

'Oh God, Charlie. Seriously? You spoke to Kelly?' Daniel checked the hallway, then stepped back into the kitchen, pushing the door closed behind him.

'No! I mean... yes, I spoke to her. I couldn't help myself. She still means... I dunno. But look, I didn't tell her any details, I promise.'

'Okay, so then there's nothing to worry about. Right?'

Charlie swallowed, his eyes failing to meet Daniel's.

'Right?'

'I... I mean... I didn't give her any details, but I may have accidentally sort of mentioned about the murders being committed by the same killers. And that they were both night-time break-ins where nothing was stolen.'

'Well, shit, okay. Not great, but still. A journo could have guessed that. It's not a major leap for her to have come to that conclusion on her own. That it?' Daniel asked. That didn't sound too bad, but he needed to know what he was dealing with, needed to be sure of his story if he was going to cover for Charlie's stupidity.

'Yes. I think so. I feel so shit. I didn't even want to speak to her. She phoned me from a new number, caught me off guard. I got rid of her pretty quickly but...' Charlie couldn't finish the sentence.

Daniel sighed. Since he'd moved to London less than a year previously, he hadn't really made any new friends. Charlie was pretty much Daniel's whole London social circle, other than Amelia, and she was his junior, not someone he could easily be friends with outside work. He hated lying, hated deceiving others, but he knew he would for Charlie. They had to work so closely together, had already been through so much. They were like brothers.

'I don't want to know all the details – just don't do it again. We don't need the extra pressure. Okay?' He shrugged, trying to make light of the situation. What could they do but deal with it and get on with things? 'And do what Hobbs said – keep your mouth shut, you dickhead.'

Charlie couldn't help laughing, the stress busting out of him with a cough. 'Thanks, mate. I mean it. See you down there.'

Daniel left the kitchen, heading for his desk to grab a smarter shirt while mentally preparing himself for the morning press conference. Great. He had two double homicides and an awkward information leak to the press that he would have to pretend he knew nothing about.

'Living the dream,' he muttered, nervous about what lay ahead.

CHAPTER NINE

I t was official. London was dealing with a psychotic killer, one who was breaking into people's houses in the middle of the night, killing them, then mutilating their bodies. Well, that was what almost every national news outlet across the UK was saying, some international ones too. None had yet mentioned two killers. That was something. A hotline had been set up and was being staffed by five people. Witness testimonies had begun to flood in, and the meeting room they had taken over was awash with printouts of recorded calls, highlighter pens and laptops with further digital records. Amelia liked the tangibility of printouts best, though.

Despite DI Graves' opinion that hotlines were a waste of time once the press got hold of a story, he had made funds for this available, on the direct order of Superintendent Hobbs. After Amelia had informed Graves that the religious angle had not taken them anywhere, she had found herself working on the hotline, unenthusiastically reading accounts given by a combination of fame-hungry idiots, people with too much time on their hands, and those who were genuinely trying to help but giving utterly useless information, slowing things down even further.

'This is a nightmare,' Hayes complained, echoing her thoughts with impeccable timing. 'I mean, listen to this.' He did bunny ears in the air as he read out a quote. 'I saw a white van circulating the area a lot over the past few days. Everyone knows what white vans mean. People use them to look inconspicuous, but I spotted it a mile away. I saw a man get out and inspect a drain yesterday evening. It was dark and I couldn't see his face, but he didn't look legit. That's why I called. He drove away after, but I reckon only because I saw him.'

'And?' Amelia asked.

'And all the bloody residents had received letters from Thames Water two days before telling them that drain inspections were going to be carried out! At the end of the transcript this idiot even concedes that he may have seen the Thames Water logo on the van!' Hayes tutted and threw the printout of the call down onto the pile in front of him. 'Waste of bollocking time.'

Amelia couldn't help but sympathise. She didn't love this part of the job, and she had acted just as Hayes was now the first few times she had been tasked with going through witness accounts. She didn't want to do it any more than he did. Neither did the other sergeants. She also knew that sometimes it worked. She felt a teachable moment coming on, and couldn't resist the chance to seize it.

'Look, Ross, I get it, I do. It's not the most fun job and it often seems pointless. You want to be out there solving crimes, arresting people. Trust me, I know the feeling. But no case is solved by one person in isolation. Cases get cracked because of teamwork. Sure, hotlines often don't amount to much, but what about the times when they have? What if in the pile in front of you is a genuine witness account by someone who actually saw something, and we missed it because we dismissed the whole lot as nonsense? It could mean the difference between catching a killer and another body turning up. So let's stick at it, okay?'

Ross rolled his eyes as Amelia smiled her best inspirational-teacher smile, but he sighed and picked up the next transcript. One of the other sergeants smirked, but Amelia let herself bask. It was a shame none of her superiors had caught the moment but still, she felt good. And maybe she would be right. Maybe someone would call in with a legitimately useful piece of information. Feeling instantly more motivated at the thought that this could be her second chance to find something and impress Graves and Palmer, Amelia took a handful of papers from her pile and began to flick through them with gusto.

It had been three days since the Rhodes couple had been found dead, and the team had made no headway. The crime scene had been fully canvassed, neighbours had been grilled, traffic cameras had been pored over, and every single statement that had come into the hotline had been checked.

For a brief moment Daniel Graves thought they had something when they saw footage of a suspicious pair of figures hanging around on the Brixton Road, not far from the Altons' house. The footage showed two men, both in dark clothing, with wool hats and gloves on, talking to each other but constantly surveying the street around them. The video timecode placed them at just gone two in the morning, so the timeline had fit roughly and their behaviour had definitely warranted a deeper dive, given their visible nerves. Everyone was eager to start looking through footage from CCTV around the Rhodes address. But things didn't go the way they hoped. They had traced the men's movements via a number of traffic cams, and this had given the suspects an alibi. They seemed to want to keep their relationship secret; they had emerged from a house three roads away and finally parted ways with a quick but intimate kiss at a bus stop a minute from where they had been standing.

So far the killers seemed to have evaded being caught on camera – or at least had managed to blend in enough not to look suspicious. There were no cameras on the roads where the Alton and Rhodes couples had lived, and even in the middle of the night both areas saw a number of pedestrians and a wide variety of vehicles passing by. It was London: there were truck drivers, drunk revellers, late-night dog walkers, even a few joggers. It would not have been hard for the killers to have walked nonchalantly past a camera in regular, non-bloodstained clothing or to have driven away in a nondescript, unremarkable car. It made Graves sick to think that perhaps they did have footage of who they were looking for but just couldn't pick the murderers out. Three assistants in the tech team had been asked to create a database of all individuals and vehicles caught on the hours of footage around the suspected times of death. They hoped to spot either a person or vehicle on more than one camera. Without a miracle, however, Daniel did not expect much. The killers, even though they had been brutal at the crime scenes, seemed to have been very careful otherwise, leaving no trace of themselves.

It was time for Charlie and Daniel to step away from finding a suspect and instead narrow down a profile of the person – or persons – who could have committed the homicides. They also still had to try and find a connection between the victims.

Once again, Martia Franklin had been brought in to help. She normally was with such violent cases. Martia was an extremely successful psychological and criminal profiler from

Texas; she still had a soft accent, which had not dissipated after more than ten years in the UK. Her track record was second to none. Daniel had worked with her before. She had assisted with the demonology case that had plagued the Homicide and Serious Crime Command only a few months ago.

Martia looked different to the last time Daniel had seen her: her hair had changed from a severe bob to a longer, softer style, with shades of honey filtering in to what had been a uniform dark brown. Martia was still all business, though, her more relaxed appearance not echoed in her personality. She was not the type to joke around in general, and especially not when on the hunt for a murderer.

'First off, we're dealing with a sociopath,' she announced, stony-faced. Detectives never liked to hear those words, and Daniel let out a sigh. Cases became so much more difficult when extreme personality types were involved.

'I'm guessing you aren't surprised at this, Graves,' she continued. Daniel shook his head.

'I can also tell you that, as you suspected, it's extremely unlikely that we're only dealing with one killer.'

That confirms the other thing I didn't want to hear, Daniel thought.

'Because it'd require more than one person to nail a body to the wall, right?' Charlie said, glancing back at Daniel with a told-you-so look. Charlie sat in a swivel chair, looking – to Daniel – far too relaxed, given the conversation. He looked as though he was ready for a cigar and whisky, not to discuss what type of person could tear body parts out of other human beings and take them home like souvenirs from a museum gift shop.

'More because I believe that the killings themselves are not the main reason these people have been targeted,' Martia said, again utterly matter-of-fact.

'What makes you think that?' Daniel asked, sitting up in his chair, not sure how Martia could have come to such a conclusion just yet. It was something he had thought about, but neither scene showed any evidence of anything being taken, or even searched for. Both houses had remained untouched. No belongings had been ransacked. Ostensibly the killers had entered both properties with the clear intention of ending lives.

'We know that our intruders broke into each house in a calm, collected manner, correct? There was no evidence of forced entry at either crime scene. Looks like the break-ins were premeditated. They had to have known and exploited weak spots in security – a window left open, keys under plant pots and such. It is well known that sociopaths are often impulsive and easily agitated. They have less tendency to spend time planning their kills, weighing up their options, and they show less constraint and caution. Yet, as I said, they got into both houses without causing any damage. We found no broken glass, no cracked window frames or drilled-out locks.'

She paused. Daniel and Charlie looked at her expectantly. It was one hell of a carrot to dangle. She had just told them they were looking for a sociopath, then in the next breath said that a sociopath wouldn't have broken into the victims' houses without leaving a trace. The air in the room suddenly felt heavier. It reminded Daniel of the way incoming storms could feel electric against the skin, a sign of something big coming. Even Martia's voice seemed to take on more gravitas as she continued.

'The bodies were moved, displayed in a clumsy way. The injuries showed very little precision or constraint but were made with clear aspirations towards the grandiose – so yes, that leads to sociopath. Granted, sociopaths are often extremely intelligent and calculating, but the type of person who would show this level of brutality is not the type of person who would plan this sort of break-in. And yes, the crime scenes were messy, but with blood, not with evidence left by the people who committed these crimes. Therefore I believe that one person is a sociopath – the person creating the horrible artworks of bodies – and another person is helping them. That person has an ulterior motive. I believe that the murders are only one half of the picture.'

'So one person kills the victims and the other takes something? Or looks for information or something specific? But the houses showed no signs of being searched,' Charlie said.

Martia nodded. 'The information they're looking for doesn't need to be material, though. And the first victims showed signs of torture.'

'Wait, though – isn't being calculated and committing crimes in such a carefully thought-out manner a classic sign of a psychopath?' Daniel asked. Could a sociopath and a psychopath work together? he wondered. It was a terrifying prospect.

'You're right – psychopaths tend to plan in meticulous detail. Their need for precision nearly always carries over into the way they deal with their victims, and there was no precision whatsoever in the Alton and Rhodes murders in terms of how they were killed. They were messy, impulsive, almost haphazard, before the bodies were posed. Which leads me back to two people again, one of whom is sociopathic. The second – well, they could be psychopathic. That's a possibility.'

Everyone in the room fell silent.

'What about the taking of body parts?' Daniel asked. It was an unusual twist to the case, to put it mildly. Katy Rhodes' eyes were missing; they had been taken as brutally as Henry Alton's heart had been stolen. Once could be seen as isolated, but twice was the start of a pattern.

'I believe these were taken as trophies – a way for our killers to prolong whatever fantasy they're playing out with these murders, or as a way to commemorate each murder. It's pretty sadistic, though, and not that common. It's far more usual for killers to take trophies in the form of personal items. But it could also be another way to make the kills more grandiose, an effort to make a true statement. I think it makes whoever we're dealing with more dangerous,' Martia concluded.

That last sentence floated around Daniel's mind. He knew they were up against it, knew they had to catch these people quickly. To hear it from Martia just made it all the more real. The case was a first for Daniel: a hunt for a sociopathic serial killer who was getting help from someone with a calculated, clearly intelligent approach to crime – a possible psychopath. They needed to connect some more dots, and fast, before the killers struck again.

———

Daniel and Charlie left the office for a breather, needing some fresh air and a change from the stifling oppression of their task force room. Daniel still felt the sting of Superintendent Hobbs' admonishment too, and the regular mentions of the case on just about every news network across the UK didn't help. The murders had caught the public imagination, and every outlet and publication seemed to be trying to get in on the action.

They headed to one of their favourites, Café Fresco, just a few minutes' walk from the Metropolitan Police headquarters. Daniel was thankful that it was after the lunch hour rush. The café felt like an oasis of calm. For a few minutes, at least, they managed not to talk about the case. Charlie waxed lyrical about a woman he was sort of seeing, a twenty-six-year-old called Molly, apparently a social media specialist from Newcastle. Daniel half listened while internally debating the pros and cons of having a salad versus an all-day breakfast with his coffee, idly pushing grains of sugar around the tabletop with one finger. He wasn't eating much. He'd had a browning banana and half a tasteless granola bar, but nothing else. Daniel had always been skinny, so he rarely felt guilty at choosing an unhealthy food option. Not having eaten much swayed him even further towards the full English. He looked out at the cold, dreary afternoon beyond the café windows and opted for comfort food.

As Charlie filled him in on how his second date with the leggy marketeer had gone, Daniel found his mind drifting to Jenny Cartwright. The word 'date' had made him feel sad. From what he had known of her, Jenny had been a vibrant, magnetic woman. He had met her at work – she had been a tattoo artist at a studio called Needlepoint Ink, and he and Charlie had been investigating a case involving a murder victim covered in tattoos and a suspect who was connected to the industry. The second he had locked eyes with Jenny he had felt something. The ground had become unstable under his feet, and he'd felt a sudden, unexpected wave of attraction to Jenny – a feeling he hadn't experienced since he'd met his last serious girlfriend, almost three years before he had moved to London.

Throughout the case Jenny had been a key source of information – which, as it turned out, had put her life in danger. Attacked by the killer, Jenny had barely escaped with her life. But she had. She had been safe. All she had needed was a little time. They had agreed that, since the case was over, they'd arrange a date.

And then the gift had shown up at Daniel's door. Beautifully wrapped, complete with a bow, but with the most horrible of surprises inside. The gift that plagued Daniel's dreams and swiftly turned them into nightmares. The gift had been Jenny's heart, taken neatly out of her chest.

What is it with cutting out hearts? An image of the messy hole in Henry Alton's chest flashed into his mind. It turned his stomach.

'... spoke to Kelly, by the way,' Charlie was saying, clearly oblivious to the fact that Daniel had tuned out. The mention of the woman's name snapped Daniel back to the present, thoughts of Jenny and hearts quickly fading as the café counter behind his partner came back into view.

'Did I hear that correctly? What do you mean, you spoke to her? Jesus, Charlie, how stupid are you?'

For a second Charlie looked insulted, then resigned. 'Hang on, I know what you're thinking but don't worry. I just wanted to find out if she knew anything else – if she was withholding any information for another story.'

'And?' Daniel asked, not entirely buying his explanation. Charlie and Kelly's relationship was clearly not history. Daniel was concerned for his friend, and about how this could complicate their work further.

'And, well... I wanted an apology from her, to be honest. For giving us a shitload more issues to deal with because of her stupid story. And for making me look like an idiot again.'

'What did she say?' In his head Daniel could hear Kelly fobbing Charlie off, flirting to distract him before dismissing him. He didn't know much about the woman, but even from when he'd seen her at the crime scene in Camberwell it was clear she knew she still had some power over Charlie. He felt sure she would use it, given the opportunity.

'Well, I didn't get an apology, that's for sure. Not that I was really expecting one, but still...'

'She really did a number on you, didn't she?' Daniel said. Charlie stared vacantly at the lunch menu before tossing it aside. He nodded, not looking up.

'Look, she's a ruthlessly ambitious journalist who you know from experience puts her career first. She's always going to go for the story, right? I don't mean to be harsh, but that might have been the reason she showed interest in you in the first place. Sure, you're a handsome guy, nice too, but maybe she just wanted the inside scoop and was willing to sleep with you to get it. If she didn't think she could get what she wanted from you, she might have tried it on with someone else in our line of work. But even if not, it's all done. You told her too much in the past, she ran a story and you got in trouble. You spoke to her again and we both got yelled at. So what have you learned? Avoid her! You need to let all positive feelings for her go and just accept the fact that she could be the type of person who will use whoever she wants to get what she wants. We aren't going to catch our killers if you're moping about over her.'

Charlie frowned at the tough love, but Daniel stood by what he had said. Charlie needed to get over Kelly, and fast. Their jobs were complicated enough without having to continually factor her in. Plus, Daniel had already told Hobbs that neither he nor Charlie would utter a single word to another journalist, beyond 'no comment', unless Hobbs specifically asked them to.

'If you speak to her again, I'll kick your arse myself. You know I can.'

With a raised eyebrow, Charlie laughed. The gloom eased. 'You can try. But yes, you're right, of course.'

'You've got the looks – it's only fair I have the brains.' Daniel smiled, glad that Charlie hadn't screwed up again. They couldn't afford any more information leaking to the press.

After they had ordered – a full English for Daniel and an unwanted but needed chicken panini for Charlie – the chat naturally found its way back to the case at hand. The mental break from it all had not lasted long in the end.

'I can't help thinking about a sociopath and a psychopath working together. What's their motive?' Charlie said.

'God knows, but given what they have already accomplished, I'm nervous at what might come next. Are they only going after couples? Is the home invasion angle deliberate? And then there's the religious subtext to the way the bodies were left. Maybe they're not choosing the victims because of religion, but the pseudo-crucifixion, the praying position – they might not be totally coincidental.'

'It's a mess, huh? And we have nothing to go on. Hobbs is going to rip us a new one if we don't hook onto something soon.'

The words hung in the air. Both men were contemplating their next steps as their late lunch arrived. As they ate, they were silent. Daniel shovelled down his food, giving his mind a few minutes off. Charlie picked at his panini, pulling pieces of chicken and cheese from out of the bread.

'I really want to know how they're selecting the victims. We need to get ahead of them. Amelia and Ross haven't found anything useful yet, have they?' Charlie asked hopefully after giving up on his food entirely.

Daniel shook his head as he swallowed his last forkful of bacon and beans. 'Nope. Amelia's built up a little team and they're looking under every stone for connections, but so far the couples seem to have lived totally unrelated lives.'

'And how the hell did the killers get into the houses without anyone noticing? No broken windows or forced locks. Did they have spare keys or what? They must be picking the locks – or God, maybe even be sneaking in and hiding while the victims were awake.'

Again Daniel shook his head. He couldn't answer that question definitively. No one could. It was starting to become a pattern, and it was frustrating as hell.

The loud honk of a car horn outside, followed by swearing, caught Daniel's attention. He looked out through the rain-dappled glass to find the source of the commotion. Then he saw something else – something past the angry cyclist, who was still waving a fist in the air at the vehicle that had honked. He saw a sign attached to a vacant-looking office building.

'Are you done?' Daniel nodded at Charlie's plate.

'I guess so. Not really feeling it.'

'Then we're out of here.'

Charlie raised his eyebrows. 'We are?'

'Yep. I think I might know how they're getting into the houses.'

The pair threw some cash down on the table, thanked the woman behind the café counter and sped out into the grey afternoon.

CHAPTER TEN

'West Kensington is such a nice area. Have you been looking for a place long?' the young man in the oversized suit asked as he dug in his coat pocket for the keys. He was visibly awkward, his short blond hair heavily gelled and his cheeks flushed.

Evening was encroaching. The wind whipped around them, ripping leaves off the poor battered maple that was trying to survive in the front garden.

The estate agent had introduced himself as Malcolm Hartly. He had launched into a barrage of chat about himself, the estate agents and the area the second they met him. Now he looked at them with anticipation for an answer to his question as he held up the front door key.

'Not long, no, but we like the area so we thought we'd start here.' Daniel put a hand on Charlie's arm and gave him a loving smile before looking back at Malcolm, on whose face a sudden new understanding had dawned.

'Well, it's a really nice part of London. And it's not too hard to get to Soho and the nightlife and stuff from here either.'

Daniel couldn't help smirking at Malcolm's awkwardness

but quickly regained his composure. He wanted to stay in character. He and Charlie had decided that it would be easier to pretend they were looking at properties rather than reveal their true intentions. They didn't want another leak to the press, especially one with details about a possible line of investigation. They hadn't even told their colleagues about it, in case they were wrong. Since articles about the murders had been plastered across the country, they knew that even the smallest amount of information would be irresistible to the hungry sharks desperate for more headlines. There was a constant press presence outside their offices, hounding everyone coming and going from the building. They had decided to pretend to be a couple looking for a new home, an innocent cover story that seemed to be working.

'Good to know, although we're not really the party types,' Charlie answered, his voice dry as a bone and his stern face giving nothing away.

Malcolm offered a weak smile. 'Shall we, then?' He turned quickly to the door, away from Charlie's gaze, fumbling the key in the lock. Daniel felt sorry for the bloke. It wasn't going well for him so far.

Inside the house was pleasant enough, with bare floorboards, mostly mark-free white walls and a dated but pristine kitchen. Malcolm pointed out the period moulding that ran around the ceiling in the living room, showed them that the water pressure was good, and mentioned the council tax banding. Daniel and Charlie simply nodded and made mildly enthusiastic comments until they had the opportunity to ditch Malcolm, using the excuse of having a few minutes to themselves to walk around again. They immediately went back upstairs to the master bedroom, which looked out over the main road.

'Well, well, well. If you aren't a smarty pants,' Charlie said as they peered out of the window. 'You can see pretty much the whole house – probably through the windows too when it's dark and there are lights on.'

'Exactly. Malcolm said the tenant just moved out a few days ago, after having only been in for a week. That's not normal renting behaviour. Our killers could have stood right here.' As he spoke, Daniel turned and scanned the empty room they stood in.

To most people who looked at it, it contained nothing of real interest. Mildly dusty wooden floors, bare walls, a pair of plain but decent curtains. Daniel, however, saw a room – a house, in fact – that would need to be locked down and searched from top to bottom for anything that would give them a clue to the identity of their killers. Strands of hair, skin cells, fingerprints, remnants of fabric and possibly more.

'If we're right about this theory, then our suspects must have spent a decent amount of time in this room. Surveying, coming up with a strategy, watching their victims. They might well have left something behind,' Daniel said, silently praying to himself that this was true.

'I think we're going to need to burst poor Malcolm's bubble. We need a team in here immediately.'

Excitement rushed over Daniel. His mind whirled. The new lead was painfully tantalising. 'Can you call them in? I'll let Malcolm and the estate agent know what's going on, get some NDAs signed.'

Charlie was on it instantly. He was already on the phone when Daniel headed downstairs to find Malcolm and break the news. The vacant house that the poor chap had hoped to rent out was now a possible crime scene.

Amelia Harding had left work for the day, taken the Tube home to Brixton and was browsing in Tesco, looking for dinner inspiration. She had only chosen some pasta and a Diet Coke when something started to niggle at her.

She and Ross had been given an update on the case, knew about the rented property near the Altons' house. They had temporarily shifted their focus away from finding connections between the victims and the ever-growing collection of supposed witness testimonials that had flooded the department since the release of Kelly Malone's story. Instead they had started to look into rentals and vacant properties in the West Kensington area, close to Katie and Lawrence Rhodes' house. They hoped there would be a place on the same street as the Rhodes house that had said goodbye to a tenant in the last few days, and therefore could have been a temporary den for their killers.

But the search had turned up nothing, with no houses for rent in any of the surrounding streets. This had felt like a real kick in the teeth. Just as they were getting somewhere, just as Graves and Palmer had turned up a juicy potential lead and everyone was eager to see where it would get them, it seemed to die again. Of course, if they were lucky they'd find trace evidence at the Kensington rental house, if their theory was correct, but locking down a pattern would have been a truly solid piece of intel. She had been chewing on it since she had started home and now, standing in the supermarket, her brain was trying to tell her something.

As she scanned the biscuits section, spotting a pack of Oreos she knew she shouldn't have but wanted anyway, Amelia went over her afternoon in as much detail as she could. She thought back through all the statements she had looked over, conversations she had had, even what she'd eaten for lunch, looking for something that would trigger her subconscious into revealing what it was hiding.

A few minutes later, eating an Oreo, Amelia was walking back to her flat when she almost collided with a scaffolding pole that stuck out onto the pavement over the kebab shop.

'Scaffolding...' she muttered, glancing up at the metal frame. Something stirred at the back of her mind. She stopped and turned back, her gaze moving up the building to rest on the windows of the flat above the takeaway. It hit her like a slap to the face.

Earlier in the day Amelia had been reading yet another unhelpful statement. The man questioned had been certain he had seen nothing, because he couldn't have. While he had been visiting the house when questioned, he was not currently residing in his property. It was about to be replastered, repainted and fitted with a new bathroom, and he didn't want to live in it while the work was going on. He had suggested asking the decorators if they had seen anything odd in the area, but maintained that he couldn't help. He'd then asked to be left alone; he was concerned about journalists hassling him, because he lived on the same street as the Rhodes couple.

'Same street, empty...' Amelia whipped around and ran for her flat, clutching her Tesco bag, all thoughts of dinner forgotten. As soon as she was through the front door she threw her shopping onto the kitchen worktop and phoned DI Graves.

'Sir, thank God I got through to you. I think we may be able to prove the pattern after all.'

It had taken far too long to get a warrant, and thus access, to the house in West Kensington. Daniel's blood was bubbling with anticipation, his heart beating faster than normal. The property owner Mark Arby, a stubborn, entitled middle-aged man, had done his best to stop them, claiming that he would lose money on the renovations if the police took up camp in his house.

After Amelia had called him the previous night about the empty property Arby had mentioned, Daniel had wanted to act on the news immediately. He didn't care about the time or that he was exhausted. In fact, the call had been like a caffeine shot into his vein. To his chagrin, his wish to inspect the house right away had been rejected by Mark Arby, and Hobbs and the CSI team. There were processes they had to carry out, legalities that had to be considered, paperwork to sign off. Daniel knew that, of course. He wasn't the kind of detective to go off book and flout the law, but it still pissed him off. To have to wait all morning and a good chunk of the afternoon was infuriating.

'Finally!' he groaned. They were at Mark Arby's front door. He pushed it open. A waft of wood dust and the scent of fresh paint billowed over him and Charlie, who stood expectantly behind him.

Arby himself had made an appearance, with one of his lawyers in tow, evidently keen on making sure his property was not compromised in any way. He looked exactly as Daniel had imagined: rotund with a red nose and receding white hair, dressed impeccably in a light-grey suit, white shirt and racing green tie. He looked rich and cocky. When he attempted to follow them inside, Charlie blocked him.

'I'm sorry, Mr Arby, but we need to survey the premises and find out if our suspicions are correct. If they are, the house will be closed off as an active crime scene. You cannot enter in case you compromise evidence.'

Charlie was a tall man with broad shoulders, but for a second Daniel thought that Arby might simply try to force his way past. With much blustering and huffing, he finally stepped back. Charlie smiled cordially and he and Daniel headed upstairs, two CSI techs accompanying them. They already knew what they were looking for: a room with a clear view of the house where Katie and Lawrence Rhodes had been killed. It didn't take them long to find one.

Unlike the vacant house they had seen the day before, Arby's property was furnished. The spare bedroom was large. The double bed, chest of drawers, wardrobe, rug and other paraphernalia had been piled into the centre of the room and covered in dust sheets, making the space feel crowded. Daniel could see the Rhodes house clearly from the window and felt a mixture of excitement and upset, sure now that again the victims had been watched before they were murdered. The idea of voyeurism had always got under his skin. He shivered.

'So we have the right room, but it's a tip.' Charlie shook his head. 'There's dust everywhere, multiple footprints from the decorators...'

'Don't worry,' one of the CSIs said. 'We'll catalogue everything we find. The other team are keeping us updated on the first house so we'll be able to cross-reference anything that stands out.'

To Daniel, she sounded a little too hopeful. He couldn't see how they could pick out anything from the mess around them – but then, she was the expert. He decided to stay positive. He and Charlie would have to trust the process and keep their fingers crossed.

'Well, I think we can assume that if the Rhodes couple were being watched, this house was the one the killers used. It's the only empty place on the street and it has a direct line of sight to their property. Let's get on to the decorators and get some statements, find out if they noticed anything. It probably wouldn't be that hard for our killers to get inside when the house was empty overnight, but maybe they moved something, left something behind, broke a lock.' Daniel's mind was racing.

'Agreed, otherwise where does this get us?' Charlie said as they stepped into the upstairs hallway. 'We can't put a squad in every empty house in London, and we don't have any connections between the victims yet.'

Daniel didn't want to admit it, but Charlie was right. They needed to find consistent evidence of the intruders in the vacant houses, otherwise they would be out of leads again. He didn't want to think about that though, not yet.

'Phone me as soon as you find anything, okay?' Daniel called back to the CSI woman who, with her partner, had started to inspect the room. She nodded and gave him a thumbs-up before switching her focus back to the task at hand.

Evidently eavesdropping from downstairs, Mark Arby called up to them. 'Are you done, Detectives? Can I have my house back now, please?'

Daniel and Charlie made their way downstairs. When they reached the front door, Daniel ushered Arby backwards down the short front path. 'I'm afraid not. We will need to close off the property while we conduct our investigation.'

'And we'll need contact details for the decorators,' Charlie added.

Visibly ruffled, Arby turned to his lawyer, ready to argue. The lawyer, a thin, tired-looking man in his early fifties, simply nodded at the detectives. There was no argument he could make. The house was considered to be a potential crime scene, and there was nothing they could do but wait until the police had finished their work.

'Fine...' Arby muttered. 'But you'll be paying for any damage!' he threw in at the last moment.

Daniel and Charlie headed past him, ignoring him.

CHAPTER ELEVEN

The case was at a temporary standstill. Daniel Graves could do nothing but wait – wait to get statements, wait to be told if anything useful had been uncovered at the crime scenes, wait to see if the voyeur pattern could be backed up with evidence, wait for the bodies to show up clues that could point them in the direction of the killers. Silver lining, though, he thought. He had finished work before day ticked over into night.

Daniel got back to his flat just after seven thirty in the evening. He was exhausted and frustrated, and the warm lights and sense of relief he felt at being home were a refreshing change from the cold, hostile world outside his front door. He had even managed to pass the threshold without thinking of the gift he had found on the step a few months ago. It was a rare day when he didn't look at the top step to check if another package had been left for him, filled with something horrifying. He'd even considered moving house, but for now things were okay. He was coping.

He had been ignoring his personal phone messages for the afternoon. When he grabbed a cold can of Kronenbourg and a plate of chicken salad from his fridge, he saw that Rachel Callahan had texted him. Rachel could always perk up his day. He still missed working with her – missed her in general, in fact. He smiled before even reading the message, and was ready to call her when he spotted another text. The sender was Amanda Graves. His sister.

Daniel's relationship with Amanda was complicated in many ways. Some of those ways were obvious and on the surface but some swam around underneath, only ever half glimpsed.

Things had been strained after the day Amanda had been attacked. The positive of Daniel saving her from being raped had been painfully undermined by him killing her attacker in the process. At the same instant, Daniel had become a saviour and a killer. It was something he and Amanda had both struggled with since. They had so many unresolved emotions – emotions that had been pushed down and diluted over the years but had never really been examined and dealt with, despite numerous sessions with therapists.

Amanda had never forgiven herself for allowing things to play out the way they had. She had told anyone who asked that she should never have fallen for Adam Spencer. She admitted she should never have been naive enough not to see how violent he could be. She felt most strongly about the statement that she should never have dragged Daniel into it and come close to ruining his life too.

Of course, no one but Amanda blamed her for those things. Daniel did not resent her. He was glad he had done everything he could to protect his sibling. The case against him had been thrown out as a clear example of self-defence by a minor, especially given Adam Spencer's volatile history, and in fact the incident had shaped Daniel's life in many positive ways. He had decided to join the police force as a direct result of that day. Despite his nightmares, his fading, but ever-present, feelings of guilt for taking a life, and his natural, but stronger than average, aversion to death, Daniel had been able to move on. Counselling had enabled him to cope with some of the tougher issues that had plagued him, to show him the good that had come out of it. Amanda had even acknowledged more than once that Daniel was likely a better man because of what they had been through.

Nevertheless, the close relationship that brother and sister had once cherished had been damaged. Small cracks had appeared after the incident, harmless by themselves but adding up to more than the sum of their parts, growing slowly bigger over the following months. Time had not healed the wounds inflicted on the family. Now Amanda barely spoke to her big brother, only getting in touch to pass on information about one of their parents or to wish him a happy birthday. Outwardly she was not exactly a fragile woman but if anyone looked closely they could still see the residual effects of what had happened to her. She distrusted men and was suspicious of new people. Her romantic relationships all ended in issues surrounding trust and intimacy. She had grown adept at keeping everything well hidden and for the most part had succeeded in being a happy, friendly person, but she had never quite managed to overcome what Adam had put her through.

And of course when she looked at her brother, even spoke to him, Adam's attack and resulting death played like a video in her head, a scene torn from a horror film. Daniel found that the same was true for him too, to a lesser extent. He found it difficult to be alone with his sister.

The message notification on the home screen of his phone just showed his sister's name, not the content of her message – a setting he had chosen so that no one could read his messages without unlocking his phone. With some trepidation Daniel unlocked the screen. Amanda's message was longer than he had expected – and surprisingly emotive. As he read what his sister had texted out of the blue, he was shocked to realise that tears were welling in his eyes.

Hey Dan – sorry, I know it's been a while. I saw your name in the paper again today about the case – the home invasions. It's so horrible. It made me think about all the stuff you must have to go through every day, all the horrid cases. Here I am stressing out over hiring new interns and dealing with my nightmare boss, yet you're hunting a killer.

Then I realised I never say how proud of you I am for what you do. Stopping people like... God, I still can't type his name even now, can you believe that? I went on your Facebook page after I read about the case, just to see what you're up to. You know you haven't posted anything in months? I don't know anything about what's going on in your life. I bet you don't know about mine either. It made me feel a little sick, to be honest. And I know it upsets Mum that we aren't close any more. I should have called, really. I guess I thought you would be too busy, but I'm probably just using that as an excuse. I think though, now more than ever, Mum and Dad getting older... we need to get back to some sort of relationship, Dan. When they're gone – well, it doesn't bear thinking about it, but you know what I mean. Anyway, as I said, I know you're probably totally caught up in the case but if you get a minute... I'd love to hear your voice again. Love you. Speak soon. A x

The messaged blurred as Daniel read it again, then he put the phone down, needing to wipe his eyes. He took a deep breath, then a swig of beer, as though he could swallow the feelings that were forcing their way up and out of him. It was somehow exactly what he needed at that moment, as though Amanda had sensed when would be best to contact him. He loved his sister. It wasn't an olive branch situation; they had never fallen out. It was, however, a huge leap forward: a message with a huge amount of power.

As he took his beer and salad to the sofa, Daniel felt genuinely shaken. He took another gulp of beer and stared at the blank television across the room. Whatever appetite he'd had seemed to have evaporated, and he let the salad go untouched.

Realising he had not answered Rachel, he messaged her to see if she was free and got a response to call her tomorrow. That wasn't what he wanted, but maybe it would do him good to let the message from his sister sit with him for a while.

The flat was silent – too silent. A sudden painful feeling of loneliness washed over Daniel. He wasn't ready to call Amanda, though, even though he was happy she had called. He wanted to let what she had said sit with him, he wanted some space to see how he truly felt about it. And as for others he could discuss his sister with – well, the list was small. One of his parents or Rachel. Technically, Charlie too, but Daniel felt he should give his colleague the night off from listening to him. He knew his parents would just get emotional if he told them what Amanda had said, and he wasn't in the mood for that either.

In a bid to add some sound to his world he switched on the television, choosing an old episode of *Friends*. Only half paying attention, his thoughts elsewhere, it didn't take long for him to start scrolling through Facebook on his phone. A few minutes later he found himself looking at Jenny Cartwright's memorial page. It wasn't even really deliberate, more an action formed out of habit. He knew the page hadn't changed in weeks.

Until now.

Daniel sat up straight. There was a new post by a clearly fake account. He instantly recognised Jenny's bluebird tattoo in the user's profile picture: the tattoo that had been cut from her body and sent to Daniel in a neatly wrapped box. Beneath it were just a few words, but they shook Daniel to his core.

Never forget, DG. I know I haven't.

CHAPTER TWELVE

A yane Matsuda slumped down on the plush sofa, a fluffy maroon cushion wedged behind her, and rested her bare feet on the coffee table. She frowned at her skinny jeans. She wished she had remembered to pack pyjamas. The trip had been a bit last minute, however, and she hadn't had much time to sort her suitcase.

'Daisy, do you have any sweats I can borrow?' she shouted, hoping her friend could hear her. A muffled yes came from somewhere upstairs and Ayane sipped her wine, relaxing.

The flight had been a nightmare. A toddler had been sitting behind her and had insisted on climbing up the back of her seat for nearly the entire journey from LAX. The two hours of interrupted sleep she had got were barely enough to keep her awake, but lazing in Daisy's living room with a large glass of wine and a plate of the best Brie she'd ever tasted was helping.

'You really did good, girl.' She smiled as she took in her surroundings. And it was true – Daisy really had done well for herself.

The women had met at USC Gould while studying law. Even though Daisy was only in California for a year as an exchange student, she and Ayane had quickly become close friends and in the ten years since they had kept in touch. Daisy had visited Los Angeles four times, Ayane had reciprocated with three trips to London, and they'd had numerous other holidays together across the world. Ayane actually considered Daisy a closer friend than most of those she had back home, despite seeing her less regularly.

Ayane had moved into public interest law after graduating, keen to follow in her mother's footsteps. Mitsuko Matsuda, while not academic, had always been a true community figure, both in Osaka and later in Los Angeles. Ayane had witnessed the respect and adoration her mother had gained in both parts of the world. Mitsuko had taken moving with her husband and young daughter to America in her stride, championing fundraising and community projects in her new home even when Santa Ana was unfamiliar and alien. She had gone on to win handfuls of awards, be featured in the press on a number of occasions and had even met the mayor of Los Angeles, but more importantly she was a cherished member of the community that she adored. Now that Mitsuko was effectively retired, Ayane was proud to continue her tradition of helping those around her. There was one downside, though. It didn't pay like Daisy's job clearly did. The house Ayane now sat in was proof of that.

Daisy's new home was actually one of the reasons Ayane was visiting. They had talked about being homeowners for years, both determined not still to be renting or living with their parents in their thirties. Daisy had bought a house in Hampstead, next to the golf club and park. Ayane didn't want to think about how much it was worth, and so far had resisted asking. It was a detached three-bed property that had just been renovated. It was stunning. Compared with Ayane's tiny apartment in Anaheim, it was a palace.

'I really should have followed your career path,' Ayane said as Daisy joined her in the living room, her dirty blonde hair piled up on her head in a bun. Daisy threw a pair of lavender jogging bottoms at her friend and went about lighting the candles on the fireplace mantel.

'Don't be silly. What you do is way more important than what I do. I just help rich people get richer and take a cut. I got most of the money for this place from working on some massive land buyout deal for a ridiculously wealthy businessman. It's caused shitloads of drama, thanks to the closure of an old library and social club on the land. It's like the exact opposite of what you do. I've helped people pull communities apart, watching them gentrify areas and fill them with delis and yoga studios.'

The scent of burnt matches filtered through the room, then was followed by the mixed berry aroma of the candles.

'Yeah, true, but look what you get as a result! I may get more points in the afterlife but I wouldn't mind swapping on occasion if I got a place like this.' Ayane stood and raised her glass. 'On that note, let's do an official cheers to you and the house.'

Daisy picked up her wine glass from the coffee table and they clinked glasses. 'God, who would have thought? This lil girl from Manchester owning a house like this in London. I mean, I have a garden. A garden, Ay, in London!' She giggled.

'It's awesome. And now I don't have to sleep on your couch when I visit either! I've already put dibs on one of the spare rooms.'

'Oh my God, I have spare rooms!' Daisy squeaked, and they burst out laughing. She poured more wine as Ayane changed out of her jeans and into the far more comfortable joggers.

'It's just so fucking cool, Daisy. I'm so happy for you. Mega-jealous but happy.' And she was. Although her friend had beaten her to the punch, was richer than she would probably ever be, Ayane was genuinely proud of Daisy.

'Now let's stick on a film for us to ignore while you tell me all about the mystery Tinder man you told me about last week.'

Outside the house, locked out from the happy glow that ebbed from Daisy Kerswell's new home, the night grew colder. Mist filled the air, soft tendrils pressing against the windows as though trying to get in.

Ayane sat up slowly, rubbing her eyes. Her head throbbed. The room was dark, and at first she couldn't work out where she was. When she found a blanket over her legs and stomach, awareness dripped into her brain and her memory lethargically kicked in. She was stretched out on the sofa in Daisy's living room. Evidently she had fallen asleep and her friend had chosen to leave her where she was. They'd been watching a film – something starring Marilyn Monroe. Ayane recalled a lot of talking and giggling but not much of the film.

Shuffling around, she switched on the lamp on the small table next to her and squinted in the sudden brightness. On the coffee table sat their wine glasses and two plates with crumbs and the remnants of the Brie and crackers. There were three wine bottles: two were empty and the third was half full. Her mouth felt dry and rough, the tang of Rioja still on her tongue.

'Gonna pay for that,' Ayane muttered, wondering what time it was. It was still dark outside; she was relieved not to have been woken up by morning light streaming in. The room still didn't have curtains. Daisy had mostly unpacked but she hadn't finished making the house her own yet. The cardboard boxes dotted around the place attested to that.

Ayane reached for her phone, which was also still on the coffee table, and checked the time. It was just past two. As she stood up, she couldn't help wondering why she had woken up in the first place. It was strange. Normally she slept heavily after drinking. A whole bottle of red should have knocked her out for a solid eight hours. A wave of anxiety ran across her and she shuddered. Around her the house was silent. Shaking her head, she dismissed her anxiety as caused by being in a new place rather than her own cosy apartment. Still holding her phone, Ayane stepped out into the shadowy downstairs hallway, her silhouette looming on the wall opposite thanks to the lamp behind her. She switched on her phone's torch, lowered the brightness and turned back to the living room to switch off the lamp. Darkness swamped her. The weak phone light made the shadows around her even darker, but she didn't want to turn on all the lights and risk waking Daisy up.

'You're not in a horror film. Stop being a dumbass, Ay, it's time for bed,' she said to herself, trying to shake off the unease. *Maybe I've already got hangover depression.*

She was halfway up the wooden stairs when the unmistakable sound of movement from the ground floor made her freeze. Thinking quickly, Ayane turned her phone torch off. Her heart pounded. The bare side table near the front door was just about visible, and there was a lump of extra darkness where she knew a decorative glass paperweight stood, but otherwise it felt like all the house's features had been stripped away with the light. Not even moonlight found its way into the hall.

Ayane pressed her back against the wall, desperately trying to convince herself that she had only heard her friend. Maybe Daisy had come down for some water or something. That had to be it, surely. But Ayane resisted calling out. Her eyes slowly adjusting to the dark, Ayane took a quiet but deep breath and leant forward against the banister. Her long hair fell around her face and tickled her cheeks like strands of a spider's web. She grabbed a handful to pull it back, and listened again. The footsteps she could hear, which came from somewhere at the back of the house, were not Daisy. She instantly knew that. They were not the sounds of someone walking barefoot, or even in slippers or socks. No, whoever was moving around was wearing shoes, maybe boots. Like a switch flicking in her head, she suddenly knew why she had woken up. She thanked God that, despite the wine, her instincts had not failed her.

Ayane had seen her fair share of scary movies about home invasions. Everything in her body was telling her to get out of the house and find help, or at the very least find a sharp or heavy weapon and prepare for a fight. She looked in the direction of the front door, but she could barely even see it.

It's locked and I don't know where the keys are. I have no way to defend myself. And what about Daisy? She was totally defenceless. Even if she could get to the door, how would she get it open? Could she risk a window? Maybe even the back door? Something told her no, no she couldn't. Everything would be locked, and the intruders would find her before she had a chance to escape. And she didn't want to leave Daisy. What could she use as a weapon? The lamp? The paperweight? Maybe the latter could do some damage, but she'd have to get up close to whoever had broken in. The thought made her feel sick. She imagined hot breath billowing over her face, psychotic eyes connecting with hers as she fought for her life.

Ayane sped up the stairs as quietly as she could, hitting the landing in a few seconds. She was instantly forced to pause again in the dark. *Shit, which is her room?*

She racked her memory for details of the tour Daisy had given her, and was pretty confident she remembered. She would go for it and hope for the best. There was no time to hesitate. Edging along the wall, her hand reading the environment more effectively than her eyes, she found the handle on the third door. She twisted it and pushed it open.

'Daisy,' she hissed, pushing the door closed before moving

over to the bed. She shook Daisy urgently. 'Daisy, wake up. Please! There's someone in the house!' she hissed.

Her friend was unresponsive, groaning at being disturbed. She muttered something that sounded like 'go back to sleep' before pulling up the covers and rolling to face away from Ayane. Just like downstairs, the bedroom did not have curtains, but a thin sheet had been draped over the rail above the window. The little moonlight that came through had mixed with the hint of a distant streetlight to cast soft ripples of grey and yellow over the scatter of boxes, suitcases and bags that covered most of the floor. A quick glance was enough for Ayane to see that there was nowhere for them to hide. They had to get out. Maybe through the bedroom window, if the drop wasn't far.

The house was worryingly silent. Ayane could hear nothing downstairs, which only served to ramp up her fear further. Her gut was churning painfully. She had no idea where the intruder was, and prayed that he or she had not yet realised the house was occupied. After all, the house had only just sold and was full of boxes. Perhaps the intruder thought it was empty.

They're just looking for things to steal, that has to be it.

'Daisy, fucking wake up,' she whispered, shaking her friend more forcefully.

'Ay, what... what time is it?' Daisy asked, her voice groggy but more alert than before. She twisted to face her friend. 'What's the matter?'

'There's someone in the house, downstairs. I heard them. We have to get out!' Ayane was struggling to keep her voice under control, even though she was terrified of being heard.

Daisy's face froze in fear and confusion. She shuffled up in the bed. 'Oh God, okay, shit, what do we do?' she asked, her voice panicked.

'Can we get out of this window?'

'Crap, no, the lock is jammed and I haven't had time to fix it yet. Wait... the back room, past the bathroom. It's over the grass in the garden – we can drop down.' Daisy's tone was lacking confidence, but her idea was all they had. Ayane grabbed Daisy's hand and dragged her towards the door.

'Hold on – you have your phone? Call the bloody police!' Daisy urged, holding Ayane back.

'We don't have time. They could be upstairs any second. And they might hear us.' Ayane pulled her again but Daisy stood firm.

'At least dial 999 – they can track the GPS, can't they?'

Daisy had a point. It would only take a few seconds and Ayane was sure she had heard the same: that emergency calls were tracked. She dialled and held the phone to her ear. A recording asked her to confirm that it was actually an emergency. She said yes. Leaving the call open, she shoved the phone into the pocket of her joggers. Her heart thudded, and she felt like she could physically hear the seconds ticking away.

'Okay, ready?'

Daisy nodded, her face pale against the dark room behind her, as though she had been replaced by a ghost.

Ayane took a deep breath, pulled the door open and stepped out onto the landing. Her eyes locked with those of the figure standing right in front of her. She didn't have time to scream – or to dodge the metal bar that swung out with a gentle whip of air. It connected with the side of her head with a painful crack.

CHAPTER THIRTEEN

B leary-eyed and as usual hoping that caffeine in huge doses would work like a miracle cure, Daniel Graves waited in a quiet corner of Whittington Hospital for confirmation that the woman was fit to be interviewed. He was not expecting her to be in any shape to talk, and he was worried that she wouldn't be able to give any details about who had attacked her. While he waited, his mind wandered into the dark territory of yesterday's nightmare, which he had yet to shake off.

His sleep the night before had been filled with dreams of Amanda. The message she had sent, seemingly out of the blue, had thrown him and had brought up painful, vivid memories from the murky depths of his subconscious. While her message was very welcome, he had realised he didn't like the unexpected nature of it. Why had she chosen that moment to send it? What had suddenly spurred her to reach out?

When he thought about it, he realised that his nightmares hadn't really been about Amanda specifically. They had been about the rainy afternoon at the construction site so many years ago when their lives had changed forever.

As they normally did, Daniel's nightmares consisted of the

sound of his sister's screams, her desperate pleas for Adam to stop, to get his hands off her, then the guttural, heart-stopping thud of Adam's body hitting the unfinished concrete floor two floors below them, the exposed metal rebar punching through his chest. The sounds were accompanied by quick flashes of visual memories, which played like a flip book made from a horror film: Adam grabbing Amanda, trying to pull off her skirt, fumbling for her bra. Daniel's hands on Adam, pulling him off Amanda, then pushing him away. He saw every detail of the skin on his fingers as though he were there; felt the woven fabric of Adam's jacket, the rain water still dripping off his fringe. Finally, the super-cut shots of Adam's body, blood pooling into the muddy puddles that covered the ground surrounding the unfinished building they had broken into. The rain rippling the puddles. Adam's leg, bent at an excruciating angle under his body. The teeth of the rebar coated with lumps of skin, still slick with blood and water.

Now, in the hospital, Daniel didn't know how accurate those visuals were and how much his mind had exaggerated them over time. The basics were real enough, though. Exaggerated or not, the story was still true.

In addition, his sleeping mind had sucker-punched him. Jenny Cartwright. That dream had been a vicious compilation of images of Jenny alive juxtaposed with images of her heart in a box on his doorstep. What made it so haunting was the same few words, which were repeated over and over again.

Never forget, DG. I know I haven't.

The voice of the man in his dream had been threatening and raspy. It had cut deep under Daniel's skin, to the point where he could feel it writhing around his veins, sliding up to his ears where it would whisper again, sending ice plunging through his body.

'Are you okay?'

The question was like verbal smelling salts. Daniel snapped back to the hospital waiting area to find a sturdy-looking nurse in front of him, mild concern on her face. He couldn't find any words.

'Detective?' the nurse continued, taking a half step towards him, her brows raised.

'Er, yes, sorry, just... I'm tired, sorry. Was miles away for a second.' He smiled to reassure her and pushed away all thoughts of the nightmares.

'Miss Matsuda is awake and willing to talk to you, but I'm afraid you'll have to keep it brief. She needs her rest and I don't want her getting worked up. She's in a lot of pain, and hours of questioning will not do her any good at all.' She turned to lead the way and Daniel followed, snapping back to the case. He knew the nurse meant it when she said he'd have limited time.

When Daniel stepped into the room where Ayane Matsuda lay, he couldn't help gasping. Ayane's face was pale, with dark rings around her eyes. A large bandage was wrapped at an angle around her head, forcing her right eye almost closed. She had a split lip, cleaned now but swollen and bruised. One leg was raised, held in a sling and heavily bandaged. She looked utterly exhausted. He was impressed that she was willing to talk to him so soon after her ordeal. It was only seven or eight hours since she had been attacked, if Daniel had his timeline correct.

'Miss Matsuda, how are you feeling? Are you honestly up to this? I can come back,' Daniel said as he pulled a chair closer to the bed.

The police officer who had been guarding Ayane since her arrival was hovering in the doorway – out of what Daniel suspected was curiosity. The nurse was still in attendance too, leaning against the wall by the door, her arms folded over her chest. Her expression was stern, the face of someone not to be crossed. She wouldn't let him continue if Ayane didn't give him the go-ahead.

'It's–' Ayane started, then began to cough. She winced. The nurse was on her in a flash, glass of water in hand. Ayane took a sip and signalled she was good to continue. 'Sorry, my throat... Yes, I mean... I need to tell you. What they did – oh God, to Daisy...' She stopped speaking and fresh tears formed in her eyes.

Slowly she recounted what had happened, every traumatic detail.

For the second time Ayane woke with a headache and blurred vision, but this time everything was so much worse. Feeling the itchy texture of carpet against her cheek, she knew she was on the floor. Even the slightest movement made her head scream in pain and she took deep breaths, trying to get some control over her sight. She could hear movement around her but was unable to discern what it was. Slowly she raised a hand to wipe the tears from her cheeks, gingerly inspecting the crusted blood she felt drying near her left eye. Her brain throbbed. She gasped when someone kicked her arm, and she pulled it to her chest.

'Don't move,' a voice warned. She remained still, scared of what might happen if she didn't follow the order. Strands of hair were stuck to her face, to the blood and sweat, but she didn't dare to try and pull them free.

She blinked to clear her vision as best she could. Shapes in the room began to emerge. Her view was mostly of the top of one wall and some of the ceiling, but in her peripheral vision she could make out the heads of two people, both featureless save for glimmers of light reflecting in their eyes. Balaclavas were pulled down over their faces. They were busy with something. With a minimal movement of her head, she could see the top of the door frame.

A weak cry came from her left, where the men were. Ayane knew the cry had come from Daisy. Instinctively she went to sit up, desperate to see her friend, but a boot lashed out again, sending pain rippling through her ribcage. Ayane recoiled into the foetal position, crying out from the hurt she felt both physically and emotionally. She didn't know what to do, could barely even fathom the situation she was in.

After a few seconds the sharper pain of the kick began to subside into a deeper, pulsing wave that she could just about cope with. Her hands pulled up close to her face, she dared to brush the hair from her eyes, as slowly as she could, her fingers inching ever so carefully in case she attracted the man's attention.

From her new position the view was different. She saw the blood first – a dark, sticky pool that stood out against the light grey carpet in the room. Her breath caught and she forced back a cough.

Pale feet, bare and bloodied, were level with her eyeline. She could see the four wooden legs of a chair. Two sets of black boots. Not wanting to but knowing she had to, Ayane tilted her head, her gaze slowly working up the chair legs to get a better picture of what was happening.

Daisy was strapped to the chair, naked save for her underwear. Her torso was covered in blood, as though her throat had been slit, but Ayane knew she was alive. Further up, she could just about make out Daisy's face. Daisy looked pale, not really there, as though she was struggling to stay conscious or perhaps allowing her mind to escape to a place where her body could not follow. Her chin was dark and looked sticky while the upper half of her face remained blood free. They had done something to Daisy's mouth. Ayane gagged as she imagined teeth being pulled out, Daisy's tongue being cut out, and she squeezed her eyes shut. The total darkness made her feel even less safe so she forced her eyes back open, relieved to be able to see at least a small portion of her surroundings again.

Daisy shuddered as one of the attackers did something to her, and gave a low, ghostly groan of pain. Ayane didn't dare tilt her head to see what, didn't think she could bear it. It was then that she realised both sets of boots were facing away from her. The men didn't seem to be watching her for the time being.

The possibilities played out in her mind. What could she do? Ayane saw herself scrabbling towards the spare room, making a desperate leap from the window and screaming for help as she fled across the back garden.

Is it possible? Do I have a chance?

Her gaze locked on to the trail of blood droplets on the carpet. Daisy gave another soul-destroying whimper.

She had to try. It was her only chance. Maybe she could even save Daisy if she found help quick enough.

As silently as she could, Ayane readied her limbs, keeping her eyes on the boots. The figures were still facing away from her. She had one precious opportunity. She had to seize it. She knew there wouldn't be another.

GO!

In one smooth movement she rolled over to face the door, pushed up and launched herself towards the hallway. Her skin iced as she heard a curse from behind her, but she couldn't risk losing her momentum. Still in a crouch she burst onto the landing. The house swayed around her as the cut on her head boomed. She felt, rather than saw, the man looming over her. As she collided with the banister, he was already reaching for her. The wooden spindles cracked against the force. Gloved fingers whispered over her right ankle but failed to get a good hold.

Ayane pushed forward as hard as she could to lurch out of the way.

'Bitch!' the man spat, his voice like that of the devil himself. Ayane scrambled across the hallway floor, struggling to get enough friction on the soft carpet. She was coming up from her crouch and about to run for the spare bedroom when something hit her back, punching her forward. She fell through the doorway into the spare room and the man leapt on top of her. She landed with a thump, her breath knocked out of her.

Screaming, her throat tearing in pain, Ayane wriggled, kicking her legs out from underneath the man pinning her. A sharp pain bit into her right calf muscle and pain exploded through her as the knife sliced down the back of her leg. She could feel blood dripping down her leg as she pulled herself forward. The man was off her, though, and she pushed up onto her knees, finding the edge of the wooden bed frame.

The window was across from the bed. So close. But already her will was starting to wane, the pain and blood loss eating away at her.

Hands around her ankles pulled her back and she was suddenly on her stomach. The man clambered onto her again, trying to hold her down. Ayane thrust her hands out, searching for anything to help. Her fingers found something solid and she grabbed it. With an agonising breath Ayane pulled the object towards her, twisted onto her side and swung the object backwards as hard as she could. She heard it connect. The man yelled, stumbling off her once more.

The window!

Ayane stood. Her leg flooded with hot pain when she put her foot on the floor. She lurched around the bed, leaving a blood trail on the carpet. Already the man was getting up, mere heartbeats from stabbing her again. Ayane once again swung the object. This time she was aiming the hockey stick at the window. The sound of the glass shattering overwhelmed her. Shards sprayed out, peppering the room, and freezing cold air broke in.

Ayane didn't hesitate. She winced as glass still lodged in the frame chewed into her hands, steadied herself on the windowsill, then pushed herself out. She hit the grass below and screamed. The sound pierced the night like a wolf howling at the moon. Then she got up and ran, her legs threatening to give way but her mind refusing to let them.

Vicious branches swiped at Ayane as she scrambled through the shrubbery at the back of Daisy's garden. From behind her she heard a man yelling. It spurred her on. With a burst of energy she pushed her way through a thick bush. The night wrapped around her as she limped down the road as fast as she could, searching frantically for any sign of safety. She could feel herself getting weaker and didn't dare look at her wounds, afraid that the sight of so much blood would defeat her.

Ayane spotted a glow from the third house down. With the last of her strength, she staggered up the driveway to the front door. She pressed the doorbell, not noticing that her blood had smeared across the bell. It buzzed. Within seconds, she heard movement from inside. She hoped whoever was on the other side would be a kind citizen, willing to help her. But before she could find out, she collapsed on the porch and passed out.

Daniel waited, listening intently as the battered woman in front of him recounted the night before. He had not yet heard the exact details of what had happened to Daisy Kerswell but he knew that she was dead, and that the scene was all too familiar. It was the first time the killers had failed – though not for a lack of trying, apparently. And Daisy and Ayane weren't a couple either – at least, he didn't think so.

Had there been a shift in the killers' pattern? He made a mental note to discuss it with Martia Franklin. It could change the profiles she was building.

Daniel tamped down his simmering tension as he waited to see what Ayane Matsuda would tell them about the men.

'As I said, there was two of them... both men. They were dressed in black so I couldn't see what they looked like, but I heard them talking. They were English. I guess that's important,' Ayane said.

'It is, thank you. Anything you can think of could be valuable, so tell me whatever you can,' Daniel answered. He was pointing his phone towards Ayane, recording what she said. Ayane leant closer to the device. Daniel held a hand out to her to suggest she stay put. He shifted nearer, allowing her to settle down more comfortably.

'Did you hear any specific accents?' he asked. Maybe that would help narrow down the list of suspects.

Ayane shook her head. 'I'm from California. I don't know British accents that well.'

'What about the time this all happened?'

'It was after two – I remember checking when I woke up on the couch. I realised when I was halfway upstairs that it must have been them breaking in that woke me.' Ayane coughed again and the nurse held out some more water, which she took gratefully. 'I think they came in through the kitchen. That's where I heard the first noises coming from.'

'Do you have any idea why they may have targeted you and Miss Kerswell?'

Ayane shook her head again. 'Honestly? No. Daisy was doing well at work – that's how she paid for the house. That was why I'm... was...' More tears came. Daniel felt awful, watching her trying to talk through everything. She had just been savagely attacked, had lost one of her best friends, and was lying in a UK hospital with no family there for support. In the same situation, he wasn't certain that he would have the resolve she was showing.

'Do you think the money could be a motive?'

Ayane was silent, clearly thinking it over, before shaking her head. 'I don't think so. I mean, she was doing well, but as far as I know she used up most of her money on the house. She only moved in, like, a week or two ago. She didn't have piles of cash.' Ayane shifted position slightly and hissed in pain.

'Oh, honey, you're really struggling. I think we need to wrap this up for now, Detective,' the nurse said.

Daniel agreed. Ayane Matsuda needed to rest. He asked if there was anything else she'd like to say, and she said no. As he made to leave, however, she stopped him.

'Wait. This could be nothing, but...'

Daniel aimed the phone back at her and pressed 'record' again. 'Honestly, Miss Matsuda, anything could help us.'

She nodded, wiping her eyes. 'Daisy said the money came from a settled land dispute or something that she had worked on – she said it had pissed off a few important people. Could that be a motive?'

Daniel couldn't say either way. It didn't seem to fit with the other murders; none of the other victims had been involved with anything similar. Still, it was worth looking into, if only to cross it off the list.

'It could be,' he said with a kind smile. 'We'll definitely look into it. Thank you so much for this. I hope you start feeling better soon, and I'm so sorry for your loss. We'll do everything we can to find the men who did this.'

Fresh tears sprang from Ayane's eyes, and Daniel could see her composure finally crumbling.

'If you think of anything else...' He didn't need to finish the sentence. Ayane nodded, her face red and cheeks wet. He offered another smile and left her and the nurse.

'I presume you've been ordered to keep watch over her?' he said to the police officer. The man nodded. 'Yes, sir. At least for now.'

'Good. I don't know if the killers will try to find her, but she's the only witness we have to any of these murders. She's vital to this case, and we need to keep her safe at all costs.'

The officer promised he would not leave her unattended.

Daniel raced down the hallway towards the lifts. He needed to catch up with Charlie and the team and get Martia building up the killer profiles even further. He also needed to attend the new crime scene.

Three crime scenes in a week and a half and no reason to indicate there wouldn't be more. There was a lot to be done and fast if they were to stop another attack. Given the speed at which these men were operating Daniel hazarded a guess at two days. The thought made his stomach churn.

CHAPTER FOURTEEN

When Kelly saw the email in her inbox, her heart started to pound. Brian needed a word. That meant she was in trouble. Big trouble. Her mind was spiralling when, as though summoned by her panic, the man appeared next to her, making her jump.

'I thought you said you were keeping ahead of the curve, Kelly,' Brian Gallagher spat. The editor-in-chief loomed over her desk, his arms crossed over his chest, his cheeks red. His normally tidy brown hair looked wild, as though it too were bubbling with irritation. Behind him a number of heads were craned in their direction, keen to hear all the gossip.

'Go on the home page for the *Guardian*,' he demanded.

Her heart still going a mile a minute, Kelly did as he asked, the clacking of her keyboard keys punctuating the tension. She knew what was coming; she had already seen it. In fact, she had been praying that Brian would somehow miss it. Her prayers had been in vain.

London Organ Snatcher strikes again! One woman survives.

As she reread the words, her stomach dropped, as if she was on a rollercoaster, only less fun. Kelly tried to brush off the piece.

'Brian, this is fluff. See? There's no quote or anything from the girl–'

'Ayane Matsuda. That's her name. Know how I know that? Because Benjamin fucking Stahl wrote about her in the bloody *Guardian*, that's how.'

Kelly tried to speak but Brian continued. 'You said – no, you promised – that you had an exclusive line into this case and that no other paper would be able to scoop any of the news. So tell me, Kelly, how the hell does Benjamin Stahl know there was another attack and that this time there was a survivor called Ayane Matsuda and you don't? Hmm? Surely someone who had access to exclusive information would know about a fucking survivor and I would be signing off on this story in our *own* bollocking newspaper!'

Kelly was about to try another excuse, but the rage on Brian's face was enough to stop her. She didn't think she'd ever seen him so mad. She was genuinely shocked, but then she had never before promised him that she could keep writing exclusive stories ahead of anyone else in the country on one of the biggest murder cases that London had seen in years either. He would be under huge pressure from his boss and she had just royally dropped the ball, possibly making him look stupid in the process.

Jennifer Khan was there of course, listening from the doorway of the meeting room closest to Kelly's desk as though she had smelled blood and had come to sink her teeth into Jenny's already badly chewed carcass.

'I'm sorry, Brian. I... I did promise. And I should have been ahead of Stahl. But I wasn't lying about having a contact. Would you forgive me if I can get an interview with this girl? The survivor?'

It was a desperate ploy, and Kelly knew it. Clearly Jennifer did too. She rolled her eyes while Brian took a breath and a moment to think about the offer. 'Yes. Yes, if you can actually do that,' he answered, his voice marginally calmer although his face was still flushed.

She wasn't sure she could achieve what she had just offered, but she couldn't think of anything else to get him off her back. She had worked so hard to get where she was and she couldn't afford to let that slide now. Brian was not a vindictive person, as far as she knew, but if she got scooped again she suspected that her career rise would be derailed in an instant.

'I can. Trust me.'

Kelly felt sick as she delivered what she desperately hoped would not be a lie. She offered Brian as confident a smile as she could muster. He didn't return it but with a sigh gave her a nod and turned to head back to his office.

'You've got twenty-four hours, Malone. Don't go breaking another promise,' he called over his shoulder before disappearing past a photocopier and large potted ficus into his office.

Kelly grabbed her handbag, locked her computer screen and bustled towards the lifts before Jennifer could stick her nose in and throw a few passive-aggressive jabs. As the doors pinged closed and the lift whirred into action to take her down to reception, Kelly's mind hummed with fear. How the hell was she going to secure an exclusive interview with Ayane Matsuda, a woman that every journalist in the UK with a brain would now be clamouring to speak to?

DI Charlie Palmer had been talking to Lucy Hastings, Katy's friend, for almost forty minutes and wasn't getting anywhere. Despite what she had claimed, Hastings was evidently still not in any state to be talking about her dead friend. She had no idea why someone would want to kill them. Her tears had hardly stopped, making her answers more sobs than words. His notes were mere bullet points on a half-page, with nothing worth checking back over later.

Charlie had been gentle and patient, of course, not wanting to upset the poor woman further, but he was beginning to think he needed to wrap things up. It was great that Hastings was willing to provide a more detailed statement, but he couldn't afford to be wasting time. He had learned very little they didn't already know. If Lucy did in fact know anything else, he suspected she was simply in too fragile a state to make sense of all the thoughts that he assumed must be rushing around her mind like a hyperactive funfair carousel.

She had been talking about what Lawrence and Katy did for a living for at least ten minutes, revealing nothing of any real use. Charlie was looking for an opportunity to thank Lucy for her time when she mentioned a name that he recognised.

It stopped him in his tracks.

'Hang on, who did you say?'

'Well, Lawrence was after this promotion at work, and–'

'Sorry, no, the name you just said.'

'Carlos Mancini?'

'Yes, that's it. How do I know that name?'

'Oh, he was in the papers last week. Some big deal or other, and now I think he's been reported missing. Such a shame.'

'Missing... yes...' Charlie's voice trailed off, and he failed to notice Lucy's eyes widening.

'Oh God, you don't think they got him too, do you? The

killers?' She reached for another tissue, her eyes welling up instantly.

'Probably not, no, but we will certainly be looking into it. What was Lawrence's connection to Mr Mancini, do you know? You mentioned a promotion.'

'Yes, he was telling us over lunch j-just the other day... he said he was working with Mancini's team because the bank had something to do with the deal... and if he did everything right he'd be a shoo-in for a promotion because of the amount of money involved. So sad – he was trying so hard to provide for him and Katy. They were thinking about children and everything.' Tears fell again, and Charlie decided to end the interview. Against all odds, Lucy Hastings had unexpectedly provided a possible new lead, and he thought it best to let her go.

Carlos Mancini. The name was circling his brain, looking for a place to take hold. He had no idea whether it was actually useful, but the fact that the man was connected to Lawrence Rhodes and had been reported missing within the same timeframe as the first murders seemed more than a bit coincidental. He jotted the name down, his pen circling the name numerous times.

Minutes after he had escorted Lucy Hastings from the building, Charlie was on the phone to DI Graves. 'I might have something new for us to look into,' he said before Daniel could ask why he was calling. 'Have you heard of Carlos Mancini?'

'Sure, he's the business mogul, right? The one that went missing last week.'

'That's him. It turns out that Lawrence Rhodes was working for him through the bank he was employed at just before Mancini went missing and the first two victims were killed.'

'And you think there's a connection?'

'I don't know, but I think it's worth looking into. The timing is a bit odd.'

Charlie heard gagging and coughing at Daniel's side of the call.

'Where are you?' he asked. 'You sound weird.'

'I'll give you one guess.'

Ah. The house of the latest victim – it had to be.

'Crime scene number three?'

'Bingo.'

'I'm going to assume it's pretty bad?'

'Understatement. Obviously the body has been taken away for examination now, but the place still smells horrific. And I've seen the photos, which you'll no doubt get to enjoy later today.'

'Was she... er... missing anything?' Charlie asked, even though he didn't really want to know the answer.

'Her tongue. So far it hasn't been found. Probably another souvenir. It's enough to suggest it's the same killers. Can I call it a blessing that there was only one body?'

'That's probably not the right word. Do we have an ID?'

'Daisy Kerswell. Thirty-three, a lawyer, single from what we know. Just moved in. Nice house off Hampstead Heath. That's why her friend was visiting from America – a housewarming of sorts.'

Charlie could hear footsteps, and assumed that Daniel was moving somewhere more private.

'Right – the woman that got away. How is she doing?'

'She's alive – quite badly hurt, but okay. Distraught too, obviously. She's only been in London since yesterday, came to see Daisy and her new house...'

Daniel went silent, but Charlie could hear his breathing.

'Dan? What is it?'

'How much do property lawyers get paid?'

'I don't know. It depends, I suppose. Why?'

'Isn't Carlos Mancini rich because he's a property developer?'

'Shit,' Charlie muttered. 'Meet me at the office?'

Suspecting that any doctor who stopped to examine her would diagnose her with extreme cardiac arrhythmia, Kelly walked as casually as she could along the third-floor corridor of the Whittington Hospital. She felt each tap of her trainers on the green-and-white checked laminate tiling reverberate deep in her chest, and fought to stop herself passing out at any moment. She was excited, though, and proud of herself for her quick thinking. Thanks to the Benjamin Stahl piece on the survivor, the car park to the Whittington Hospital was busy enough to give the impression that Beyoncé herself was being treated there, but Kelly had got in nonetheless. All it had taken was a bottle of fake blood and a horror make-up set from the pound shop and she had been allowed past the throngs of other journalists with relative ease; the policemen at the door had assumed she needed medical attention. She had never been so grateful that Halloween was around the corner, a holiday she had never cared for in the past.

Dressed in casual clothing she would not normally be seen dead in outside her flat, Kelly made her way into the main waiting room of the hospital, gave a fake name to the receptionist and was told to take a seat. She had chosen one next to the doors the doctors kept coming through. It had taken almost an hour for an opportunity, but she had seized it without hesitation. She had never done anything quite so risky before. Sure, she was always pushy, but this time she knew she would be in serious shit if someone caught her. But Kelly had decided it was worth it. If she was going to advance beyond being a little fish in a pretty big pond she needed to grow some bigger fins.

After a further twenty minutes of ducking and diving in and out of stairwells and behind plants and pillars, plus cleaning her face surreptitiously in one of the bathrooms, she had found her way to the third floor. She could see the police officer on guard from down the corridor.

'Now what, Kelly?' she whispered, fingering the zipper on the worn-out hoodie that she normally reserved for hungover Sundays on the sofa. She edged closer to the policeman outside the door of the room and, pretending to be inspecting the contents of the drinks machine in an alcove that housed two armchairs and some old magazines, she watched him for a moment. He yawned and looked her way. Quickly she looked back at the drinks, tapping her finger on the Dr Pepper button as though she was close to making a decision. She waited for another few seconds, then risked another glance. The man yawned again and an idea popped into her brain.

Seriously? It'll never work!

Ignoring the voice, she dug in her jogging bottoms pocket for a few coins and slotted them into the drinks machine. She chose two cans of Coke. Her throat was dry, but not from thirst, as the machine dropped the cans into the collection tray.

Okay, here goes nothing...

Making sure the policeman wasn't looking, she retrieved the cans and shook one as hard as she could before starting the show.

'Ha!' She giggled loudly. 'My lucky day!' She made a show of holding up both cans, then shouted along the quiet corridor, 'Anyone want one of these? I don't need two.' She made a point of looking at the policeman. He smiled but shook his head.

'You sure? You look like you could do with the sugar,' she said, walking closer to him, holding one can out in front of her.

He deliberated for another few seconds. 'Sod it. Go on, then. Thank you.' He licked his lips. He had clearly been standing there for a while. He looked almost lasciviously at the cold can as he took it from her. He popped the ring and, as expected, fizzy liquid sprayed out all over his face and chest, soaking him.

'Oh shit, I'm so sorry!' Kelly exclaimed.

'Shit indeed...' The man frowned as he wiped his eyes.

'Crap, your radio,' she continued. 'I'll get tissues. I'm so sorry!' She started towards the sign for the ladies down the hall.

'It's not your fault; you were just trying to be nice,' the policeman said. He was holding the dripping radio away from him. 'Don't worry about tissues. I need to clean this off properly.'

Kelly pulled her best apologetic face and continued slowly down the hall, waiting for the man to move. It took a second. He clearly didn't want to risk leaving his post but the drink had really drenched him and would soon become sticky. He followed her towards the men's toilets. She got to the end of the hall before he vanished into the toilets, then doubled back quickly. The coast was clear. After checking through a slit in the door that Matsuda was alone, she ducked into the room and closed the door behind her.

I've got a minute or two, tops. Got to make it count! Her heart sank as she took a proper look at the woman in the bed. Ayane Matsuda looked like absolute hell – and, worse, she was fast asleep. Kelly guessed she had been given something to knock her out. For a second she considered trying to wake the woman, but knew that would be intensely cruel and it probably wouldn't work anyway.

She sighed, not sure what to do and annoyed that her hard work had been in vain. *Not quite*, her inner voice piped up again. *There is still one way to avoid this being a total waste of time.*

Kelly pulled her phone from her pocket, unlocked the camera and snapped a range of photos, from a distance and close-up. After checking to make sure she had enough and that they weren't blurry, she pulled up her hood, waited for a nurse to walk past the door and darted back out into the corridor. She was getting in the lift when she saw – out of the corner of her eye – the policeman heading back to his station. The lift doors closed, and she let out a huge sigh of relief. She hadn't secured the interview she had promised her boss, but even Benjamin Stahl wouldn't be able to beat front-page photos of the bruised, battered sole survivor of London's most wanted killer lying unconscious in her hospital bed.

Brian was going to love her.

CHAPTER FIFTEEN

Daniel Graves had called an all-team meeting. It was almost seven in the evening by the time everyone was available and had made it in. The topic was something everyone needed to be present for, though, and he had been willing to wait. He prayed that they all agreed with him when they'd heard what he had to say.

They were back in the meeting room that they had taken over for the case: its walls and windows featured even more printouts and sticky notes. The room was a decent size but stuffy nonetheless. Daniel felt sweat break out under his arms, and was thankful that his shirt wasn't grey.

Other than Charlie, no one else knew about the potential lead that had come from the interview with Lucy Hastings earlier in the day. They agreed to tell the team en masse. Everyone had arrived full of anticipation, hoping to hear about a breakthrough. Looking back at him were Charlie, Sergeant Amelia Harding, Junior Sergeant Ross Hayes, Martia Franklin, Superintendent Peter Hobbs and another three junior officers there to help in any way they could, none of whose names he knew. Hobbs' assistant Isabelle was also present, laptop open and ready to take notes. Even Patrick Marsden, the digital specialist who led the IT team, had joined. Nerves were quivering in his gut, as though he was about to stand up in front of the classroom and give a presentation he hadn't prepared for but would be graded on.

'I'm on the edge of my seat, Graves,' Hobbs said, as though reading Daniel's mind. 'I hope this is good. This case has been spinning its wheels for too long already.'

'It is,' Charlie answered quickly. 'Go on, Daniel.'

Daniel took some comfort from the fact that Charlie sounded so confident.

'Okay. I'll get to the point. We think we've found a common denominator between the victims. Have any of you heard of Carlos Mancini?' Daniel started in.

Half of people in the room nodded; the other half looked back at him, confused.

'Isn't that the businessman who went missing last week?' Martia said. 'A super-rich property guy or something similar.'

'Yes, that's the one. He was reported as missing by a family member ten days ago. It was a pretty widely covered story because of his wealth. He still hasn't been found, but our killers have taken over the front pages since, so there hasn't been as much coverage of his case in the last few days.'

'What does he have to do with our victims?' Hobbs asked bluntly. Although Daniel knew that Hobbs was still pissed off at him and Charlie for what had happened with the journalist and the story leak, he felt pretty sure that all would be forgiven with what he was about to say.

'He first came up when Charlie questioned Lucy Hastings, the woman who discovered and reported the Rhodes victims. According to her, Lawrence Rhodes, who was employed by a bank in Canary Wharf, had been working on the finances for Mancini's team on a large property deal that the bank was managing. By itself, not that useful, but it struck a chord when we found that Daisy Kerswell, the latest victim, had been a property lawyer and her firm had recently won a sizeable new client.'

'Property lawyer,' Hobbs said, his eyebrow raising.

'Exactly,' Daniel continued, pleased that Hobbs was connecting the dots. 'Her firm was representing Mancini in a dispute over a large piece of land in south London he wanted to develop on. They won and it seems that Kerswell bought her house with help from her bonus, according to her mortgage paperwork.'

'Some bonus!' Ross Hayes said with evident envy. Amelia shot him a look to shut up.

'On that,' Amelia interjected, 'I had a look into vacant properties near that one. There weren't any listings even remotely close to Kerswell's house, currently or in the last few weeks. Unlike both of the other crime scenes. Could it be a break in the pattern?'

Daniel was thinking about it when Martia answered the question. 'I believe the pattern still stands. The house that became the third crime scene was vacant before Daisy Kerswell bought it, correct?'

A murmur rippled through the room as everyone cottoned on to what Martia was pointing out.

'So this time there was no need to rent a nearby house to spy on the victim as she moved things in or get the lie of the land – the victim's house served the same purpose.' Charlie said out loud what everyone was now thinking.

'There's a good chance they may even have sneaked into the house when she was there, while she had boxes and stuff delivered,' Daniel said.

'That's a terrifying thought,' Amelia admitted with a shiver.

'And they probably knew that her friend was visiting and

timed it because it's part of the pattern to attack two people – right, Martia?' Daniel asked.

'We don't know if it's just a coincidence,' the profiler responded, 'but I suppose it's possible.'

'Let's bring this back to Mancini,' Hobbs said with a hint of renewed energy. 'First of all, what did the first couple have to do with him? Do we know? Second of all, where the hell is he? If he's been killed by this pair, why don't we have a body? And third, what's the motive?'

'We don't know where Mancini is, but I've reached out to the missing persons team dealing with the case,' Charlie answered.

'And we don't have a connection yet between Mancini and the Alton couple, but we're looking into it next.'

'And motive?' Hobbs pushed.

'Hopefully that will come out when we find out more. That's all we've got right now.' Daniel hated giving such a weak answer, but there was no point avoiding the issue. Hobbs would simply call him out on any excuses or bullshit. And really, if Mancini did prove to be the connection, Daniel was sure that the motive would reveal itself in due course. Finding out who was committing the crimes was ultimately more important than why they were doing it. He would happily wait to discover the motive after the killers had been caught.

'Okay, get me answers as soon as you can,' Hobbs said. 'You've got more resources on the case now, but if you need extra manpower let me know. Patrick, get your team back on CCTV duty. I want to know if anyone appeared on any footage around even two of the crime scenes, let alone all three. Right, let's get cracking, team.'

Patrick gave the superintendent a silent salute and Isabelle frantically typed something before shutting her laptop. As though that were the signal he was waiting for, Hobbs immediately stood up and left the room, gifting Daniel with a shoulder pat as he went. Charlie smiled at Daniel once their boss was gone.

'See? Told you he'd forgive us.' He grinned.

'Thank God. Him being annoyed at us was just adding to the pressure,' Daniel said with a sigh. He looked at his watch. 'Want to order some food? We need to establish if the Altons had any link to Carlos Mancini and time is of the essence, as they say. I reckon it's another all-nighter. Two linked crimes could be passed off as a coincidence but three will be nigh on impossible to argue with.'

'True, and it could narrow down the list of possible future targets for these sickos too. Anyone working on large deals for his company, like the ones that Lawrence Rhodes and Daisy Kerswell contributed to, could well be next on the list,' Charlie suggested as they headed out of the meeting room, back to their desks. He pulled out his phone and opened an app for food deliveries as they walked.

'Pizza?'

Charlie was reading through reports on all the Mancini Estates deals currently under way – a lengthy list that would take some time to work through. One of the women working at the UK Missing Persons Bureau had given it to them. Charlie was extremely thankful that they had employees working late over at the Berkshire headquarters. He had expected to get a recorded answering machine message, but someone called Angela had picked up his call after just two rings. They'd discussed the Carlos Mancini case for a while, Charlie providing only enough information to get her to co-operate. He put on his most charming voice in an attempt to seal the deal. Angela had instantly called him out on it but had thanked him for the effort nonetheless. Twenty minutes later she had emailed over some of the files they had for the report.

'I can't find anything here,' he groaned, flicking through some of the papers he had printed out from the PDF on his computer screen. 'If either of the Altons had a connection to Mancini, it's invisible to me.' He dropped the printouts on the table, irritated, and reached for a cold slice of ham and mushroom pizza.

'I refuse to give up on this yet, Charlie,' Daniel said, his voice terse in the quiet office.

'Don't worry. I didn't say anything about giving up,' Charlie mumbled around a mouthful.

Daniel looked up from the laptop he was using and gave Charlie an apologetic look. He looked exhausted.

'You know, I think you really need a girlfriend,' Charlie said, bellowing with laughter when Daniel glared at him. 'Well, something anyway – something to pay some attention to other than dead people. I've said it before and I'll say it again: your surname is too perfect.'

'Not funny, Charlie.' Daniel turned back to the computer, looking pissed off. It took a second for Charlie to realise how much he'd just put his foot in his mouth.

'Shit, Dan, sorry, I didn't mean Jenny... I didn't think.'

Daniel's lack of response cut right through Charlie, who wasn't the kind of person to deliberately upset people. In fact, he went out of his way to be nice, to be considerate of others, often carefully choosing his words. People often made assumptions about him when they saw his good looks – mostly that he'd be an arrogant prick. Many people treated him as such, not bothering to find out what he was really like. He had been told on numerous occasions how much kinder and funnier he was than one would expect, how refreshing it was that he was self-deprecating and not a cocky git. Even Daniel had said as much, assuming he'd been lumped with an obnoxious, arrogant partner when he had moved to London. It hurt Charlie deeply that Daniel might have thought he had been a dick deliberately. He sighed in relief when his partner spoke up again.

'It's not you, Charlie. I know you well enough to realise you were joking. You actually have a point, to be honest...' He took a swig of the energy drink he'd ordered with his meal.

Charlie looked closely at him. 'Good, I didn't mean any offence. But something's clearly got to you. What's going on?'

'It's to do with Jenny,' Daniel started. Charlie wondered if his colleague would open up to him, a feeling that left him simultaneously happy and guilty. They had been working together for almost six months, were always in each other's company, and Charlie had started to really enjoy the bond they were developing as friends and as partners in solving crime, but still he knew that Daniel held back a lot of the time. Sure, he had eventually told Charlie what had happened with his sister, about killing that kid, and he had opened up about his feelings for Jenny a few times, but he had actually confided in Amelia first. That had annoyed Charlie, upset him, in fact, more than he would care to admit. More often than not Charlie got the feeling that Daniel preferred to remain a fairly closed book with him. He knew that the best detectives had partnerships based on strong connections, of openness and trust. Somehow that still seemed slightly out of reach with Daniel, and it unsettled him.

'Okay, lay it on me. What's going on?' he said, hoping Daniel would not just give him the headline but would actually confide a bit more.

'Someone posted on her Facebook wall, on the memorial account, and it was aimed at me. I'm pretty sure it's the same person who left that gift on my doorstep. It's completely fucked me up.'

Charlie coughed, choking on a bite of cold pizza. He swallowed it painfully and took a breath. 'God, I wasn't expecting that! Are you sure it was aimed at you?'

Daniel picked up his mobile phone from the desk. A few taps later he offered it to Charlie, who took it tentatively, as though it would bite him if provoked. The phone screen was filled with the Facebook app. And there it was, the post, clear as day.

Never forget, DG. I know I haven't.

'Okay, yeah,' Charlie admitted. He was sure there were other things the initials could stand for, other people, but it seemed like in this case the most obvious answer was also the correct one. 'Shit.'

'Exactly. I mean, I've been struggling with all this anyway. I'm not... not over her, not over what happened. And the nightmares are pretty regular still. Then of course one of our current victims had their heart cut out. Everyone knows how squeamish I am. The homicide detective who gags at the sight of an actual homicide. I felt like I'd been punched in the stomach when I saw Henry Alton's body, that hole in his chest...'

Charlie felt a knot in his throat as Daniel said that. He had never experienced it, but he thought he could imagine the impact it must have had. He had never experienced something as horrific as receiving a body part in a box, but he could still imagine how traumatic it would be. To be reminded of that at another gruesome murder not long after would send him over the edge, he was sure of it. He was surprised, and impressed, that Daniel had held it together as well as he had.

'Come on, Dan, even the strongest stomachs would have churned at any of the murders on this case. Mine certainly did. I bet everyone has felt sick at all of the victims' houses. Well, maybe not Stephanie Mitchum, since she's clearly a robot, but everyone else.'

Daniel snorted a laugh at that, but Charlie knew his words had done little to comfort his partner.

'And yes, I know I keep telling you to move on from Jenny and her death, but I would be a mess too if I saw this post aimed at me. It has made me a little shaky.'

'I was a mess before the post, but it's made it so much more – well, raw, I suppose. After all that time looking for a clue to the person who killed her, I'd sort of given up hope. And this not only ignites hope in me that we still can catch this person, but it also scares the actual fuck out of me. I mean, what am I supposed to do with this? This nutjob could be anyone, and anywhere, and has clearly not forgotten that Cassandra Salinas was killed thanks to me.'

'Okay, wait, you know that wasn't your fault, though. Right? Seriously, mate. You are not the reason she is dead.'

'Yes, of course I know that. I feel guilty, but she was crazy and trying to kill Jenny, had killed others. I don't think she would have handed herself over. But obviously whoever murdered Jenny doesn't give two shits that it wasn't technically my finger on the trigger. They've decided I took someone from them and are determined to continue to make me pay for it. It terrifies me that I don't know what that means. They've already taken Jenny. What next? Or who next? You? My sister? Anyone they think I'm even remotely close to? You wouldn't believe the nightmares I've had, Charlie.' Daniel spoke quickly, getting more and more agitated, his cheeks flushing and his breaths shorter and faster.

'Mate, breathe, okay? You're not going to do us any good if you have a panic attack.'

Daniel frowned but attempted to do as Charlie instructed, his breathing becoming slightly calmer with some effort.

'I know this must scare you. It scares me. And it isn't specifically happening to me. But we're a team, Dan, a dynamic duo. If this was a movie, we'd be the buddy cop leads, Starsky and Hutch. I'm in this with you. We'll figure it out. Maybe Patrick can track something through the post, figure out where it came from. Who knows? But we'll get this bastard. With every step he takes there's a chance he'll make a mistake, and when he does we'll be there to kick him in the nuts so hard he'll be chewing on them.'

Again Daniel gave a weak mutter of a laugh. Charlie sensed it was probably as cheery as Daniel was going to get, given the circumstances. He pushed over the pizza box to Daniel, changing their focus.

'Thanks, Charlie,' Daniel said, and Charlie knew it wasn't gratitude for the pizza.

'No problem.'

In a weird way, Charlie found himself feeling satisfied. They had just experienced a moment where their bond as not just colleagues but also as friends had grown a little tighter. Charlie's awareness of the situation, that his brain had actually stopped to think about it in this way, should have made him feel guilty. He did a little, to be fair, as though he were somehow making it all about him. He was satisfied, though. It might not have been much but it was something, a good something. Daniel had opened up a little more than normal and Charlie was happy that Daniel had felt comfortable enough to choose him. He couldn't help feeling pleased, whether that was childish or not.

'Anyway, back to this mess...' Daniel gestured towards the files and paperwork they had been going through. 'I feel like we're going about this the wrong way. I think we need to look at them as people again. Find out more about their day-to-day lives. No official records and files can tell us who they really were. Do we have the digital footprint report for Henry and Jane?'

Charlie pulled his keyboard closer, knowing that he had the details somewhere in his inbox. An online behavioural specialist from Patrick's team had sent them over a few days ago with an accompanying summary stating she had found nothing of note. He found the email and opened the attachment.

'Their profiles and search histories and stuff were looked into but nothing useful was found. Of course, that was before we had three more bodies and a survivor. Are you thinking that maybe now, with hindsight, there could be something there?'

'I think it's a possibility, sure.' Daniel scooted over next to Charlie and they began to go through the links to the Altons' social media accounts. They started with Jane. She had a Facebook profile as well as a selling page that she used to sell various knitted things – evidently a hobby business. Her posts went back to around a year ago. Her personal profile showed very little, apart from a few photos at parties and other social gatherings. No familiar faces appeared, and there was certainly nothing about Carlos Mancini. In fact, Jane had barely ever posted. She had no other social accounts either. She had clearly only used social media to try and build her start-up.

Henry's online persona was not vastly different. There was less knitting, but otherwise he too posted briefly and similar things, or was tagged in other people's photos. He had a Twitter account with nine followers and even fewer tweets, and an Instagram account that had never been used yet somehow had thirty-three followers.

'Anything else?' Daniel asked with a sigh.

'He had a LinkedIn account.' Charlie clicked on it and waited for the page to load. After a few seconds a blurry thumbnail of Henry Alton appeared; the photo was evidently old, given its poor resolution. Henry had been an electrician, had worked for a small family-owned business in Camberwell, just down the road from where he and Jane had lived. It was not new information. Amelia Harding had already spoken to someone at the company to get some background information on Henry and to see if they knew of anyone who may have wanted him out of the way. The page didn't give them anything they weren't already aware of.

'So that's that.' Daniel slumped back in his chair, eyeing the cold pizza but not taking a slice.

'Yeah, I suppose so, but...'

'But?'

'I think I just had a brainwave.' Charlie opened a new browser tab and googled the name of the company that Henry had worked for, Camberlectric Ltd. The results brought up the company website, its social pages, then other similar businesses.

'What are you looking for?'

'Just hang on a second...' Charlie checked out the company Twitter account, clicked 'media' and started to scroll down the posted images.

'Boom!' he whooped suddenly before tapping an image on the screen, tweeted a month ago.

Daniel craned his neck for a better look. 'What am I looking at?'

'You don't get it? Where are they standing?'

'On a building site.'

'And?'

'Guess who has an unfinished project in Peckham, just down from Camberwell? I saw it in the papers that Angela sent over.'

'So we're thinking that Camberlectric Ltd was contracted to work on one of Carlos Mancini's developments?' Daniel said, wide-eyed.

'Yes, we are. And Henry Alton is listed as a project lead on his LinkedIn, so there's a very good chance he was working closely on it all. Amelia wouldn't have known to try and connect Henry's workload with Mancini's company at the time, but maybe we can now.'

'Looks like we need to pay a visit to Camberlectric first thing in the morning, find out some more info on their projects.' Daniel's face fell as he spoke, and he paled.

'What's the matter? Isn't this a good thing? New lead?'

'Yes... yeah, that part's great. It's the... er... building site part that is less ideal.'

'Of course. I can go by myself if you want, catch up with you after?'

Charlie thought about what Daniel had told him about his sister, about the teenager who had tried to sexually assault her, and what Daniel had done to stop it from happening. It had made him queasy at the time. The thought of Daniel killing someone was odd and hard to digest.

He had come to the conclusion, though, that he'd have most likely done the same as Daniel had. He'd worked on sexual assault cases and had often thought that the world would be infinitely better off without the perpetrators of such crimes in it. They thought they could do what they wanted if someone they fancied even looked at them.

'No, it's okay. I'll be fine. And I do want to go. You may just have to keep an eye on me!' A thin smile accompanied Daniel's words – the first time he had smiled that night. Charlie felt his own mouth curve in a matching grin.

This was more than just a coincidence. Surely this was a concrete lead. If he was right, then all three sets of victims had a tangible, provable link to missing property mogul Carlos Mancini. Charlie didn't know why this would be a motive for murder yet, but he could feel his body humming with anticipation again. They'd catch those psychos soon, he knew it.

CHAPTER SIXTEEN

For once Daniel Graves was not feeling the need for copious amounts of caffeine, despite the fact that he and Charlie had met before eight in the morning. He felt alert, fresher than he had in some time.

As he looked around the already bustling Peckham site, which featured men in hard hats lugging horrendously heavy-looking items around and noisy machinery chewing through metal and cement, Daniel felt surprisingly positive despite his natural trepidation at being back on a construction site – the first time he had dared to go near one since he'd been a teenager.

The connection between the three sets of victims was so visible now, like a new penny glimmering at the bottom of a fountain. He was ready to risk getting his hand wet in order to seize it.

Daniel had a hunch that they were about to get the proof they needed to give to Superintendent Hobbs. That was more than enough reason for him to force his nerves aside at being at the site. If ever there was a worthy justification, this was it. In the back of his mind the worry was of course still there, irrational or not, but he was succeeding in managing it and was proud of himself for doing so. He'd spent most of his adult life crossing the road to get away from building sites, to subdue the mental images of a dead Adam Spencer. This was a big moment for him.

Charlie Palmer was dodging the patches of mud peppering the huge plot of land as he went to find the site manager, while Daniel waited and took in the scene. The morning was cold but for what seemed like the first time in weeks it wasn't raining. The winter sun gave the scene in front of him a comforting sense of life.

The foundations of what was to be a new block of luxury flats was already finished: a wide concrete L-shape with a skeleton that reached five floors high. Thick metal girders and concrete columns gave the building a sense of solidity, even though no walls were in place. On a more dreary day, the presence of so much grey could have been miserable. Instead Daniel let the sunlight invigorate him, taking the chilled air as bracing rather than unwelcome.

'Watch out!'

A jarring crash of metal made Daniel jump, and he whirled round to find the source of the sudden commotion. It was just a few poles of rebar toppling over. The warning had been more of an admonishment than a call to signal danger. It didn't matter. Daniel's heart leaped at the shock. He felt stupid, and hoped that no one had seen him startling like a small child. Even as logic told him there was nothing to worry about, his body was telling him that really it would prefer not to be there. He glanced at the open gates nearby that led out of the site.

'Dan?' he heard from behind him.

His chest still not quite steady, Daniel turned around to see Charlie returning.

'You okay? You look a bit pale.'

Daniel made an attempt at a reassuring smile. 'It's just this place. I heard the workers drop something and, you know, associations...' Daniel grimaced. He felt like an idiot and was annoyed that Charlie had spotted that he was spooked. He pulled at his shirt collar.

'Makes sense,' Charlie said, looking around. 'Do you want to sit this one out? I can meet you afterwards. Honestly, go grab a coffee or something.'

Daniel straightened up. 'No. I'm okay, honestly, just overreacting.'

'Flashback?'

'Something like that.' Daniel laughed off some of the adrenaline. 'Anyway, I need to be here. Did you speak to the site manager?'

Charlie nodded. 'He was irritated that we're here, said it's bad for business. At any rate, he confirmed that Camberlectric Ltd are working on the project. The contracts were signed a few weeks ago – seems they've only just started. The guy who runs the business is here somewhere. Amir Mittal.'

'Then let's go find Amir. We need to be certain that Henry Alton was involved in the project,' Daniel said, who had recovered from his jump scare.

It didn't take them long to find Mittal. The second builder they spoke to pointed out the man, standing, clipboard in hand, in front of one of the temporary office units that had been set up on the edge of the plot.

Amir Mittal was a short man with a paunch that stretched the front of his shirt. His chubby face sported a tidy beard and a friendly expression as Daniel and Charlie approached.

'Hi,' he said with a smile, seeming unfazed that two strangers clearly not dressed for a building site had come to talk to him.

'Amir Mittal?' Daniel asked, though it wasn't really a question.

Mittal nodded. 'What can I do for you? I'm pretty busy but I can spare a few minutes if it's important.'

'It is,' Charlie answered. 'I'm Detective Inspector Palmer and this is my partner Detective Inspector Graves.'

Daniel saw Amir Mittal smile to himself at the surname, though the man didn't say anything. Daniel was relieved. He was not in the mood for the usual jokes.

'So it is important. Is this to do with Henry, by any chance? Do you want to go into one of the offices? Much warmer,' Mittal said, gesturing behind him to the units.

Daniel said yes and the three of them moved the conversation indoors. Inside the rectangular box of an office it was undeniably cosy, heated by an electric fan in the corner and with the scent of fresh coffee in the air. The walls and desks were covered in papers, building plans, bits of wiring. Amir took a seat next to one desk after pulling up two other chairs.

'So what can I do for you? I'm pretty sure I said all I know about Henry to that officer the other day.'

'We won't keep you long, but we wanted to ask you about Henry Alton's projects,' Daniel started.

'Terrible loss. The team still can't quite believe it. What... what did you want to know?' The cheery expression had faded from Mittal's face. Daniel suspected that Henry's murder had hit him hard. There was a good chance they had been friends too. It was a family business, after all, and he suspected everyone was fairly close.

'We just wanted to confirm that he worked on this project, and to find out a bit more about what that may have involved.'

'Yeah, he did – he was managing a large chunk of the job. We've not done much on the site, obviously, it not being a finished building, but we've already planned a lot of the systems that need to be integrated and where power will run through the structure. Henry is – shit, *was* – great with that sort of work, the planning. Making sure nothing was missed out at the start, avoiding headaches later on. Great project manager.'

'I take it you knew Henry well?' Charlie asked.

Amir nodded. 'He has worked with the company for, what, six years now, I think. It's... we're all feeling the loss. Not just because he was good at his job.'

'Standard question, but do you know of anyone who had any issue with Henry?'

'You mean anyone that would want him dead? Like I said to the officer who called up, I honestly can't. He was a decent guy. A good manager for the team here and well liked. Him and Jane were happy, had a good life from what I know. Maybe you could chat with Mark and Phil – they worked with him more than I did. I'm only on site two days a week. I own the business so I like to check in, but I'm not here or at the main office every day. I doubt they'll say any different, but they're both here today so maybe it's worth your time talking to them. I don't think they've spoken to anyone about him yet.'

'Could you take us to them? If you wouldn't mind,' Charlie said.

Mittal nodded, offering a smile with no real happiness behind it. In silence they left the office unit and headed around the front to an adjoining block. The men they were looking for stood at the foot of a metal flight of steps, papers in hand, discussing a technical plan of some sort.

'Guys, two detectives here to speak with you. About Henry,' Mittal said, his voice solemn. His initially cheery disposition had well and truly evaporated. Daniel thanked him as they stepped past him and greeted the two men. Amir Mittal left them to it and the workers introduced themselves as Mark Schriver and Phil Attwood. They both wore thick coats and yellow hard hats.

'Wantin' to know about 'Enry, right?' Phil said, his East

London accent thicker and deeper than Daniel had expected from his thin frame and baby face.

'That's right. Can you think of anyone who didn't get on with Henry, might have a grudge against him?'

The men shook their heads. 'No, Henry was a stand-up bloke. Such a fuckin' shame,' Mark said, quickly apologising for swearing.

The pair looked uncomfortable and awkward. Not used to speaking with the police, Daniel assumed.

'He was a solid bloke,' Phil added. 'Gave good banter. Good boss too.'

'So he got on with everyone?'

'I fink so – as much as anyone does at work, ya know? We all been down the pub a few times, played pool and that. He was decent. Don't think I ever saw him get aggro,' Mark informed them. Phil nodded.

'And had he ever mentioned anything about any troubles outside of work? Over a pint, maybe?'

Both men were silent for a moment, mulling the question over.

'I don't think he liked his dad-in-law much, but that's about it,' Phil answered. 'He was pretty chilled overall.'

'Were there any issues with this project? Anything at all?' Charlie asked.

'Sod all. No drama yet, being as we just started on it. I mean, a few people were pissed off that he got to meet that mega-rich Mancini guy, but it was nuffin' really. Just jokes and stuff,' Phil answered.

Daniel and Charlie looked at each other, wide-eyed.

'You're saying that Henry Alton met Carlos Mancini in person? When was this?' Daniel asked, his heart racing again but not because of his surroundings.

'Er, maybe just over a fortnight ago? It was like 'aving a celebrity visitin'.' Phil looked at Mark for confirmation.

'I fink so, yeah. No idea what they chatted about. The job, I s'pose. It was a big deal, though, someone that loaded and important comin' by in person.'

'And you said a few people were jealous of this?'

Phil looked wide-eyed now, clearly realising where the questions were leading the conversation. 'Yeah, I mean we all were. Mancini is a big deal in our profession but, like I said, it was all just banter. No one would have—'

Phil Attwood stopped short but Daniel knew what he had not said: that Phil didn't think that was enough reason for someone to kill Henry Alton. Daniel had to agree that jealousy over meeting Carlos Mancini didn't seem like a realistic motive, but someone else had clearly thought differently.

Movement nearby caught Daniel's attention and he swivelled, locking eyes with a man not twenty metres from where they stood. The man, who was wearing a green and yellow jacket and carrying lengths of wood, froze. The wood clattered to the ground. Before Daniel could process what was happening, the stranger was running.

'Charlie!' Daniel yelled, sprinting after the runaway, not waiting to see if his partner was following. The guy had a head start on him, was dodging around workers, yells of shock erupting as he shoved past a group of men who had stopped for coffee. Daniel registered one of the cups hitting the dirt and spilling, but didn't stop.

The main gates to the site were coming up fast. Daniel had begun to run towards them when the runner shot left unexpectedly, heading for the looming frame of the building. Daniel followed, skidding in a slick patch of mud but managing to avoid falling, barely losing momentum. The man lunged past a stack of wooden pallets and into the structure itself. Shadows fell over him as he turned again. For a second Daniel lost sight of him behind a thick concrete pillar, but quickly spotted his coat. Glittering sparks from a saw to his right shot out with the screech of blade meeting metal. Daniel flinched, ducking past the machinery in the direction of the runner.

As the space opened up, an empty cavern with only more pillars blocking the view, Daniel realised he couldn't see the man any more. He came to a halt, his breathing heavy as he scanned his surroundings. In seconds Charlie was next to him.

'Where'd he go?' Charlie gasped.

Around them workers had started to gather, watching them, unsure of what they were witnessing.

'Fuck!' Daniel bellowed, anger ripping through him as he desperately looked for the man they were chasing. His voice echoed around them, bouncing between the pillars and escaping out through the gaps where no walls yet existed.

'There!' Charlie shouted, starting to run again. Daniel too saw the green and yellow of the man's jacket. The man was already off the foundations, sprinting towards a second gate in the fencing that surrounded the site. Daniel threw himself after Charlie and pounded across the concrete. He wished he was wearing trainers, not stiff leather brogues.

'The gate!' Charlie yelled from just ahead, jumping off the concrete platform and back into the mud. Daniel saw the van before Charlie did and dodged sideways even as it blocked his partner's way, the driver oblivious to what he was getting in the way of.

The runaway was almost at the gate. Daniel's lungs were burning. He could not let him get away; he forced himself to run faster, despite his body's complaints. The gap was getting smaller and suddenly Daniel could almost smell the runner's sweat. The man in green and yellow made an attempt to push past two workers near the gate, stumbling as he misjudged the space. Daniel saw the moment as though time had frozen: the stunned, terrified face of the man as he struggled to regain his footing. Daniel tackled him hard and they went down fast, mud squelching underneath them. The man struggled, pushing to get up and away from Daniel's grasp, but Charlie, red-faced and panting, now stood in between them and the gate. The runner seemed to give up then, dropping once more to the ground.

Even as Daniel chugged in fresh air, out of breath, he smiled at the sight of the handcuffs in his partner's grasp. 'Got you, you fucker,' he muttered to himself as he got up off the ground, not caring that he was covered in mud. 'Got you.'

CHAPTER SEVENTEEN

While they had a sense that they were making progress, there was one key ingredient missing from the mix that had the whole team on edge. Motive.

Sergeant Amelia Harding was leading the internal research team to try and find a motive – a daunting project that was making her anxious. For the last two days she had been constantly rubbing clammy hands on her trousers, horribly nervous each time one of the detective inspectors asked her for a status report. Finding a motive should have been made easier now that the team knew how the Alton couple were linked to Carlos Mancini. Unfortunately this had illuminated very little. Connecting the victims to Mancini would only take them so far without the motive, making the challenge of identifying possible next victims just as difficult as picking out suspects.

Sitting at her desk, feeling stifled from being stuck in the office despite the harsh winter chill and spitting rain outside, Amelia looked through the current profiles of the killers that Martia Franklin had put together. They made for macabre, stomach-churning reading. The very existence of anyone capable of committing such cruel acts of violence was terrifying.

The profiles detailed what sorts of personality types were most likely responsible for the serial killings, and gave Amelia something to reference against any suspects that arose. On their own, however, they did not help to suggest a motive any more than Mancini being the link between victims did.

Amelia was still utilising Junior Sergeant Ross Hayes as her main resource for the case. Others dropped in and out when they were able to help, but she had made sure his was a consistent presence. He was sitting across from her and she had emailed him the profiles. She was hoping for a different perspective from Ross. Her own thoughts were not proving to be particularly successful, and she hoped that their combined brainpower would provide better results. Amelia watched him scan the email, chewing the baguette he had brought with him. Amelia had not eaten anything since forcing down a semi-stale croissant for breakfast, and found herself staring hungrily at the remaining section of his baguette on the desk – chicken and freshly sliced tomato.

'You can have it if you want,' Ross said. She was immediately embarrassed that he had noticed her salivating and offered up a token protest, but was secretly glad when he pushed it over to her anyway, then went back to the profiles. He sighed as he finished reading. 'Nothing is jumping out at me. At the moment it's just traits on a page, not like a real person I can imagine. Also there's something I don't understand. The profiler said that the killers are probably sociopathic, right? But she said that sociopaths kill because they need to, not because they have a specific reason, like revenge or something. If that's true, then why are the victims apparently being chosen because of a connection to Carlos Mancini? It doesn't fit.'

Amelia swallowed a bite awkwardly and brought a hand up to cover her mouth as she answered. 'Martia also said that one is likely a sociopath and the other a psychopath. So maybe the psychopathic one has his reasons and the other one is just along for the ride?' As she said it, a chill whispered down her spine. It was a frightening combination.

'You mean one has a motive and the other doesn't?'

Amelia nodded, biting another chunk of baguette that was loaded with chicken, hoping that Ross wouldn't notice that she was eating as though she had been starved for a week. She liked to present herself in a certain way at work, and shovelling food into her face undermined that somewhat. At least it wasn't Daniel or Charlie sitting across from her watching baguette crumbs stick to her chin. She was technically Ross's senior, which made her feel better. Being a slob in front of a DI would have been mortifying – not the image of someone always keen to get noticed and bumped up a rank.

'That's so fucked up,' Ross said to the killer duo theory.

She nodded again. It most certainly was. 'I guess our best approach is to start looking through Carlos Mancini's past. It's likely that the one with the motive has a prior connection with him, otherwise what the hell could the reason for the murders possibly be?'

'So, someone Mancini screwed over, you think?'

'I reckon so. Maybe through work, or personally. He's a powerful man with a lot of money and I bet he's done a bit of stomping over others to get what he wants.'

'That could be a long list,' Ross said, screwing up the empty baguette wrapper and throwing it into a nearby bin. It hit the rim then went in, and he fist-pumped.

'I know. But I'm not sure where to begin.'

Amelia thought for a moment, trying to pick a sensible approach. She knew of course that solving the case wasn't resting solely on her shoulder – she was part of a team and by no means near the top of the hierarchy – but the pressure felt very real still.

'Why don't you start by looking for any negative news stories on Mancini?' she asked Ross. 'If he's pissed someone off on any major scale, there's a chance that the press would have covered it. He's often followed by journalists. I'm actually quite surprised that someone like him could go missing.'

Ross nodded, pulling his laptop closer. 'And I'll start going through his public records, contact his secretary and family members again.'

Breaking the job down between them would help, but Amelia was concerned nonetheless. She knew they were working to a deadline. The killers could choose their next victims at any moment; they could already have been lined up for the chopping block.

Suddenly the thought of the responsibility seemed painfully heavy.

'Graves, a minor find but not something that's going to rock your world, unfortunately,' Stephanie was saying into the phone. Daniel watched Charlie escort the man they'd arrested at the building site into an interview room. The guy looked terrified. Daniel had no idea of what would come out of grilling him, but was eager to find out.

'Graves? Are you listening?' he heard Stephanie say, and forced his attention back to the call.

'Sorry, yes. Busy morning.'

'I'm calling from the coroner's office. We found some trace evidence at the vacant property the killers used to spy on the Rhodes couple.'

'Wait – you found possible evidence of our killers and that's something I shouldn't be excited about?'

'It really isn't much. A few strands of hair and some skin cells.' Her voice was flat.

'It's better than nothing. What can you tell me?'

'The hair is European in ancestry, brunette and short, so probably from a male. No root pulp was found, so we can't run DNA tests. The skin cells seem to be from two different people, but we haven't been able to create any meaningful profiles. At any rate, there's no definitive way to tell if they are from the killers. Both hair and cells could have been left by previous inhabitants.'

'Well, we suspected that our killers are men, so the hair sample backs that up.'

'No, it doesn't, Graves. I said probably male and we can't be sure. Hence not being very useful.'

'Okay, but I'll take it as a start anyway.'

Daniel heard Stephanie tutting quietly to herself but chose to ignore it. He wouldn't win a science argument with her. Technically she was right too. He knew full well that, when it came to rented properties, getting useful DNA evidence was a tall order. The number of people who came and went in rentals made it very difficult to prove anything. What they really needed was something to compare the samples to.

Stephanie seemed to read his mind. 'Regardless, we will need comparable evidence traces for this to be of any use. I'll chase the forensics team. The previous crime scenes have not provided anything but the house belonging to the latest victim is still being worked over.'

'Great – thanks, Stephanie. Keep in touch.'

The line went dead without any further response from the forensic anthropologist.

'Well, that was pointless,' Charlie said, suddenly behind Daniel in the hallway.

It took Daniel a second to realise what was happening. He

put his phone away and stepped towards the investigation room door, stopping as his brain caught up with what Charlie had said, his hand resting on the door, about to push it open.

'Wait, pointless? Our runner?'

Charlie nodded, brushing his fringe off his forehead. He looked frustrated. 'Yep, he has nothing to do with our case.'

'So why did he run?' Daniel asked.

'He thought we were there to bust him for selling weed to other guys on the site.'

Daniel couldn't help laughing. The truth was frustrating. They had wasted time chasing the guy and arresting him, and now Charlie would have to fill out all the relevant paperwork. And they had better things to do with their time... His irritation came out as a laugh. Charlie responded in kind, smirking out of exasperation.

'And here I was wishing I could join in the questioning!' Daniel admitted with a smile.

'So the site visit was a bust?'

'I suppose so, although we confirmed the link between Carlos Mancini and Henry Alton, and we know that Alton spoke to Mancini before he died, so that may be something. I'm not sure how we can find out what they talked about, but we can check in with Mancini's team to see if they have any notes of their meeting.'

'A half bust, then,' Charlie said.

Daniel had to agree. With the runner proving unrelated to the murders, they were no closer to identifying any suspects. 'I really thought we had something more concrete,' he muttered. 'Stephanie called just then, by the way. They found evidence at one of the vacant houses.'

Daniel could see Charlie's face lighting up and stopped him. 'Don't get too excited. It doesn't tell us much. But we have something for comparison, at least.'

'Another half bust,' Charlie said.

'Okay, you need to stop saying bust,' Daniel warned with a smile. 'Let's go update Martia and the team, and then I think we need to start hounding anyone close to Mancini.'

Kelly Malone stared at her reflection in the large wall-mounted mirror above the sinks in the women's toilets. The bright lights that surrounded the mirror were harsh and unforgiving. She swore her skin was regressing to teenage status, patchy and spotty.

One of the junior editors, a young woman called Anneka Stroup, stepped out from a cubicle behind her, tucking her top into her jeans. In front of other colleagues, Kelly might have stopped what she was doing and attempted to look more put together. Not Anneka. While they didn't often have to work closely together, they had become accidental buddies after a raucous Christmas party that had involved them both dancing on a table and singing a Britney Spears song at the top of their lungs. They had since formed a decent friendship and a mutual understanding that they didn't have to follow the unspoken rule in the office to always be as on-trend and fashionable as possible.

'You shouldn't poke at your face, Kel, you'll make it worse,' Anneka warned as she washed her hands, then leant in to inspect her own reflection, running her fingers through her long, black, impossibly shiny hair. Kelly thought she looked like she had just finished a shoot for Pantene, but kept her jealousy to herself.

'I know, I know. I thought I was too old for this shit. I may no longer be blessed with youth like you, but I had assumed that one of the few perks of ageing was not to get spots any more.'

Kelly dug in her handbag for concealer and powder and spent a minute or two trying to make herself look more presentable.

'Stress, probably,' Anneka answered, still finger-combing her hair. Her own face was make-up free except for some mascara, Kelly noticed. Anneka could look truly amazing when she wanted, but Kelly somehow felt better that most days she decided not to bother, today wearing faded skinny jeans and a plain cream top. She still looked good but an achievable good. High-street good.

'Most likely,' Kelly muttered as she hunted for her Rimmel lipstick. 'I certainly feel more stressed out at the moment.'

'Who are you making this effort for? Besides me, obviously?'

Kelly looked around to check that the other cubicles were empty before turning back to Anneka. 'Technically Brian, but really Bitchface McSlutbag.' Kelly frowned, sighing when she found the lipstick and discovered that it was almost finished. She applied a thin layer.

Bitchface McSlutbag was the unimaginative but oddly satisfying nickname Anneka had come up with for Jennifer Khan. She had told Kelly about it one Friday over after-work wines at the All Bar One round the corner from their office. It had come about after Anneka had been speaking to a new guy in the design team regarding a project. Jennifer had shunted her way into the conversation, pushed her chest out and had taken the designer for her own apparently far more important job. Anneka had resented Jennifer's rudeness at interrupting, and Jennifer's use of her looks to get what she wanted. The nickname therefore seemed appropriate. Kelly had been inclined to agree. Now they rarely referred to Jennifer by her actual name unless she was present.

'Ugh, yeah, that cow would stress me out too. But why would you try to impress her?'

'I'm not, really,' Kelly answered. 'But we have a meeting

with Brian in half an hour about the evening news cycle, and I don't want to look like Primark next to her Prada. I know Brian doesn't really pay attention to what we look like, but still, I need to come across like I'm a decent competitor.'

'I thought you weren't trying to compete.'

'So did I, but here I am. I've got an amazing piece on the survivor of the home invasion in Hampstead and I need Brian to choose it over whatever crap Jennifer has.'

'I heard she's working on an exposé of a WAG, so I think you're good.' Anneka laughed.

Kelly prayed her colleague was right. She had risked a lot to get the photos of Ayane Matsuda, and she would be damned if she didn't score the front page of the evening edition and a huge headline on the website. She couldn't wait to see the look on Jennifer's face.

'Fingers crossed it's not a famous WAG!'

Together they left the toilets, Anneka heading off to the right, her typical peppy self, and Kelly heading left, her heart thumping and butterflies tumbling in her stomach.

CHAPTER EIGHTEEN

Superintendent Peter Hobbs was under a lot of pressure. Gang crimes were up, with stabbings and fights between machete-wielding teens horribly regular. Tourists were reporting muggings and thefts more than ever; the city seemed to be full of chancers on mopeds speeding past unsuspecting people and snatching phones and bags so quickly that their shocked victims couldn't react. This last week alone, there had been twenty-three fights in bars and pubs across the city, and numerous people had ended up in hospital. And there had been an acid attack just yesterday at a club in Clapham.

Sitting in his office, the door deliberately closed to give him some space for a few minutes before the office came to life for the day, Hobbs couldn't help feeling as though London was far more chaotic than usual. And that was without factoring in the serial killers.

He loved his job, was proud of his career, wouldn't change it for the world, but sometimes he couldn't help looking forward to the day he retired, when someone else would take up the mantle. The job was incredibly rewarding and worthwhile, but it was also often exhausting and depressing.

He sat back in his chair and closed his eyes to take a few slow, calming breaths. A knock on his door broke the quiet like a bullet through glass.

'Come in,' he said with a quiet sigh.

His personal assistant Tim gave him a wary smile as he stepped into the office, a coffee in one hand and a wad of printouts and post in the other. Tim put Hobbs' coffee down and handed him the printouts.

'Thank you,' Hobbs said.

Tim nodded. 'You may want to check the top newspaper. There's new coverage about the serial killer case. Have a read and let me know what you think. We might need to hold a press conference.'

Hobbs felt his neck stiffen as he shuffled through the pile and stopped at the newspaper Tim had referred to. 'You have to be kidding...'

Tim grimaced.

'Get everyone on the case in the task room as soon as they come in.'

Tim hurried out of the office and left Hobbs alone. Any chance of a moment of respite had left with Tim. Hobbs could feel his blood boiling already.

It was severely painful déjà-vu, but this time it wasn't just Daniel and Charlie who felt the burn from the dressing-down. Everyone sat shell-shocked even after Hobbs had left the task force room in a rage. All that was missing was cartoon steam coming from his ears and nostrils. Daniel knew it wasn't their fault that the policeman at the hospital had made such a stupid mistake, but Hobbs had been right: this was their case, and they needed to be on top of it.

The newspaper sat in the middle of the table. A picture of Ayane Matsuda asleep in her hospital bed filled the front page. It was all over the news and social media. Nothing made the public more interested in a serial killer case than photos of a beaten, but breathing, survivor.

Daniel knew he should say something to defuse some of the tension, but he wasn't sure what. Amelia and Ross looked dumbfounded and Martia just seemed uncomfortable.

The heavy quiet seemed to stretch on forever until finally Charlie stood up, grabbed the paper and dropped it in the bin in the corner. 'I can't say we entirely deserved that, and there's not much we can do about it now, but he's right. We need to make some headway on this – and fast. I know everyone is working hard, but we need to crack this.' Charlie had his hands on his hips and looked confident and encouraging.

He'd done what Daniel had not. A flash of something like jealousy streaked through Daniel before he admitted that Charlie displayed a quality that Daniel was not sure he himself possessed. Authority. He knew he had the respect of his colleagues but even now, when he'd been in his job almost a year and had worked on a number of homicides, he still felt pangs of insecurity.

The sergeants and profiler nodded, looking slightly less on edge.

'Don't worry, guys,' Daniel said. 'This wasn't our fault. We just need to keep on working to crack the case.' He hoped his words sounded as confident as Charlie's.

'I'm going to head off, if that's okay,' Martia said, standing and retrieving her jacket from the back of her chair. 'I'll pull together an update on the profiles based on what forensics threw up. Amelia, email me the narrowed-down list of Mancini associates and I'll see if they fit who we're looking for from a psychological perspective.'

'Sure thing,' Amelia said, jotting a note.

'Thanks, Martia.' Daniel smiled at her as she left the meeting room, no doubt relieved that she was escaping to the outside world. Daniel wished he could too. A week off, even a weekend off, would be welcome. He needed to slough off the pressure he was feeling. But he knew that now wasn't the right time. They were hunting two serial killers, and Daniel putting his feet up and cracking open the wonderfully aged whisky his dad had given him for his birthday was not going to result in any arrests.

'Okay, guys, walk us through what you've found.'

Amelia and Ross had compiled a list of eight names of people who could feasibly have had something against Carlos Mancini – enough to perhaps want him to go missing or to seek some sort of revenge upon the man. First up were two journalists who had written articles about Mancini, only to have to redact nearly everything they'd said due to a range of legal issues and impending lawsuits. Neither journalist seemed to have much career success since, but Daniel didn't think they were good candidates. He would have them brought in for questioning, but his gut was ruling them out for the time being.

The other six had all been wronged by Mancini from a business perspective: outraged landowners powerless to stop Mancini building where they didn't want him to. A man who worked for the Greater London planning committee who hadn't approved any of the projects Mancini's company had proposed. Competitors who had lost out in various ways.

'No one on this list screams "serial killer" to me,' Daniel said after he had looked through the brief bios that Amelia had added for each person. 'Can you get contact details and addresses for them all, though? We should at least talk to them.'

Just then, they were interrupted by Patrick Marsden.

Patrick had flushed cheeks and was visibly distressed. 'Graves, we need to talk. Now, if you have time.'

'Guys, call me when you have details,' Charlie said to Amelia and Ross before following Daniel and Patrick out of the room.

Daniel's stomach churned as they quickly made their way downstairs.

'I thought I should show you this, rather than just tell you,' Patrick said as he dropped awkwardly into the swivel chair at his desk. Daniel stood so close to him, he could smell Patrick's aftershave. He didn't care. He needed to see what Patrick had found. The anticipation was painful. He shook his head in an attempt to clear it, and focused on Patrick's screen.

'A map?' he said, confused.

'I traced the IP address of the post that appeared on Jenny Cartwright's Facebook page the other day. This is the address that came back.'

Daniel was studying the map. It only took him a few seconds to see where the map showed. 'That's–'

He couldn't finish the words. His breathing became short and fast and he realised his hands were shaking.

'Breathe, Daniel.'

He could see and hear Charlie in front of him but it felt as though he was at the bottom of a swimming pool: he could make out his partner leaning over him but the water was muffling his features and words.

Even as he tried to do as Charlie instructed, his mind continued to scream, over and over again.

That's my house, that's my house, that's my house.

Once he had recovered from the panic attack, Daniel had been forced to take the rest of the day off. Superintendent Hobbs had even suggested he take more time off but Daniel had refused. There was no way he was letting someone else take his place on the case. He was too far in. He'd be fine tomorrow, he promised, hoping that it wasn't a lie.

Now he sat on the sofa in Charlie's living room. Charlie was still at work, and the house was eerily quiet around him. He was staying there overnight while a team swept his own flat. Charlie had suggested that someone must have broken in and used Daniel's computer to post on Jenny's Facebook wall. Two crime scene workers were looking for any evidence of the intruder, another tech specialist was sweeping for bugs, and a security company was changing all the locks on the doors and windows, as well as installing a new alarm system. It was costing Daniel more than he was comfortable with but, given the circumstances, he wasn't sure he had a choice. He didn't want to move if he didn't have to, and he definitely didn't want any more uninvited guests.

Charlie's house was perfectly nice, but Daniel wasn't convinced he felt any better being there than he would have in his own house. He had said to Charlie that surely anyone clever enough to get into his house undetected could simply find out where Charlie lived, if they didn't already know, and do the same, but Charlie had insisted it was a better option than Daniel checking into a hotel. He had promised to bring home a takeaway and a few beers, adamant that Daniel would feel better staying with a friend than in a hotel room on his own.

Surprisingly, Daniel had never been to Charlie's house before. He sat in the living room, looking around. It was well decorated, nothing like a typical bachelor pad. He didn't really know what to do with himself. His thoughts were in a whirl: Jenny and her death, who wrote on her Facebook page, that person had written the post from inside his house, the implications of the intrusion, the intruder must have known that Daniel would find out where they had posted from, the case, the killers, possible leads, his sister, Adam Spencer... It was exhausting.

He had already called Rachel, who had insisted on coming down to London the next day to stay with him for a while. She had framed it as a good excuse for her to be a London tourist again, listing some things she wanted to do: a new exhibition at the V&A would allow her some culture, some shopping around Bond Street and Columbia flower market would tap into her need for a splurge, and she wanted to visit her sister. They both knew that these activities were simply a cover for her to come and stay and make sure he was okay.

Rachel was one of the few people that Daniel truly confided in. He had known she would come and, though he hadn't asked her, was glad.

In a bid to distract himself, he turned on Charlie's PlayStation. He wasn't much of a gamer but figured it would pass some time. He stuck in the disc for a horror game before deciding that horror was the exact opposite of what he needed, so he ejected it in favour of the latest *FIFA* instead. After half an hour, during which he discovered that he was as terrible at digital football as the real thing, he turned it off and booted up Netflix instead. He scrolled through the menu for a good ten minutes before choosing a comedy show featuring a stand-up comedian. He hadn't heard of the guy but found him funny nonetheless. The first half of the show, anyway. Despite his overactive brain, his body had decided it needed rest and he fell asleep on the sofa.

It was dark when he woke up, his neck sore from having slept awkwardly. The living-room curtains were still open and he could see that evening had arrived, the winter sky pretty much black. With a yawn he reached out to grab his phone from the coffee table. It was just past seven. He had a few messages: Charlie saying he'd be back by eight. Amelia checking in to see if he was okay. Rachel informing him she had booked her train ticket and would arrive tomorrow afternoon. Amanda had messaged too. He hesitated about opening it, then thought back to her last text. If she was trying to make an effort, then so should he.

He regretted it immediately.

Can we talk? I need your help. Call me.

And there it was. The real reason she had contacted him the other day. He had known there would be something besides reconnecting, but he'd decided to take her first text at face value. He hadn't called her because he had been stressed from work and emotional; he hadn't felt up to it. Now he just felt annoyed. And fatigued. He didn't have the energy to deal with Amanda. Sighing, he dropped his phone on the sofa. A minute later he realised she would see that he had read her message and not answered. He quickly replied, saying that he would try to call her tomorrow and he hoped she was okay before dropping his phone again.

For a few minutes Daniel sat in the dark, trying to relax. It wasn't to last. His phone lit up with a notification. He was about to curse his sister for hounding him when he saw that it was Charlie ringing. 'Hey, mate, what's up? You home soon?'

'Dan, we... Shit, we have a situation.'

Daniel frowned. 'What situation?'

'It's... Ayane Matsuda, the survivor from the last attack. Sh-she's dead, Dan. Someone got to her.'

Daniel was suddenly alert. 'What? How? How the hell did that happen?'

'Dunno, mate, but listen, I'm going to the hospital now. I'm afraid you're going to have to get dinner alone.'

'Like hell I am. Come and get me! I'm coming with you!' Daniel realised he was shouting, but he didn't care. 'I've slept all afternoon. I'm fine – and I need to be doing something. Come and pick me up.'

'Are you sure?'

'Yes. Hurry up.'

'Well, that explains how they got to Matsuda,' Charlie said grimly. He and Daniel stood side by side in Ayane Matsuda's hospital room. It had been left untouched while hospital staff waited for the detectives. The sergeant who had been guarding the room lay on his front. Blood pooled underneath him. The back of his uniform was red, and several wounds were visible through the torn fabric. A scalpel lay discarded not far from him.

'Poor guy. The copper who let the reporter in and got suspended will be glad he did when he finds out about this,' Daniel responded. Making sure he didn't step in any blood, splashes of which dotted the linoleum-tiled floor, he made his way around the bed for a closer look at Ayane Matsuda.

The room was a little messier than it should be, with a chair askew and some of the bed sheets pulled half off, but the main thing he noticed was that it was nothing like the crime scenes at the houses that had been broken into. The body hadn't been positioned and no body parts were missing, as far as he could tell. Matsuda, like the dead police officer, had been stabbed multiple times, mainly in the chest. The alarm button that had hung by the bed lay on the floor, its wire cut.

'This was quick. Efficient. An in-and-out job.'

Daniel turned back to Charlie, who moved aside to allow the crime scene photographer access to the room. Flashes of sharp light glowed for a few seconds, highlighting the pools of blood around the bodies. 'I don't think we're dealing with both of our killers here. This is the work of the one who plans – otherwise the room would be a lot more bloody.'

'Right. We need to work out the timeline and check the hospital cameras. The killer must have been caught on one somewhere.' As Charlie spoke, he looked around the room. So did Daniel. There were no cameras, but Daniel figured that the hallways, stairs and lifts would have them.

'Where's the nurse who found the bodies?' Daniel asked, looking back at Matsuda, focusing on her face rather than the fatal wounds. He thought that at least she looked fairly peaceful, had probably been asleep when she was stabbed and would have died quickly. A small saving grace, if it could be considered that.

'She's waiting for us down the corridor. Probably still recovering.'

Daniel and Charlie went out into the hall, signalling to the waiting crime scene staff that they could now access the scene.

They identified the nurse easily. She sat alone in the waiting area just down from them, gripping a glass of water. Tall and slim with a short afro, she was pretty and had a kind face. At that moment, however, she looked ill, her forehead clammy and her skin washed out. Daniel wasn't surprised. Even working in a hospital wouldn't prepare someone for walking in on a double homicide.

'Detectives? Sorry I'm not more together. I still haven't got over the shock...' Her soft voice was filled with anxiety and sadness.

'That's okay,' Daniel said, immediately sympathetic. 'So you found the victims, Miss...'

'Nenge – Afia Nenge. And yes. I was doing my rounds and I saw that the policeman had gone – he wasn't outside the room. The woman in there, she's not... I mean, she wasn't on my list to check, but I thought it was weird. I mean, there's been someone on guard all the time. That's why I went to look. I wasn't expecting... I mean, I've seen dead bodies before, but...'

'Okay. Can you tell us what time it was when you saw that the officer wasn't outside the room?'

Afia looked at the small silver watch clipped to the pocket of her shirt. 'I found them... about... yeah, about an hour and a half ago, so that would make it around quarter to nine. My rounds started at seven this evening. I don't know how long the policeman hadn't been there. It was just, God, such a shock.'

'And did you see anyone suspicious around here at all today? Anyone you didn't recognise, anyone acting oddly?'

She looked thoughtful, then shook her head.

Daniel nodded. He hadn't expected her to have witnessed anything, but it was a shame she hadn't seen even a glimpse of a suspect.

'Do you know if any other nurses or doctors could have witnessed anything?' Charlie asked.

Afia shook her head straight away. 'It's not likely. This part of the hospital is quiet, away from the other busier wards and buildings. Miss Matsuda was put here for security reasons, as instructed by you guys, actually. Only a few people are allowed up here. I checked with the nurse on shift before me and the doctors who have access to this floor while I was waiting to speak to you. I'm sure you'll want to ask around yourself, but they all said everything was fine when they were last here.'

'That narrows it down to after seven and before quarter to nine,' Daniel said, more to Charlie than the nurse, although she nodded anyway. 'We presume the hospital has CCTV?'

Afia nodded again. 'Yeah, in all the main communal areas.

None of the rooms with patients have cameras, obviously, but yes, corridors, lifts and stuff.'

'Do you have a security team?' Charlie asked, frowning.

'Erm, yeah. Their office is on the ground floor in the A&E building.'

That would be their next stop. Daniel was about to thank the nurse for her help and give her his card so she could contact him if she thought of anything else when Charlie spoke up.

'You said this part of the hospital is only accessible to a small number of people, right?' he asked Afia.

She nodded and showed him a plastic access card attached to a retractable clip on her hip. 'Yes, you need one of these cards to get in.'

'So whoever got in needed to steal an access card from someone.' Daniel thought back to when they'd arrived. The doors that faced the lifts had been opened for them by another nurse so he hadn't noticed that they had gone through an electronically controlled door.

'Let's check to see if anyone has lost their card when we get down to the security office. One could have been stolen.'

Charlie raised his eyebrows at Daniel. A shiver skimmed over him. He knew what Charlie was silently getting at. Sure, maybe the card had been stolen. Or there might be a dead security guard somewhere in the hospital.

'Let's head down there now,' Daniel said calmly, despite his racing pulse. They thanked Afia, Daniel gave her his card, and they hurried back towards the lifts.

CHAPTER NINETEEN

By the time Daniel and Charlie had spoken to the hospital security team and gained a copy of all the CCTV footage from the time of Ayane Matsuda's death, it was too late to do anything with it. They had headed back to Charlie's house to crash.

Daniel did not sleep well. He couldn't switch off; his brain sped through different case-related trains of thought. Nevertheless, as he and Charlie sat waiting for the team to arrive the next day, he felt alert. He was too amped up to give in to fatigue.

The plastic clock on the wall said it was just past seven. They'd already been in the office for almost an hour, but Daniel wanted to wait for Patrick, and he wanted Amelia present before they kicked things off. So he and Charlie had picked up emails, checked to see if they had any useful updates, which they did not, then moved into the task force room.

Daniel had received a confirmation email from the security company that the work on his flat had been completed, but he'd decided to ignore that issue for now. He didn't feel comfortable with the thought of going back to his own home, but he had to focus on the case at hand. He decided to think about his situation when Rachel arrived. Being with her would make it easier for him to go back to his flat. He could talk to her about Amanda too – another thing he still didn't have the mental capacity to deal with. Rachel knew Amanda fairly well and was normally pretty good at knowing what to say to her. In fact, on a few occasions over the years she had handled Amanda's outbursts with much more authority and confidence than Daniel had.

'Okay, here I am and I'm good to go,' Patrick Marsden announced with gusto as he bustled through the door to the meeting room, laptop under one arm and juggling a coffee and a box of croissants. The door swung back and almost caught Amelia in the face as she came in behind him, still in her coat and bobble hat.

Charlie smirked.

'Don't you dare, Charlie Palmer. I know the bloody hat has a kitten on it. It was on sale and I was in a rush,' Amelia said defensively, pulling the hat off and flicking her hair back.

'I didn't say a word.' Charlie grinned.

'Yes, because I stopped you.' Amelia frowned before returning the smile. 'Sorry I'm late.'

Patrick handed her a croissant as she took a seat at the table, and she bit into it eagerly.

'Amelia, it's not even half seven. You're not late,' Daniel said. 'We just couldn't afford to wait on this. Patrick, you got the link to the CCTV footage, right?'

'Yep, it's all downloaded onto the server.' Patrick took a swig of coffee before pulling a cable out from the centre of the table and plugging it into the side of his laptop. Almost instantly his laptop screen was shared onto the wall-mounted TV. They all swivelled round to get a better view.

'I've not watched any of it yet, but Alistair and Natalie came back in overnight to work on it. They've isolated all the footage from the part of the hospital Ayane Matsuda was in.'

'Sorry if you've already told me this, but how did they get into the ward?' Amelia asked as Patrick loaded the footage. Four video rectangles appeared on the screen.

'One of the guards' key cards was stolen. We're not sure how, but that's better than another body.' Daniel was watching the screen like a hawk.

They watched in silence for a while as Patrick let the videos play. Daniel quickly felt his frustration building. 'Are these the only camera angles we have?' he said. 'This is a waste of time if we can't see half of the place because of privacy regulations.' He tore off a piece of croissant and popped it into his mouth.

'I'm afraid so. Sorry it's not what we were hoping for,' Patrick answered quietly.

'It's not your fault. I'm just pissed off. How are we supposed to find our killer with this?'

'Patrick, can you rewind that shot in the top right?' Charlie asked, ignoring Daniel's question. Patrick nodded. Daniel frowned.

'Give it up, mate, there's no sign of this guy on the footage. There's barely a sign of anyone with these angles.'

'I think there is. Patrick?' Charlie nodded at the man again, ignoring his partner.

On the big screen, the videos rewound, going back a few seconds for every real-time second. Charlie sat silently, staring at the video. Daniel's irritation grew as he watched various hospital staff walking backwards down hallways and through doors. He was annoyed that the hospital hadn't had a camera on Matsuda's room.

They sat in silence for another few minutes.

'Charlie, seriously, what did you think you saw?'

'That!' his partner exclaimed with perfect timing, pointing at the television. 'See? Top right.'

Everyone leant forward.

'Do you mean the reflection?' Amelia asked.

'Yes – see the colour and pattern? On the torso? It's a checked pattern. A lumberjack shirt or jacket, maybe.'

'Vaguely, yes, but come on, that image is way too blurry. It could be anyone,' Daniel responded. He was surprised to find he was now determined to prove this was a waste of time. *Maybe I'm just sick of getting my hopes up on thin leads*, he thought.

'Yeah, sorry, Charlie, but we can't really do much to enhance that. The video quality is pretty shit,' Patrick said.

'Okay, sure,' Charlie answered back, 'but that pattern is fairly recognisable, so how come we've not seen anyone wearing a jacket or shirt like that in any of the other footage?'

Amelia's eyes widened. 'Because they were deliberately avoiding the cameras?'

'Exactly! Any regular person – a guard, nurse, visitor, whatever – they would walk down the middle of the corridor. The angle of these cameras may be bad, but they're set up to ensure that you can't really avoid being on a few of them. I know I didn't see that pattern of shirt in any other shots, and I don't think that's by chance. I'm willing to bet that that's our killer, that they were deliberately avoiding the cameras. If we look at other CCTV footage, from around the rest of the hospital or the neighbouring streets, we might be able to spot them. They can't have avoided every single camera around, unless they're some sort of super-spy.'

'Shit,' Daniel mumbled. Charlie was right. So far each new lead was like that glimmer of blue sky you saw on a crappy grey morning that you desperately hoped would turn the weather sunny and somehow salvage the day so you kept an eye on it, monitoring its progress, and just when you thought that the day would brighten up it poured and you got soaked. But as Daniel stared at the screen, where the blur of pattern was paused for all to see, he knew this lead felt slightly more tangible.

'Enough to feel like we've not wasted our time, then?' Charlie asked, a slight smugness on his face.

Daniel nodded begrudgingly. 'Patrick, you know the drill. Get as much footage from around the hospital as you can. Traffic cameras, CCTV, everything you can get your hands on.'

Patrick nodded and plucked his phone from his pocket, making a call as he quickly unplugged his laptop. 'I'll get the team on it now,' he said over his shoulder as he left the room.

Charlie's phone rang.

'You have to be fucking kidding.' He groaned when he looked at the screen, before turning it around so Daniel could see.

'Kelly? As in nightmare, pain-in-the-ass, causing-us-constant-headaches journalist Kelly?' Daniel asked. Amelia pulled a face at his description of the woman.

'That's the one.'

The phone kept ringing.

'She's erm... determined,' Amelia said.

Another few rings.

'Just answer it and get rid of her,' Daniel advised. 'But if you say one word about the case to her, I'll kill you.'

'What do you want?' Charlie said curtly into the phone.

Amelia and Daniel leant in, trying to hear Kelly's half of the conversation. Daniel could just make out her voice, but not what she was saying.

'Come out with it, Kelly. I don't have time for the bullshit and I'm not giving you any more ammo for your bloody articles. You've caused enough trouble... An update? Which is? Just tell me. No, I don't want to do it over drinks. If you have something I need to know, just say it. No more manipulation.'

There was a pause. Charlie's expression shifted from irritation to something else – surprise, maybe.

'Wait... are you telling me the truth? Why did you call me? Couldn't you just make this another exclusive, fuck us over even more? Say that again?' Charlie pressed his phone screen and put Kelly on loudspeaker.

'Because... a few reasons. One, I feel bad, I suppose, for what I did. I know I used you in the past. But also, I'm sort of scared. If Mancini isn't missing after all, then why are these killers targeting their victims?'

Amelia rocked back in her chair and shock rippled across her face.

'What did you just say?' Daniel said, unable to help himself.

'Fuck, Charlie, you have me on speakerphone?' Kelly said.

'You called with info about the case, Kelly. It's not just for my ears.'

'Mancini has been found?' Daniel asked. He looked at Charlie, feeling suddenly helpless. 'How do you even know there's a connection between him and the victims?'

'Because I'm good at my job! I was hoping it would turn into a solid new lead for my articles. It didn't take too much digging to find out that all the victims had a connection to Mancini – one that you obviously found too. And apparently yes, he has been found. A reporter in Italy had been following a rumour that Carlos Mancini had been seen in Sicily. There's no concrete proof yet, but there are a few apparent eye-witness accounts, plus a photo. A blurry, long-distance one, sure, but I've seen it and it does look like him. It's not one hundred per cent definite that it's him, but...'

'But it's pretty damn likely,' Charlie finished.

'I'm afraid so. Look, I know this case has been like gold for me but, like I said, it scared me and I thought you should find out sooner rather than later. It changes things, surely.'

'Yeah, it does. Okay, well, I suppose... thank you,' Charlie said. 'I appreciate it.'

He hung up before she could say anything else. The three of them sat, dumbfounded, for a moment as they tried to comprehend what this new information meant to the case.

'It... can't still be... I mean, all three sets of victims – it's too much of a coincidence, right?' Amelia broke the silence.

'Honestly, I don't know,' Daniel said, which was the truth. 'If Mancini really is fine and dandy and not missing or dead then he's either responsible for the murders or has nothing at all to do with them. Coincidences do happen.'

'But this is a big one,' Charlie said.

'So we don't drop it. Maybe the killers are trying to get a rise out of him. Or like I said, maybe he's behind the murders.'

'If the first is true, it doesn't seem to be working,' Charlie said. 'And if the second is true, I don't even know how to prove that a billionaire property mogul swanning around Italy is behind six murders in England.'

Again they were silent.

'So... we continue as we were?' Charlie asked. 'Look for this person in the checked shirt?'

'I don't see what else we can do. But God, this is going to cause even more of a press nightmare. The speculation that will get thrown our way...'

After some discussion they resolved to keep on track. Patrick and his team were looking for other CCTV footage, so maybe they would find something that would help. And they had the list of people wronged by Carlos Mancini to cross off still – even though this held less promise than it had before the call from Kelly Malone. And maybe the coroner's office would turn up something else. The reports of Ayane Matsuda and the police officer's death were due in. Perhaps one of those bodies would provide a clue.

As they got up from the table, ready to get to work, Daniel felt the heavy grey clouds pulling in over his head.

———

At the end of the day, they were no further forward.

Rachel had arrived at Euston. Daniel decided he needed a break, so he had left Charlie manning the fort. His partner would call if anything urgent came up, but for once Daniel hoped there would be no developments in the case, just for a short while. Some time away from it would not be the worst thing in the world. He needed some headspace.

He'd agreed to meet Rachel outside Kennington Tube station, which was near his flat. He'd only been waiting a couple of minutes when she arrived. The tight hug she threw around him was like a kiss of life, helping to revive him.

'You're looking... well... bloody knackered if I'm honest, Dan,' Rachel said as she stood back to look at him, hoisting her bag over her shoulder. 'It's good to see you though – so good.'

'You have no idea, on both counts. I'm so glad you're here, Rach.'

They linked arms as they walked towards Daniel's flat. Tendrils of dread wound their way through him as they walked closer to their destination. He shivered, and knew it wasn't just because of the weather.

'Chill out, babe. Your knightess in shining armour is here!' Rachel joked.

'I don't think knightess is a word,' he said with a smile, trying to push his nerves down.

'I assure you it is, and I am she!' Rachel said in an affected fake-posh accent.

Daniel felt a flood of relief. He was more than glad that Rachel was walking beside him, her arm entwined with his. It felt as if a weight had been lifted off him – as though by her presence Rachel would help him get through everything. In some ways, she would. She could definitely help with Amanda, and she could offer her thoughts on the case – at least, of the details he could share with her. Her experience in the force more than qualified her to do that.

She couldn't help on the case, though. She also couldn't help him to find the person who had killed Jenny Cartwright and who had broken into his house. Somehow, though, he felt that he could deal with everything a little better with Rachel nearby. He didn't know how long she was planning on staying, but his best friend was here with him now. He planned to enjoy that, to make the most of it.

'Okay then, knightess, what do you want for dinner?' Daniel asked as they crossed the road. The shallow light of the afternoon was already fading, promising a sharp snap of cold to come.

They stopped at the Tesco by Daniel's flat, bought two large oven pizzas, two bottles of wine and some Haribo for dessert. When they reached Daniel's front door, it occurred to him that they had made it here without him falling apart. The fear came the second he focused on entering the property. He held out the new keys, which had been delivered to him at work, then froze.

'Allow me,' Rachel said, taking the keys and unlocking the door. A shrill beeping started as she pushed open the door.

'Shit, the alarm,' Daniel said, pulling his phone from his pocket. He unlocked it and found the email from the security company, which contained the passcode to shut the system off. After he'd found the wall-mounted unit tucked into a space to the left of the door, he punched in the code. The beeping stopped.

'Thank God. It would have been embarrassing to have the alarm company calling in backup already.' He had to admit, the alarm made him feel more secure. He shut the front door, locked it and set the alarm again. It would signal if anyone tried to break in through the door or the windows. There was also an extra bolt and lock on the door.

He stood still in the small hallway and gathered himself.

'Good to be home?' Rachel asked as she moved into the open-plan kitchen/living room and switched on the lights.

'I'll get back to you on that,' he answered as he reluctantly followed her.

He turned the oven on and slid in the pizzas, and Rachel poured them both a generous glass of wine. Daniel tried to ignore the discomfort that snaked through him. His home, his sanctum, had been compromised, and now he wasn't sure it offered the same feeling of safety it had prior to the break-in. A random burglary would have been bad enough, but this was worse: it was personal, someone had done it to rattle him.

'You'll be okay,' Rachel said as she handed him his drink. 'I'm sure it's weird and unsettling, but the security team has turned this place into Fort Knox, right? And I'm here now. I'll kick the arse of anyone who tries to get in here again.' She smiled as she sipped her wine.

He nodded, not sure what to say, and decided it was probably time to tackle the other matter that needed to be dealt with. He pulled his phone from his pocket.

'While the pizza cooks, I'll ring Amanda. Get it over with.'

Rachel opened the pack of Haribo and took out a few sweets. 'Good plan.'

Rachel couldn't make the call for him, but she might be able to help if things went awry. He called Amanda's number, then put the phone on speaker, placing it on the grey kitchen counter and gulping his wine. Rachel held out the sweets and he took a few. He was chewing when his sister answered.

'Daniel, hi, thanks for calling me back. You okay?'

'Yeah, I suppose. Tired and stressed, but okay. I have wine.'

'A good one, I hope. You sound weird. Am I on speaker?'

'Yes, sorry – I'm cooking so it's easier,' he lied. He wanted Rachel to be able to hear both sides of the conversation, but knew that Amanda would get funny if she knew Rachel was listening.

'Okay, sure. How's the case going?'

Daniel suspected she was trying to delay the real reason she wanted to talk to him. 'It's tough. We have some leads. I can't discuss it, though.'

'Oh, I know. That makes sense.'

There was a tense silence. Daniel took another gulp of wine and looked at Rachel, who shrugged.

'Have you spoken to Mum or Dad lately?' Amanda tried. She sounded like she had been trapped by someone at a party and was doing her best to offer polite chat.

'No. Dad texted me about some film the other day, telling me to watch it, but that's it. I've not spoken to Mum in weeks.'

'You should. They would like to hear from you.'

Daniel knew she was right. He was terrible at keeping in touch with them, and was well aware that it bothered his parents. There wasn't even any real reason he didn't speak to them much. They just seemed to have fallen into a pattern of not getting in contact often; they only really caught up on birthdays or at Christmas or if something major happened. They never talked about their day-to-day lives. They knew very little about him now, beyond the basics. They didn't seem to be that interested, and in return he didn't bother to keep them abreast of anything. His father didn't like the fact that Daniel had moved away from them, and his mother hated hearing about his work, claiming it worried her too much. He knew it was a shame, but the thought of doing something about their relationship made him uneasy. As a child he'd been quite close to his mother, but as an adult he couldn't help feeling that she judged him for his decisions. He rarely had the energy to deal with her. Everything was a negative to her, and he doubted he would change her mind or give her a more positive outlook on life, so he avoided having any deep and meaningful discussions with her these days.

He decided to cut to the chase. 'So what's up? Your text said you needed to talk.'

'Right. Yeah.' Amanda sounded different immediately, her voice lower and more serious. 'It's... well, I've been seeing this guy, and I'm not sure he's exactly what he seems. Like he's too good to be true.'

Rachel mouthed 'here we go' at Daniel from across the counter. They'd heard this one before.

'Okay, but why did you need to talk to me about it?' He realised after he'd said it that he sounded a bit too blunt. He winced, then shrugged.

'Why do you think, Dan? You know I have trust issues, especially with men, and I thought you might... might be able to look into him for me. I read about Clare's Law – you know, where you can ask the police to check out your partner if you think your partner poses a risk.'

Rachel coughed on a sweet. Daniel quickly put a finger to his mouth. She mouthed 'sorry'.

'I see. Hang on a sec, I just need to check the food.' Daniel pressed 'mute' on the phone. 'Is she kidding? She wants me to be her PI?'

'It would seem so,' Rachel said flatly, clearly not that surprised.

'I guess her just wanting to try being my sister was too good to be true after all.' He pulled open the oven door and turned the pizzas to keep them cooking evenly. They smelled good. He wanted to be off the phone so he and Rachel could get back to catching up.

'Can you help her? I mean, if you wanted to.'

'Technically, yes, probably, although it's a bit of an abuse of power, and Clare's Law doesn't cover this situation. Amanda said he's too good to be true, not that she's worried he might be a threat to her. I'd need a good reason.'

'Maybe you should see if you can help her. Might be easier than arguing with her. Get it out of the way and then it's one less thing to stress about.'

'Yeah, except it adds more stress to me, which I don't need right now.'

'Dan? You still there?' Amanda asked.

Daniel screwed up his face before unmuting the call. 'Yes, sorry. The, er, the food needed stirring.'

'So? What do you think?'

'Honestly, I think if you're not sure about this guy you should just steer clear of him,' Daniel answered, his tone blunt. He was annoyed and felt he had the right to be. Amanda never contacted him, never even texted unless he did first, yet she had pretended to be a doting sister who wanted to reconnect with him simply so he could help her with some random man she was seeing.

'It's not like that. This guy, he's nice. I really like him.'

'Yet you want me to dig up his files to see if he's as good as he seems?'

'He is. I mean, I hope he is. Please, Dan, you know I struggle with this. I haven't had a successful relationship in forever. Surely you want that for me.'

The guilt trip was blatant. She had dropped the act entirely. Rachel rolled her eyes and swigged her wine.

'You know, I really don't need this right now. I'm already dealing with enough. This guy isn't Adam.'

At the mention of the name both siblings fell silent again. Daniel felt a pang of guilt. That nightmare had been a barrier between them for so many years. Rather than bringing them closer together, as sharing a traumatic event sometimes did, it had actually weakened their relationship and left them barely more than strangers tied by blood. They were both guilty of avoiding the other in a bid not to deal with their feelings.

He wasn't sure what to say. Amanda stayed quiet too. He could feel the tension crackling out of the phone.

'Just help her,' Rachel whispered.

Despite everything else in his body telling him otherwise, a small part of him knew that his friend was right. It was a shit situation. It hurt that this was the only reason Amanda had wanted to talk to him – and his hurt made him want to say no. But if he did, that would probably increase the distance between them, if that was even possible. At least if he helped her then he could take the moral high ground and avoid making things worse. At best, maybe it would actually bring them a little closer. Possibly.

'I'll see what I can do,' he said at last, another gulp of wine not taking away the bitter taste in his mouth.

'Will you? Oh thanks, Dan, thanks. You won't find anything, I'm sure. He's lovely. I just... I need to be sure.'

'Okay. Text me his details.'

'Amazing.'

'But I can't promise anything. This case is my priority. I might not have time to help right away.'

'Of course, I get it. Thanks, Dan. I'll text you his details soon, okay?'

'Sure. Speak to you soon.'

Amanda hung up and Daniel felt his shoulders sagging. 'Fuck my life,' he muttered.

'Nope, none of that,' Rachel said. 'You did it, you dealt with her, sort of. Now it's time for pizza, more wine and some shit television. No more serious chat.'

'Okay, deal. Although I might pick your brains a bit about the case.'

'Pizza first. Then maybe.'

'Thank God you're here,' Daniel said again. Rachel raised her glass.

'I'll drink to that!'

They clinked glasses. Daniel smiled, and finally allowed his mind and body to relax.

CHAPTER TWENTY

There was subdued excitement in the air the next morning. Patrick Marsden had made all of his available team members work on the case. They had nicknamed the job Operation Plaid, a simple, self-explanatory moniker.

Getting more footage from the hospital had been easy and quick. From street cameras it was not quite as speedy, but still fairly straightforward. One social media specialist was even going through social media posts that had been loaded around the time of the murders at the hospital, tracking geotagged posts as well as any that had used hashtags that related to the hospital and the surrounding area.

Going through all this proved to be a monumental task. That had not deterred the seven-strong team, however, and Daniel was now racing down the brightly lit corridors of his building to get to the tech department, trying not to get his hopes up but at the same time feeling spikes of adrenaline.

One of the team had found the checked jacket.

Daniel spotted Patrick and a couple of the IT specialists. 'Show me, show me!' he said as calmly and politely as he could.

'I think you might owe us a round of pints, because we

actually have a few shots,' Patrick answered, gesturing towards the bank of enormous screens lining the wall. 'This, my detective friend, is the best one.' He was smiling – grinning, in fact. Daniel's gaze locked onto one of the larger monitors. His insides flipped.

The video had been paused. The image was, while not perfect, remarkably clear, even though it had been captured at night. The man was right in the middle of the frame, looking over his shoulder. A streetlight highlighted him in a neat yellow circle. The patterned jacket that they had spotted in the reflection of the metal lift doors at the hospital was unmistakable.

Daniel stared and for a moment lost himself in the image. The man had been caught on one of the cameras that overlooked one entrance to the hospital car park. His face was slightly blurry but his eyes still seemed to shine with cruelty.

'Shit,' was all Daniel could manage. 'This is brilliant. Do we know who he is?'

'We ran his face through our database and it spat out three likely results,' one of the men standing next to Patrick answered.

'Three?'

'Afraid so. Unfortunately the best image is still not sharp enough for the system to be one hundred per cent sure. It has a favourite, though, as do I.'

Patrick picked up a tablet from the desk behind him and tapped the screen a few times before directing Daniel's attention to one of the smaller screens. 'I think it's him.'

The mugshot showed a white man in his late twenties. He had short, wiry black hair, patchy stubble, mild crow's feet and a cold expression.

'Calvin Cavendish,' Daniel read out aloud. 'Known for his involvement in drugs and break-ins – now off the radar, I presume, given the last charge against him was seven years ago.'

They looked at the other two options as well. David Kowal, brought up for assault a few years back but with no other apparent offences. Alex Masters, charged with indecency as a teenager.

'It's interesting that none of them have recent charges, nothing that would point to them being sociopathic or psychopathic. Perhaps whichever one it is got smarter over time, has somehow managed to stay out of the spotlight. We need to get these profiles to Martia. I'll get the team to do some digging into them too. Amazing stuff, guys.'

There was a moment of celebration before work mode took over again and Daniel rang Charlie with the news.

'Mate, I've been waiting for your call. Got pulled in to consult on another case by Hobbs. Please tell me it's good news,' Charlie said.

'We have three suspects. There's a very good chance it's one of them. God knows what their motive is, but I'm getting Martia in as soon as possible to go through their profiles.'

'Are Amelia and Ross in already? Get them started on more background checking.'

'I think Amelia is. I was planning on going upstairs to tell her right now.'

'Great minds think alike,' Charlie answered. 'I'll be in the office by lunchtime. Call me if you find anything else before then.'

Daniel promised he would before bounding towards the lifts, feeling refreshingly confident.

He could feel the crusted blood in the folds of skin around his eyes, clumping his lashes together and making his right cheek feel stiff and tight. As consciousness finally came to him, he was not surprised to find that he was still in the same place.

A weak grey light lanced through the shadows where it found cracks between the boards that covered the windows, illuminating the dust and decay of the old building. Faded bits of paper, a few rotted slats of wood, a rickety-looking table and a dilapidated armchair were pretty much it in the way of contents – besides, of course, him and the sturdy oak chair he was tied to.

The room was cold, visually and literally, though he suspected that at some point it had been a nicely decorated space in an equally nice building. He could hear traffic close by and wished he knew where the building was. Not that it would help him. Even if he somehow escaped his bindings, he feared his legs would be useless, at least for a while. He was only allowed up to go to the bathroom, which was at the other end of the room. Otherwise he had to stay sitting down: his knees had stiffened and sores had developed on his backside and underneath his thighs.

He was thirsty: the coarse, thick rope gag in his mouth stole away any moisture and chafed the inside edges of his lips. It was almost bad enough for him to welcome the return of one of his captors. Almost. Being thirsty and brutally uncomfortable was still better than what they brought with them.

While he had been imprisoned there he had seen one of the men four times, the other one six times. They had only visited him together once. That time had been worse than any other, and he was thankful that they seemed to want to interrogate him separately for the most part.

He had learned quite a bit about them, which he prayed would come in handy at some point, but he was starting to doubt that there would be a happy ending for him. He knew their names, thanks to an argument he had heard between them a few days back. Sound carried in the old building with no furnishings to absorb it, and evidently they had not realised that. He had discerned that the smaller man was the one in charge, though they bickered about this regularly. He also knew what they wanted and why they had kidnapped him in the first place.

So far, he had managed not to say anything of any consequence. He was aware that they wanted him alive for now, and that the second they thought he was no longer essential they would kill him. He gave them leads, threads of information that would keep them occupied.

It was getting harder, though. They were cruel, vindictive men, and they enjoyed causing him pain. They had beaten him every time they visited, no matter what he said to them. He was fairly sure one or more of his ribs was fractured. Two of his back teeth had been unceremoniously pulled out; his gums were only now firming up again after a few days. The taller man had truly relished that moment. He was clearly crazy. The smaller one was more reserved, more careful perhaps, in what he did and said, in how he moved. They were a terrifying pair.

As well as the injuries he had sustained, he was deeply worried that he would run out of things to tell them that would keep him safe. He was already sending them on what he knew were wild-goose chases, and it was only a matter of time before they noticed. He didn't think the tall one minded, but the smaller one had already shown signs of irritation. The ruse would be up before long; it was inevitable.

And one other thing made his trickery harder and harder to stomach. The other victims. This was where the taller man truly came alive, explaining what had been done to each person, how they had been killed and mutilated. It was harrowing, and made worse by the fact that it was his fault these poor people were being killed. He was literally giving the killers targets. But couldn't stop. These people were dying so he could live. As it turned out, this was true in more ways than one.

Yesterday his dinner had been a bread roll filled with a fried human tongue. Yet he had eaten it quickly, spurred on by painful hunger. It hadn't even made him gag, not like the heart had – or, worse, the eyes. Sure, each body part had been cooked in some way, but the eyes had been a struggle nonetheless. He had thrown up that time and received a punch to the side of the head for wasting food.

And now they were out looking for their next victim, which would no doubt result in his next meal. He had given them another name: someone who was vaguely connected to him. He wondered what body part he would have to eat when they returned, disturbed by the fact that his stomach rumbled and his mouth salivated at the thought of more cooked human. It was so wrong, so troubling, on top of everything else. But if they refused to give him anything else to eat, what choice did he have? He needed whatever sustenance he could get, to allow his body to attempt to heal after each time they hurt him.

He expected it would take them another day, maybe. He'd not seen them since the night before. The taller one had brought him water, and the smaller one had escorted him to the toilet. He thought they had probably scoped out the poor person he'd put in their crosshairs by now, which meant more blood on his hands, depending on how he looked at the situation. Sure, he wasn't the one killing people, but could he be considered innocent?

Still, if there was one thing he now knew, it was that he was made of strong stuff. He had worked damn hard, had thrown everything he had into becoming a success, had dragged his way up after a less than fortunate start in life. Determination had always been – and still was – Carlos Mancini's personal mantra.

And he knew he would do anything he could to stay alive.

CHAPTER TWENTY-ONE

I t had taken a long time to track down the three men who were now prime suspects. They had found Masters first. He had moved to Glasgow and set up a motorcycle repair shop. After a few calls to check out the legitimacy of the business and his registered address, they were happy to cross him off the list.

Initial enquiries still placed the other two in the Greater London area, but – as good as Patrick's team were – they had struggled to find much concrete information on either of the men. Both seemed to have succeeded in disappearing entirely.

Facial recognition software and internet spiders had found a few images of Cavendish posted on Facebook at a barbecue in Rotherhithe in 2013, but they had not been tagged to a profile and he seemed to have no social media presence himself. Kowal had been listed as an employee at a hardware store in Watford a few years ago, but they had called the shop and discovered he no longer worked there, and he had given the shop owner a mixture of true and false details. Occasional addresses appeared for both over the course of the last decade but since 2014, there was nothing. They had disappeared.

Martia Franklin, still working on the evolving killer profiles, had been quick to point out that fading into the background was often a core characteristic of psychopaths. The man who had killed Ayane Matsuda and the policeman in the hospital had to be the psychopath of the duo, not the sociopath, because the murders had been planned, efficient and restrained. Therefore the man they were looking for had probably found a way to blend into the world around him without leaving much of a ripple.

'Why haven't we at least found the sociopath, then?' Charlie asked. 'According to known indicators, they struggle to acclimatise and adapt to normal societal behaviour. That's the opposite of blending in.'

'That person has no doubt been convicted of something in the past, Detective, or may have come up related to a previous case somewhere, but it's possible that the psychopath is, for now, maintaining some control over the sociopath to remain out of sight. It's also possible that the sociopath has actually not been a member of the general public for some time – perhaps they have spent time in prison or a treatment facility of some sort.'

Daniel had immediately asked Sergeant Amelia Harding to look into recent releases of patients from mental health hospitals across the UK.

'It's also possible they have changed their identities. In fact, it's highly probable. The psychopath is a planner, meticulous, remember?'

That had thrown up another research project. The rental records for the houses that had been used to spy on the victims had been pulled back out of the files. Daniel had checked through them when the pattern of renting properties had first appeared and had found no connection between any of the names on the short-term leases. He had dismissed it at the time, for the same reason Martia had brought it up. Multiple identities would not help them, and some of the estate agents had been less than stringent at checking that paperwork had been filled out properly when letting properties. Daniel had needed to utilise his team's time elsewhere, on leads with more substance. Now though, with a face to connect to a fake name, maybe they had a chance.

An agency called SoLo Lettings came back with something positive. Daniel and Charlie leaped into Daniel's car and sped across the river to SoLo Lettings' office in Kennington to meet with one of their estate agents, Mya Rimini. Now, as they sat opposite her cheap-looking desk, which was stacked with paper, empty coffee mugs and a range of nail varnishes in garish colours, Daniel was eager to get as much as possible from the woman.

'Thanks for agreeing to see us,' he said. 'I know you must be closing up soon.' He looked around at the quiet office, empty except for the three of them.

'It's okay,' she said, her tight smile indicating that she hoped the chat would be quick.

'I know you said you recognised the man in the photo we emailed over, but can you just confirm that for us?' Daniel asked, handing Mya a printed photo of lead suspect Calvin Cavendish. She took the picture carefully, her bright blue nails a stark contrast with the dull printout, and pursed her lips as she inspected it again. Her free hand twirled a long curly strand of jet-black hair.

'I mean... I'm, like, ninety-nine per cent sure we rented to him. I see a lot of people every day and it was a while ago. But yeah, I'm pretty sure.' She passed the photo back to Daniel.

'And do you know what property he rented?' Charlie asked.

'Not for definite, we don't take pictures from customers, but I got out a few possible ones while you was driving over.'

She handed them a pile of prints. Daniel was impressed that

she had been so prepared for them. He flicked through the property details, stopping at the sixth one in the stack.

'Recognise this?' he said to Charlie.

'Shit, that's the one by the Altons.'

Mya's eyes widened. 'Wait, the Altons? Aren't they that couple what got killed last week? I seen it in the *Metro*. That serial killer. Oh my days...'

'We can't give any details on that,' Daniel said quickly. 'This, though, this was rented by a Callum Davis, right?' He handed her back the papers, now with the Camberwell house on top. 'That's the name against the property.'

Mya typed something into her computer and nodded, pulling her cardigan tightly around her as though she was cold. Daniel could see that she was anxious. He was glad he had brought paperwork for her to sign to prevent her talking to anyone about any of this. They had already had enough press nightmares to deal with. Another one would surely make Superintendent Hobbs' head explode.

Mya informed them that in person Calvin Cavendish, pretending to be Callum Davis, was polite and friendly but quite pushy, from what she recalled.

'He was well specific about what he wanted. Made me show him that flat the same day he called, and signed for it instantly. I can't believe it...'

Mya signed the non-disclosure agreement with a shaky hand and took Daniel's card so she could contact him if she thought of anything else.

As Charlie drove towards Daniel's flat, where Rachel was waiting to take him out for dinner, Daniel called Patrick to get the team onto the next CCTV job. They needed footage of Calvin Cavendish near to, or at, the scene of the crime. Maybe they could follow him, find out where he lived. Daniel could feel excitement humming in his body.

CHAPTER TWENTY-TWO

The blissful high that Kelly Malone had felt after landing another headline exclusive for the *City Post* had not yet fully dissipated, but she knew it wouldn't last much longer. Like any great high, it was fleeting. The bottle of champagne her boss Brian had given her had been a real treat, and the look on Jennifer Khan's face had been so good that Kelly wished she could have Instagrammed it.

It had been almost a week since then, however, and the stories about the London Organ Snatcher, as many of the dailies had started calling the killer, were drying up. The interest was there but the facts were not. She had nothing to write about, nothing to say that would even come close to the image of Ayane Matsuda in the hospital. And to make matters worse, the *Daily Mail* had beaten her to the punch with an article on Matsuda's murder. Brian hadn't said anything to her about that, but she knew he wouldn't be impressed. Sure, she didn't have exclusive access or rights to write about the case, but already her name had started to become synonymous with coverage on the hunt for the murderer. Being beaten to the punch again had been a real blow.

She realised that she needed new tactics. The story was so widespread that the competition for breaking news had really heated up. Everyone was on edge, the public were terrified, people were constantly being interviewed on TV for talk pieces about home safety and what to do in the event of a break-in. The country was waiting to see what would happen next. She needed to tap into it all somehow, but how?

For a brief moment, Kelly considered phoning Charlie Palmer. He seemed like the obvious choice. Maybe she could wrangle some more dirt on the case from him. She quickly dismissed the notion, however. He wouldn't fall for her tricks again; that bridge was too badly burnt. In fact, he had barely been willing to speak to her even when she had called about Carlos Mancini. Talk about frosty. She thought that had probably earned her a few brownie points, but not enough for him to forget that twice she had used information from Charlie to write stories. The trust was definitely no longer there.

Her next tactic was to find Steven, the office exec, and hit on him again in an attempt to get any titbits that had come in through the hotlines. She had cornered him in the kitchen as he waited for the kettle to boil. Five minutes of blatant flirting later, she had nothing new to report except a potential date next week that she didn't really want.

Returning to her desk, Kelly had a moment of self-doubt. Was her only tactic to hit on men to get information? Was she a journalist?

'No, Kel. You just landed a front cover. You got this,' she said quietly to herself, keen not to be overheard. With a deep breath, she started to research. But by the end of the day, having tried every avenue she could think of, she was no better off. She had written the first paragraph of a possible thought piece on the killer, but it was crap, and now that Brian was expecting better, there was no way it would fly. She deleted it and sank down in her chair, staring at nothing and feeling more frustrated than she had in weeks.

'Maybe I'm just a shit journalist,' she whispered to herself, the pep talk long forgotten. Try as she might, her mind kept going back to Charlie. It annoyed her that she couldn't speak to him. Really got under her skin. She wondered for a hot second if there was more to the irritation than that, but now was not the time to reminisce or get distracted by romantic feelings – if any still remained. Anyway, his partner would be sure to keep her away even if she wanted to get close to Charlie again.

She needed an inside scoop, though, that much was clear. She couldn't be beaten to a story again or her hard work would be forgotten. Bribery was a possible option, but she didn't exactly have cash to spare. Plus, who would she bribe? And that seemed too morally bankrupt – worse than getting information through flirting.

More Jennifer's style, the sleazy cow, she thought snidely, wishing Anneka was around to join in the bitching. So what else was there? How could she gain access to information that only the police knew? Then she sat up straight. She'd had another morally bankrupt idea, possibly worse than the idea of paying shady police officers for information, but if no one ever found out then did it really matter?

She pulled her keyboard towards her, typed quickly into Google, then selected an item to purchase from the shopping tab. After another quick search she had ordered a second item. Both would arrive at the office tomorrow morning. She had made sure of it, for once willing to pay for express delivery.

If she couldn't get information from Charlie by asking, then she would damn well get it another way: by using a GPS tracker to follow him and a directional microphone to listen in on his conversations.

Putting her bank card back in her purse, Kelly felt oddly

satisfied with herself – and mildly surprised at what she was willing to do to get ahead. First the trick with the fizzy drink at the hospital, now this. She chose to ignore the quiet voice in the back of her mind, the one warning her about the slippery slope she seemed to have started down.

The IT team had found success much more quickly than during the hunt for the patterned jacket, mainly because the job Patrick Marsden had given them was more straightforward.

The area of Camberwell that the Altons had lived in was not exactly littered with cameras, which meant less chance of spotting Calvin Cavendish on a recording, but also a much smaller pool of footage to go through. It had still taken a while, but now they knew the face of one of the men they were looking for, it was a lot quicker to rule out other people who had been caught on camera.

After a few hours one of the team spotted someone who looked very like Cavendish walking into a takeaway on Denmark Hill, not far from King's College Hospital. After another two hours, they had their hands on footage filmed inside the takeaway. The camera was a security feed recording customers, set up by the owner to deter late-night robberies or drunken misdemeanours.

'It's him all right,' Patrick confirmed to his team after looking at the grainy, but well-lit recording. He'd called Daniel and Charlie immediately.

'He stopped to buy fried chicken? After murdering two people?' Charlie had asked incredulously. 'And why wasn't there blood on his clothing?'

'Perhaps he took the jacket off when he attacked Matsude

and the officer. Any chance you spotted someone else with him? His possible partner in crime?' Daniel had asked.

He thought that a man could fancy fried chicken and chips not long after stabbing two people to death was astonishing, but he needed Patrick to focus and not get side-tracked into a chat about ethics. He'd seen Charlie and Patrick do that before, and he didn't want to waste any time.

'Afraid not. We tried to follow him back to the Alton house but he wasn't spotted on another camera between the house and the takeaway.'

'Please tell me you could follow him, though. Preferably to his front door?' Daniel urged.

'Again, no. Sorry, Graves. We do think we know the rough area, though. We're trying to narrow it down, but it seems likely to be out Lewisham way. He got on a bus. Most of them head that way, but we couldn't get its number or licence plate, so we need to dig in a little more, check the bus routes around the area. I'll get back to you when we know more. Don't you worry. My guys will find the little fucker, I promise you.'

Daniel had hung up, then realised he'd had his fingers crossed the entire time. He trusted Patrick. They were getting close now, he could feel it. He just hoped they were close enough to avoid more bloodshed. It wouldn't be long before Calvin and his accomplice struck again.

———

Kelly had been sitting in her Astra for what seemed like hours. She'd given her nails a file and a new pale pink polish, eaten a salad, half a pot of hummus and two chocolate bars, and run out of lives on every match-three game in her phone. She'd also looked up new cars in case she managed to get a promotion and could say goodbye to her beloved but battered vehicle.

It wasn't until almost eight – the night thick and cold outside of her little blue bubble – that she'd had a notification that Charlie Palmer was on the move.

It had surprised her how easy it was to set up the GPS tracker. She already knew which car was his, had spent many nights in it going to dinner or the cinema while they had been seeing each other. Locating it in the car park of Charlie's office had been easy. She had simply walked up to it, bent down to tuck the tracker under one of the wheel arches, and walked away. No one saw her and she was back in her own car three roads away within a few minutes, phone in hand.

Now the small blue dot was moving across the map of London in the tracking app. She started the engine, put trainer to pedal and started to follow the detective, her stomach bubbling, knowing she was breaking the law.

'Where will you take me, Charlie boy?' she said aloud, a grin plastered across her face. She switched on the radio and began singing along to an Ariana Grande song, her gaze flicking between the tracker and the dark, rain-slick road ahead.

Charlie pulled up to the kerb and switched off the engine. Daniel peered out of the window and up at the block of flats their suspect had been traced to.

'Let's hope Patrick was right, otherwise we're fucked,' Charlie said as he unbuckled his seat belt.

'Ever the optimist, hey?' Daniel answered.

'Oh, you're one to talk!' Charlie laughed.

'Fair point. Shall we?'

The men got out of the car. Daniel pulled the collar of his coat up against the cold drizzle as they jogged across the street and entered the small car park that served the flats.

From where she had parked, her view was lousy, but Kelly knew the detectives would spot her if she got any closer. She was only at the end of the closest side road, though. Plus she couldn't recall if Charlie knew what her car looked like. She'd had it for years, so he would definitely have seen it when they were together. She doubted he would notice the vehicle and know right away whose it was; nonetheless, she wanted to be careful.

Her windscreen was dappled with raindrops, and tall, spindly trees with dense, jagged branches grew up in front of the block of flats, so while Kelly had just about been able to see Charlie and his partner go through a door into the flats – thanks to the building being set back from the pavement and having grass and a shrubbery out front – she couldn't see which floor they were going to, despite the external balconies on each storey.

'Fuck this,' she muttered. Grabbing her phone and handbag, Kelly clambered out of the car. Keeping her gaze on the building, as she got closer she saw movement. The detectives emerged onto the fourth floor, walking to the sixth front door along. They stopped and Charlie knocked on the door. Pulling her phone out as she walked, Kelly unlocked the camera. She paused, aiming it up at the building, then tutted when she saw that neither the men or the door could be made out. She pinched the screen to zoom in and took a shot, but it was blurry. Not even vaguely useful for a story. She had to get closer.

The road was silent apart from the wind, which whipped the rain around her face, but she checked for cars anyway. None came and she ran across the road, narrowly missing a puddle. A few seconds later, she was on the pavement outside the building. Her heart was racing. If either detective looked down, they would see her immediately. Kelly ducked into the shadow of one of the trees.

Charlie didn't seem to be getting an answer. He knocked harder, loud enough for Kelly to hear. She raised her phone again and took another photo, smiling at the outcome. It was much clearer. She didn't know why they had come to this building, but she already knew the story she'd write to go with the photo.

Could the Organ Snatcher be your neighbour?

It would be perfect – a great talking point. She could put the photo up, list the address, everything. Sure it would be controversial, but she reckoned Brian would sign off on it. It would be a huge exclusive look into the work the police were doing on the case – and if it turned out to be true, even better.

Realising she was forgetting something, she dug into her handbag and pulled out the directional microphone she had bought. It was smaller than she had expected, but she'd tested it and it seemed okay. She plugged it into the headphone jack on her phone, put the setting on maximum, and aimed it up at the balcony. She made sure her camera was still on the men and pressed 'record'.

She couldn't hear much. There was sound, much better than had she aimed her phone by itself, but it was still quiet. Nevertheless she kept recording until the detectives gave up. Maybe one of them had said something useful and, if not, the photo was still a good one.

Unplugging the microphone and stuffing it back into her bag, Kelly turned. She was about to run back to her car when she spotted something odd. Across the road was a man, standing totally still, looking directly at her. Instinctively, Kelly ducked back into the shadows. Peeking around the tree, she saw that he was dressed in black, with a hood that covered his features. She also saw that the man was not looking at her. He was looking up at the building. She turned and saw Charlie and Daniel Graves walking back along the balcony in the direction of the stairwell.

Shit!

She felt trapped. She glanced back at the creepy man, whose head turned slowly as he followed the detectives. Then he turned unexpectedly and, walking much quicker than normal speed, headed down the road she was parked on.

For a second she was confused about what had happened. As soon as she was sure the man in black would not notice her, she ran back to her Astra. She jumped into the car and closed the door, feeling safe again, letting her breathing slow.

Then it dawned on her.

I think I may have just seen the killer.

Shit!

She could run back and tell Charlie and David. She should tell them. But that would ruin her story – and expose the fact she was following them. No. Plus, she could get in real trouble; she might even be arrested.

There is another option.

Her hands shaking, Kelly started the car. That man could not have gone far, not yet. If she followed him instead – well, imagine the story she could write...

The question had been floating through Kelly Malone's mind for the last hour but now it was urgent and unremitting. *What the hell am I doing?*

The idea of following the man had seemed like a no-brainer. It had been one of those decisions made where the alternative would have been eternal regret. At least that's what she thought when she made it.

After spending the last sixty-seven minutes trying to hide her car behind buses and trees, ducking down below her steering wheel if the man looked her way, she was starting to think she had made a bad decision. The roads around her were still busy, but she felt startlingly alone. The night pressed down on her, almost overwhelming her, and rain constantly washed over her windscreen, heavier than it had been when she had hidden behind the tree.

There were no pedestrians – clearly they were avoiding the weather – save one. The man she was following, the man that Kelly's recording of Charlie Palmer, which she had played on loudspeaker as she drove, told her was Calvin Cavendish. He had walked from the block of flats on the west side of Lewisham to here. He'd taken a circuitous route, clearly attempting to ensure he wasn't followed, but she had managed to keep an eye on him nonetheless, even though it was an absolute pain to follow a pedestrian in a car and she had lost him a few times. Then he had disappeared into a boarded-up old building on Lewisham High Street, a building that looked abandoned, despite being shrouded in rickety-looking scaffolding and six-foot-high wooden panelling.

A quick search on her phone told Kelly that it was the old Lewisham Temperance Billiard Hall. Google also told her that the building was up for renovation, and bids were being invited for the project. One name stood out.

'Carlos Mancini. That can't be a coincidence,' she muttered.

Even when she had been told that Mancini had been seen in Italy, even after seeing the photo of him, she hadn't been entirely convinced, not deep down. All the murder victims so far had connections to Mancini, and she had known from Detective Graves' tone alone that they had been looking into it too. She had called Charlie because she had been trying to earn brownie points, and who was she to comment on the legitimacy of a photo? But this couldn't be just another coincidence. Only three bids had been registered for the plot, her initial search told her, and one of them was Mancini? That could not be ignored as a fluke.

She gathered her thoughts while she decided what to do. She could go to the police, to Charlie, and reveal that she knew where Cavendish was. That would gain her a lot of trust with the police force – something she was currently severely lacking. It could lead, in time, to more exclusives, more stories. She could write about how she had followed Cavendish and knew it would make a good piece.

But she had a second option. She could play detective herself, follow Cavendish, maybe even find out who the next victims could be – presuming he was not finished killing yet. Who knew what that could lead to?

This is big. Fucking huge. The biggest homicide case in the country in years. Internationally famous. I've broken exclusive info already, and now I'm sitting on a journalistic goldmine. Do I want to pass on that?

Under the cover of night, protected from the elements in her faithful little Astra, the second option didn't seem totally unrealistic. Was it risky? Sure. But as soon as she felt she was in danger, she could contact Charlie.

Imagine if I break an exclusive on the killer. Name, face, everything. It would make my career. Every newspaper editor would know my name. And that's what I've always wanted.

She had managed to land in the middle of the scoop of the century. She couldn't just hand it over.

'Well, Kel, time to think up a plan.' She turned on the engine and pulled out of the parking space, ready to head across the city to her flat. It wasn't that late, only just past ten, and although she was tired, she doubted she could sleep. She was already thinking of ways she could get into the abandoned building that Cavendish was using as a hideout while he was not there. If she played it as safe as possible, the rewards could be huge...

CHAPTER TWENTY-THREE

'Steven, for fuck's sake, how many times do I have to tell you to pick up your own stuff?' Aaron Hudson shouted from the bathroom. 'I'm not your maid.' He waited for a second but got no response. He wasn't surprised. Steven had very selective hearing, not seeming to catch anything he didn't like or didn't deem worthy of a response. Aaron stared at himself in the mirror, running a hand through his hair and wondering if there was something more interesting he could do with it style-wise. A generic short cut with a bit of spike was so boring.

'Maybe I should grow it out,' he mumbled, leaning in closer to inspect the pores on his nose.

With a sigh Aaron picked up the dirty socks, marched down the hallway into the living room, and threw the socks at Steven. One went wide; the other landed perfectly on Steven's head. Putting the Xbox controller down, Steven slowly and deliberately removed the sock, flashed a quick smile and lobbed it back at Aaron. Then he resumed his game.

'You can't get out of everything with a smile, you know. You're not that cute.'

'Yes, I am,' Steven answered, flashing another grin before returning his attention to the car on screen.

'Pick up your shit,' Aaron said again but with less heat.

Unfortunately Steven was right. Aaron *did* think he was that cute. The way his dimples popped in, the tuft of black hair at the back of his head that always seemed to appear at the end of the day after his hair product had lost its control, his eyes, which lit up with love and mischief in equal measure. He would probably let him get away with murder. It was a dynamic that Aaron wasn't entirely keen on, and now that they lived together he didn't think it would cease any time soon. He would do anything for Steven. He'd complain about it, sure, but he'd still do it.

'Can we go to bed now?' he asked, slumping on the sofa next to Steven. 'It's almost two.'

'One more race then we can, promise.' Steven paused the game, gave Aaron a quick kiss, then resumed playing. Aaron knew what that meant. He should go to bed by himself and Steven would come when he was finished, meaning that Aaron would be lying there, wide awake and waiting. Annoyance flashed again but he realised he was too tired to make a thing out of it.

Aaron decided to read in bed while he waited. He had been feeling guilty for not reading more regularly, so it was a good opportunity. That's what he told himself anyway.

As he entered their bedroom he shivered in the frosty air. He went over to the window to check the radiator and close the curtains. The moon was high and clear now that the rain had stopped, and its light glowed on the tops of the trees that edged Highgate Wood, which started at the end of their garden. But the trees were not the only thing the moonlight illuminated. Despite the shadows, Aaron could swear he had seen someone standing at the end of their garden. Instinctively he jumped backwards to avoid being seen.

'Steven,' he hissed, as though the person outside would hear him. Slowly, hunched down, he edged back to the window to peer around the curtain. The figure was gone. He straightened a little, trying to get a better view. There was no sign of anyone down there, just the trees waving in the wind, leaves shimmering with moonlight and residual raindrops. His initial fear faded and Aaron wondered if he had imagined the dark silhouette.

'What's Annabelle doing up at this time?' Steven asked when he finally joined Aaron in bed half an hour later – longer than he had promised.

'What?' Aaron said, putting his Kindle on the bedside table.

'Annabelle. Just heard her banging around downstairs. Thought she'd be asleep at this time.' He shrugged, took a swig of water and went to turn the lamp off.

'You know she's not there, right? She flew to Adelaide last week to visit her parents. She's gone for the whole of this month.'

'Oh. Weird,' Steven responded with another shrug.

'Babe, she's not in, which means she wasn't banging around, which means – shit!' Aaron sat up, feeling the blood drain from his face.

'What is it?'

'We need to call the police.'

'Why would we–'

'Because I saw someone. I fucking saw someone in the garden, maybe half an hour ago. I knew I didn't imagine it!'

'You think it could be...' Steven started. Aaron glared at him.

'Don't even say it. It's probably just a regular break-in. You know she leaves a spare key under the bloody pot by her back door? Such a fucking stupid hiding place.'

Jumping out of bed, Aaron pulled on a pair of jogging bottoms and a T-shirt he'd left on the floor. His phone was charging and he unplugged it, dialling 999. He pressed 'call', but nothing happened.

'Okay, freaking out here. My phone is dead, got no signal. Check yours.'

Steven took his phone from his side table to check it. A second later he shook his head. 'Nothing. How is that possible? Have they got some sort of EMP device? What do we do?'

'Get the hell out of here?'

Steven nodded and clambered out of the bed, shoving on a pair of jeans and his old Abercrombie hoodie.

Then the lamp went out, drenching them in darkness.

'Ow, fuck! Why'd you turn the light off?' Aaron hissed.

'I didn't,' Steven answered, his voice shaking. 'I think the electricity went out.'

Aaron stumbled round the bed. Steven took his hand and together they edged out into the hallway – a normally safe space that Aaron suddenly found unnervingly threatening.

At their front door they shoved on trainers and Steven grabbed a set of keys from the hooks by the entrance. He went to open the door, jumping as Aaron reached out to stop him.

'Wait a second. Can you hear anything?'

They stood silent in the darkness, listening for signs of movement in Annabelle's flat below them.

'No. Come on, let's get the hell out of here and call the police,' Steven urged. Aaron nodded, watching his boyfriend unlock the door. His heart pounded.

The door opened with barely a creak. Steven peered out into the shadowed hallway that led to the stairs down to the communal front door on the ground floor. The house was quiet. Holding hands again, they edged out of their flat. Aaron pulled the door shut behind him, feeling sick. He was overwhelmed by a sharp sense of vulnerability and forced himself to keep breathing steadily.

They had made it to the top of the stairs when Steven stopped. Aaron bumped into him.

'Oh God, what is it?' he whispered.

'I thought I heard something.'

They stayed frozen for another few seemingly endless seconds before Steven nodded and they continued. They were halfway down the stairs when a figure, cloaked in black, turned into the stairwell and looked up at them.

'Fuck, go!' Steven yelled, spinning around and shoving Aaron back up the stairs. Aaron stumbled up them as fast as he could, charging towards their front door, Steven right behind him, keys in hand.

As Steven fumbled to open the door, Aaron turned to look behind them. His heart pretty much stopped as the man reached the top of the stairs and sprinted towards them. Aaron fell backwards as the front door opened and watched in horror as the intruder charged, barely registering that Steven was pulling him backwards and into the flat.

'Aaron, the door!' Steven yelled. In a flash of clarity Aaron kicked out, slamming the door shut just inches from the man in black's face. Over him Steven reached out to lock the door before stepping backwards, breathing heavily.

As Aaron scrambled up off the floor, he registered the terror in Steven's eyes. It was the first time he had ever seen such an emotion in his partner. The world threatened to fall out from under him. They hurried back into the bedroom and Steven immediately started pushing at the wardrobe. Aaron followed his lead and they managed to push it in front of the door.

Steven collapsed on the bed.

'We really should have kept up our gym memberships,' he sputtered.

'Seriously? It's not the time for jokes. What the hell are we going to do?' Aaron lurched towards the window, pressing his head against the glass to see what was in Annabelle's garden below them.

'Sorry, nervous tension,' Steven said. 'Can we jump?'

'Maybe, but it's paving slabs below. If we land wrong...' Aaron couldn't bring himself to finish the sentence, images of bone poking out of splintered shins and broken ankles running through his mind.

'Phones are still dead. He must be jamming them somehow. Do you think it really could be the guy? The Snatcher? The one in the papers?' Steven asked.

'I really hope not,' Aaron answered, thinking about some of the murders he had read about. 'But if it is, why us? What the fuck did we do?'

Steven was silent, leaving Aaron to pace around the bed, looking for something to use as a weapon. Digging in the back of the wardrobe he pulled out his old badminton racket, and turned to show Steven.

'Better than nothing, I guess,' he said, though he could barely imagine himself using it to hit someone. Would it do any damage? He sat next to Steven, flipping the racket in his hands, when something awoke in his brain and rose to the surface. 'Oh no... I think... I think I know why. Oh fuck. Fuck, fuck, fuck!'

Suddenly it all made sense. The stories he'd been following for the past fortnight about the murders, about the possible killer. There had been an update redacting a headline but still, he knew he was right. It was because of Carlos Mancini.

'That job, that fucking contract I took for Mancini Estates. Fuck!'

'Quiet!' Steven hissed. 'I thought the papers said that was a false lead. Why would that be a reason, anyway? You only did that job for six months.'

'Yeah, but I was in charge of all the hiring on that huge build project, wasn't I? What if this guy is some sort of pissed-off former employee? Oh shit, what if I know him?' Aaron could feel his pulse rocketing again.

'Okay, but seriously, I swear the news said Mancini was found alive and had been ruled out as being connected.'

'Yeah, it did, but here we bloody are, with someone trapping us in our flat at three in the morning, and here I am having worked for Mancini. You think that's a coincidence? I don't. God, that fucking job! I only took it for the pay. Now we're going to get murdered and it's my fault!' He could feel the tears coming, and was thankful when Steven grabbed him in a strong hug, kissing the side of his head. They sat for a while, racking their brains for a way out of the situation. Aaron felt helpless, adrift. At least he had Steven, though. He couldn't even begin to think how he would cope alone.

'Do you think we could wait him out?' Steven asked, his voice booming in the quiet despite him whispering. 'Maybe you're wrong and he's just, like, a regular burglar or something. I can replace the Xbox.'

Aaron wanted to believe that the man was just an opportunist breaking in, but somehow that didn't feel right. The way he had been standing in the garden watching their house; it was too unsettling. He wasn't creeping around looking for a house to take a chance on. It seemed too deliberate.

'Maybe,' he said weakly.

There was a crash from the hallway, then another. They jumped. The sound was instantly recognisable. The man had smashed the front door in.

'Oh God!' Aaron gasped, clamping a hand to his mouth. Steven took the badminton racket from the bed and stood like an aggressive mannequin, posed as though ready to strike. Light footsteps moved down the hall, getting closer before stopping.

Steven looked at Aaron, his eyes wide. The intruder was outside their bedroom door. Aaron stifled a sob as the door handle rattled. The door did not budge, held firmly closed by the wardrobe. A few seconds later, the footsteps continued towards the living room, kitchen and bathroom.

'We need to move now,' Steven whispered. 'Our flat is too small. He'll know we're in here any minute.'

The fear that Aaron could hear in Steven's voice was like ice through him, but his boyfriend was right. He moved back to the window, looking down into Annabelle's garden again. Moonlight seemed to glow off the concrete paving, as though deliberately highlighting the bone-breaking surface.

'Maybe if I hang down and then drop?' he said, turning back to Steven, who nodded.

'I think it's our only choice.' He joined Aaron, checking the drop himself, then unclicked the clasp and pulled up the window sash. Cold air shot through, rippling the curtains. Behind them, the man slammed against the bedroom door. The wardrobe rattled.

'Okay, babe, you go first. I'll help you,' Steven said.

Aaron clambered up onto the windowsill, awkwardly pivoting so that he was facing Steven, who held on to him to keep him steady. Aaron felt sick and he was sweating, despite the cold air. He lowered one leg, and the feeling of having nothing underneath him threatened to undo his balance.

'You can do it, I've got you. Keep hold of my arms and get as close to the ground as you can, okay?' Steven's voice was remarkably calm. Aaron simply nodded, his heart lurching when he slipped as he lowered his other leg. His fingers dug into Steven's hands. From the hallway came another booming crash.

'Shit, Aaron, you have to drop, he's coming in!' Steven's calm tone had gone, replaced by terror, but Aaron couldn't let go. It was too far, he knew it. What had they been thinking?

They should have stayed, they could have stopped the guy between them, surely – two against one.

'Aaron, come on!' Steven's voice was flooded with panic as another crash came from inside the flat. Aaron knew it was the sound of the wardrobe being kicked from the back. It would topple over, and in seconds the man would be closing in on Steven.

'Oh God, fuck, okay...' Aaron lowered himself as far as he could, his chest pressing against the rough brick, his toes reaching down for the earth. Then he released his grip on Steven.

The fall was quick – much quicker than he had expected. He hit the paving slabs feet first. His ankle twisted and he fell backwards, scraping his palms on the concrete. He hissed in pain. He had made it.

'Ste, come on, quick!' Still on the cold paving, Aaron watched, heart in mouth, as Steven got one leg out, gripping the edge of the frame.

'That's it, come on!' Aaron got to his feet, ignoring the murmur of pain in his ankle, automatically shifting his weight onto his other foot to compensate. Then Steven was pulled backwards into the flat, into the dark.

Aaron screamed. 'Steven! No, Steven!'

His voice punched through the night like an alarm going off. It was all he could hear. Frantic, yet totally frozen by what had just happened, he failed to see the figure that came up behind him from the deep shadows that surrounded the garden. Something hit him hard across the back of the skull, and he dropped like lead to the grass.

His first thought was that he didn't know where he was. The second was that he wasn't alone. The third was how painful it was each time his heart beat. His head throbbed. He became aware that his hair felt different at the back – was it sticky with blood?

Even though the room was dark, it was somehow familiar. Aaron blinked through the searing headache to clear his vision. Eventually his eyes adjusted. It was a kitchen. He was in a kitchen. It wasn't his, though. Whose was it?

Annabelle's.

He and Steven weren't exactly close to the woman who lived below them but they had been to a few of her parties, had gone to the pub together a couple of times. They were friendly enough neighbours and enjoyed a chat when they saw her. He recognised the pink Smeg fridge, the heart-shaped noticeboard on the wall above the small table in one corner.

His memory clicked back to the second thing he had realised. Someone else was in the room with him. He knew it: his body sensed a presence. The hairs on his arms rose at the prospect of coming face to face with his attacker.

He attempted to get up but found he was tied to the chair in which he was sitting – one he assumed was usually pushed under Annabelle's table. Shifting around, he found that he was in the middle of the room, away from any countertops or drawers, anything he could use to free himself. Away from the body slumped against the cupboard under the sink. The other person in the room.

'No...' he mumbled weakly through the fabric gag over his mouth as his mind tried to process what his eyes had seen. Tears rolled down his cheeks and his chest began to heave. He felt an overwhelming sense of defeat. The man he loved was unconscious, possibly dead, just a few metres from him, and there was nothing he could do. And if Steven was dead, then what was the point of Aaron escaping from this nightmare? Bile rose in the back of his throat and he choked, feeling the acidic liquid spatter over the gag and down his chin.

It took him a while to recover, to get his breathing and sobbing under control, but when he did he silenced himself and listened.

Somewhere in the flat a clock ticked – maybe in Annabelle's living room. The fridge hummed gently. The wind outside traced its fingers over the back door that led to the garden. There was something else – a sound he struggled to pinpoint at first. From somewhere in the depths of his mind it came to him. Breathing.

'Steven?' he attempted to whisper around the gag, staring at the unmoving body of his boyfriend. For the first time he registered the blood – a dark splash spilled down the front of Steven's grey hoodie. It glimmered in the little light that came through the windows into the kitchen. Aaron's body shook, threatening to spew up more than just bile, but he fought it back, his throat burning. He couldn't be sure, but he thought he could see Steven's chest rising and falling ever so slightly. He prayed he was right.

Something else was off, though. Was that the breathing he could hear? His mind decided no, but then the truth sank in slowly, like a drop of black paint mixing in with water, filling his mind. He turned his head slowly, shifting in his chair, until he had a view of the door that led out to the hallway. A man stood there, perfectly still, watching him. His eyes shone against the black balaclava pulled down over his face.

A scream got caught in Aaron's mouth.

'Hello, Mr Hudson,' the man said, stepping over the threshold and into the kitchen.

Hearing his name, Aaron's mind raced in a million

directions at once until another name floated up to the top. *Mancini.* That had to be it. Carlos fucking Mancini.

Even though he was strapped to a chair, even though Steven lay on the floor just out of reach, Aaron couldn't quite believe that this was really happening, that he would be the next victim of the London Organ Snatcher. For a few seconds he felt like he was having an out-of-body experience, or was watching the plot of a nasty film unfold, one that Steven would force him to watch through his fingers. And yet he knew the actors – two of them, anyway. Reality snapped back like a whiplash as the man in black stopped in front of Aaron and leant down until their eyes were level. He gave a smile. It was the most terrifying thing Aaron had ever seen.

'Time to pick your brain,' the man said, straightening up and leaning against the kitchen counter. Steven was propped up on the floor next to him.

Aaron could feel himself shaking. He had never felt totally helpless before, but now he knew the concept all too well. The footsteps behind him somehow took that helplessness to a whole new level. He had forgotten that there was another attacker, the one who had knocked him out.

'And if you don't tell us what we want to know,' the man continued, his voice horribly jovial, 'then lover boy here is going to start losing pieces.'

Aaron's heart skipped when the man kicked Steven's shoulder. A low, barely-there moan came from Steven, the smallest of silver linings to Aaron. He was still alive, at least.

Tell them what they want to know, his mind warned him, although he knew that, no matter what he said, they might kill him and Steven anyway.

'What do you want?' he attempted to ask, his voice muffled by the gag. He jumped when a pair of gloved hands landed heavily on his shoulders from behind, the fingers moving up to wrap gently around his throat. The man's laugh made him squirm. Not being able to see who was behind him was even worse than having to look into the eyes of the psycho across from him.

I just have to get through this. He tried to convince himself but the silent words weren't working. He didn't think that there was any getting through this. If he messed them around, they would torture Steven, then kill them both. If he told them everything he knew, maybe he and Steven would at least be killed quickly. But they would still be dead. The outcome was the same. Aaron didn't even entertain the idea that maybe they would escape with their lives intact. He needed a miracle and, sitting bound in a chair in a dark kitchen opposite his unconscious boyfriend with the night outside covering all bad deeds, it didn't seem likely that one would find him before it was too late.

'Carlos Mancini has done some bad, bad things, Mr Hudson,' the man in front of him began. 'He ruins lives. Breaks apart families. And I want him to pay. But no one listened to me. No one believed me and no one cared. So now, I'm making him care. That's why we're here, that's why I'm talking to you now. See, I know some things about Carlos, but I don't know everything. You had access to the man – privileged access. So maybe you can help me where others have failed.'

Aaron's heart sank. What did he know? God, he had only met Mancini a few times. What on earth could he know that would be useful? He'd heard rumours, of course, that the mogul was not exactly a nice man, but was that it? Clearly there was some truth to the rumours, at least according to the serial murderer standing opposite him.

But what the hell do I know that's helpful?

'I'm sure you'll have heard about the other victims by now,' the masked man said matter-of-factly. 'I mean, we're famous, right?' He smiled at his partner, still positioned behind Aaron, his white teeth in the darkness chilling Aaron's blood again. 'But none of them were very useful. They claimed to know nothing, refused to tell me what I want to know. It's like you've all ganged up together to cover up the truth.'

His tone of voice changed in the last sentence. In a heartbeat the jovial quality was gone, his words edged with anger. 'And I'm not going to let that happen again, Mr Hudson. Do you understand?'

Aaron nodded instinctively, panic building inside him as he racked his memory for anything relevant.

'Tools,' the killer in front of Aaron said to the other man. A shuffling came from behind Aaron before an outstretched arm appeared to his side, offering a bag.

'You see, Aaron,' the smiling man continued as he knelt down and began to rummage through the bag, 'I think you know more than you think you do, and I need you to co-operate.'

Moonlight shone off the bolt cutters the man held as he walked over to Steven. Aaron watched in horror as the man opened the bolt cutters and manoeuvred one of Steven's fingers between the blades.

The smile came again. 'So tell me. What do you know about the blood on Carlos's hands?'

Blood? As Aaron tried to process the information, desperate to think of anything that related, the man behind him whispered *tick-tock* into Aaron's right ear. Aaron could feel the heat of the breath on his cheek.

'I... I don't...' Aaron mumbled.

'Yes you do, Mr Hudson. I just know it. Don't be shy.' The bolt cutters closed a little more, the blades closer to skin.

Aaron felt faint, his pulse racing. What the hell did this man mean? Blood? He figured Mancini was shady, had done some criminal stuff, but no one knew any details. It was all just gossip.

People chatted shit about the billionaire all the time, but it was just that, shit. Made-up stories most likely way more exciting than the truth. Rumours of swindling money, running smaller companies out of business, roughing up people who wouldn't do business, and—

'Snip!' the man with the bolt cutters said with excitement. Aaron heard the crunch of bone and one of Steven's fingers fell to the floor. Blood dripped onto the laminate tiles.

'No!' Aaron choked, tasting bile yet again. His vision blurred.

Steven groaned but remained unconscious.

What the hell did they do to you?! Aaron's mind screamed, his eyes fixated on the growing pool of dark liquid under Steven's hand, the blood like ink on the pale floor.

'Can't have hurt that much – didn't even wake him,' the man with the bolt cutters said with a laugh, as though he was pranking a friend, not disfiguring someone. 'Thought of anything yet?'

The shock of seeing the man hurt Steven had temporarily wiped Aaron's memory, and he dug back into his thoughts, trying to remember the rumour he'd heard. Someone had got hurt, maybe, or there had been an accident. The blood dripping from Steven's hand wasn't slowing, and Aaron fought to focus.

'An accident...' he mumbled, more to himself than to his attacker, as though saying the word out loud might jog his memory. It was all so hazy, though. He had met so many people during that contract, had so many conversations about a huge range of things.

'An accident, you say. Could we be on to something here, do you think?' the man in black said to his accomplice. 'Anything else?'

Heart thudding and sweat beading on his forehead, Aaron began to run through all the people he had met while working for Mancini. Who had said something about an accident? And what had they said?

FUCK! Why can't I remember?

'You're taking too long, Aaron, and guess what? I'm bored of fingers.'

The words were like a charge through Aaron's chest. Uselessly, he lurched in his chair as the man lifted the bolt cutters again. He lifted the blades to Steven's head, hovered them by his face, then picked a spot. The man grinned at Aaron before turning back to Steven and closing the blades together, severing Steven's left ear.

Aaron screamed, the noise loud despite the gag. Steven's eyes opened and his body shook with the pain charging through him. He began to roar in agony, louder than Aaron, his eyes wide. The man swung the bolt cutters through the air and connected with Steven's head. He toppled onto his side. Blood streaked across the floor. Steven looked as if he was struggling to remain conscious. He was silent again other than the sounds of his rasping breath.

Aaron felt darkness taking over to protect him from what he was witnessing. A gloved hand slapped him across the face, forcing him back into something resembling awareness.

'That spurred anything in that little brain of yours? He's not dead yet. I can do much more to him while you watch, you know. I'm sure you've read the papers. We're – what is it? Oh yes, escalating. I think that's what the detectives said.'

Aaron swallowed painfully. He felt utterly drained of hope. Tears flooded down his face as he stared at Steven's shuddering body. His only option now was to speed things along, get it over with.

The accident... think!

The man in black raised the cutters, this time horribly close to Aaron. It was like a match being lit, illuminating a recollection of the conversation in the depths of Aaron's mind.

'Four men... they died. At a construction site. It was his fault.' His words were sputtered, the rag impeding his speech. The man behind him lifted a gloved hand to Aaron's mouth, making him flinch. The man pulled the rag from his mouth. Aaron coughed.

'And who told you this? The news sure as hell didn't blame him; he got away scot-free. So who told you it was his fault? That person knew, so they must have helped cover up for him.'

The man's voice was full of venom, his words growling out with force. Spittle flecked Aaron's front, the man's face was so close to his now.

'It... she... Clara...' Aaron shuddered as an image of the woman flashed into his mind, as well as the horrible realisation that he was about to sign her death warrant and it wouldn't even save him.

'Last name, if you please!'

'Clara Michaut. She knows all about it,' Aaron said, the words falling out, his energy expended.

'Atta boy,' the man in front of him said, his voice instantly calmer, the change so swift it was almost like a different person speaking. He stood straight and confident even as Aaron collapsed in on himself in the chair. Aaron felt his vision fading once more as the man hovered over Steven's battered body, the cutters resting casually on his shoulder.

'Of course, you knew this and didn't do anything, just like everyone else. Yet another cog in the machine protecting that man. Mancini will get what's coming to him, fear not, but I'm afraid you have to too.' With a grunt the man swung the bolt cutters in front of him, pointed the blades down and jammed them deep into Steven's neck. Dark blood spurted out from the ragged, pale flesh where the blunt blade tips had forced their entry. Just before Aaron's body gave out entirely, his vision going dark, he heard one last sentence that sent a shiver of pure horror through him.

'Your turn. Do what you want to them.'

The man still behind him laughed before the night took Aaron into its grasp.

CHAPTER TWENTY-FOUR

Blindly thrusting an arm out from under his duvet, Daniel Graves grabbed his phone, trying to shut it up. His sleep-filled eyes registered the time. Confusion washed over him. His alarm wasn't due to go off for another hour. A second later, his brain realised it wasn't in fact the alarm that had woken him up. He answered the call.

'DI Graves,' he mumbled, pushing himself up to a sitting position. He listened, his heart sinking.

'Thanks. On my way shortly,' he said before hanging up. He felt exhausted, but the call sure woke him up. Bad news could do that in a way that even coffee couldn't, and he felt anxious about the day ahead. He turned on a lamp to break up the darkness of his room. He had just put the phone back on his bedside table when it rang again. It was Charlie.

'You got the same call, then,' he said by way of a greeting.

'Yeah. See you there? I can be there in about half an hour.'

Daniel padded through the flat and found Rachel still fast asleep on the sofa. Relieved that he hadn't woken her he headed into the bathroom for a quick shower, hoping the hot water might give him some more energy. He had the feeling he was going to need it.

The night had not yet given way to the approaching dawn. The road dripped in shadows, the edges of houses and trees and shrubs only lit by the weak moonlight and the ugly yellow streetlights stationed at intervals down the pavement.

The man shut the front door behind him, pulled his coat more tightly around him and trudged down the steps towards his car. He didn't even glance at the Range Rover parked across the road; he didn't see the person watching him through the windscreen.

Traffic was quiet and Daniel was making decent time. Glancing in the rear-view mirror before he took a left, he saw a familiar black vehicle again. His stomach lurched.

'You've been tailing me for an awfully long time...' he said. He'd noticed the Range Rover five minutes ago, tucked in behind him a few roads from his house. Looking at the road ahead, he thought about his route. Instead of heading up to Elephant and Castle, he took a right onto Penton Place. It was an experiment. He sped up slightly to add some distance between him and the Range Rover, then checked in his rear-view again. The Range Rover turned into the side road and followed him.

Not convinced he was correct, Daniel decided to try again. This time he took an awkward circular route around Pasley Park, knowing it would not be a normal route for anyone who was actually trying to get somewhere. Still, the Range Rover remained in his rear-view mirror.

It was too much of a coincidence for Daniel.

'Shit...' he muttered, planning his next move.

Ahead of him, a small van was waiting to reverse out of the entrance to an estate. Its brake lights came on and Daniel realised it was letting him go. He put his foot down and shot past the van, glancing in the mirror again. The van had reversed less than a metre out onto the road, then had stopped. The Range Rover appeared, swerving around the back of the van and coming close to hitting it. The car was going fast, too fast.

'Shit!'

Daniel floored it. His car surged forward and he racked his brain for a way out of this. His evasive driving training had been so long ago. He knew that stopping to confront his pursuer was not a sensible option, not when he was alone. They also wouldn't simply follow him forever; either they would try to ram him off the road or they would give up. The Range Rover was a big machine. Had they been looking for an opportunity? Hoping one of the quieter roads he was taking would trap him? His imagination was going crazy.

Using his hands-free set, he called Charlie. With each ring he felt himself getting more tense.

'Dan, what's up? Are you near? I'm just pulling up to the house.'

'Charlie, I'm in trouble. Someone's following me. You need to call it in!' Daniel practically shouted, his voice booming in the confines of the car.

'What? Where are you?' his partner asked, sounding on edge.

'Walworth, heading for Bermondsey... I'll be hitting Old Kent Road in a minute, I think.'

'Great. Get on a main road – the busier the better.'

'Seriously? Are you crazy?'

'Daniel, you need traffic, witnesses. As soon as you're somewhere busy there's a very good chance this guy will drop off your tail. Can you describe the car? I'll put the call out now.'

'It's a black Range Rover, fairly new,' Daniel answered, shooting across a junction, his heart in his mouth when he realised he hadn't even checked to see if his way was clear. He flicked a look up to the mirror. 'Number plate is... EC44... shit!'

A woman was crossing the road ahead of him. Without thinking, he swerved. A screech of metal told him he'd clipped a parked car.

'Dan? Daniel! You okay?' Charlie sounded panicked.

'Fuck...' Daniel was breathing heavily as he straightened the car out. He checked his mirror again and saw the woman waving a fist at him, her face twisting in shock as the Range Rover shot past her.

'What happened?'

'Sorry, I'm fine, though someone is going to get a shock when they find their car. This bastard is not giving up!' Daniel jerked the steering wheel and took the next left, terrified that he was going to hit someone.

'Okay, well, you staying alive is more important. Did you catch the rest of the number plate?'

'I don't want to risk taking my eyes off the road again, to be honest, mate!' But Daniel chanced a look, saw his pursuer closer than before. 'Who the fuck is this guy?' Something sparked in the back of his mind, and his stomach dropped. 'Oh God...'

Daniel could hear Charlie ordering someone to put out a bulletin for the Range Rover, sounding only marginally less frantic than he felt.

'Okay, the call is out. The area will be swarming with police in minutes. They won't get away.'

'Charlie, I think...'

'Yeah?'

'I think this could be Jenny's killer. They've been teasing me from a distance – now they've decided to make an appearance.' As he said the words his body chilled – a feeling he had not experienced since the morning he had opened the box containing Jenny Carpenter's bloody heart. The note inside the box had said that her death was just the start. It had been a warning. And then that message had appeared for him on Jenny's memorial page, then his flat had been broken into. It had all been building up to something. Was this the climax? Was the killer finally making himself visible, ready to strike?

'Daniel, don't even think about it, just pay attention to your driving. You must be at Old Kent Road by now, surely?'

Daniel checked his surroundings, bringing his mind back to the task at hand. The road ahead was busy – too busy. In seconds he would be stuck in a line of cars trying to turn onto John Ruskin Street, a wider main road.

'Yeah, I'm almost there, but I can't stop!' he yelled. A burst of shouts and beeping blasted out behind him. A glance in his rear-view showed a car stopped at an awkward angle in the road and the Range Rover swerving round it.

'Just get onto the main road, Dan. He'll give up, I know it.'

'Shit...' Daniel muttered. He had reached a queue of cars. He was forced to slow, but his follower loomed in his mirror. He desperately looked for a gap, then shot forward. More horns blared. He prepared to swing out onto Old Kent Road. And then the gap was gone. A double-decker bus had turned into the oncoming lane. Daniel pulled the wheel right, the car's undercarriage protesting as he mounted the pavement.

'Fuck, fuck, fuck!' he chanted. Two teenagers jumped out of the way as he crossed the corner of the pavement and bounced onto the main road. Another queue. All the cars were going in the opposite direction to him and he yanked the wheel again, shoving his car's nose into the left-hand lane. He could hear chaos breaking out behind him as the Range Rover tried, and failed, to get past the bus.

'Yes! Lost the fucker!' Daniel whooped, his heart pounding but a grin spreading across his face nonetheless. Charlie said something back, but Daniel didn't hear it over the sound of crunching metal as something ploughed into the side of his car.

CHAPTER TWENTY-FIVE

Charlie watched as the man in high-vis and an orange jumpsuit attached a hook to the front of the battered car, then pressed a button to heave it onto the recovery truck.

'So depressing,' Daniel muttered next to him. He sat in the back of the ambulance, picking at the butterfly stitches on his forehead. 'I know it wasn't the best car, but it's totally mangled.'

'Just be glad you aren't totally mangled too,' Charlie said. 'It could have been a lot worse.'

'Yeah. I feel like crap, to be honest. And I still don't know what happened, not really.'

Charlie stepped sideways to allow one of the ambulance team past. The chaos was already starting to dissipate as the emergency services worked to clear the scene.

'That old man drove right into the side of your car. You probably came out of nowhere.'

Daniel craned his neck so that he could see the old man in question – a fellow in his early seventies, bald except for a tuft of hair at the back of his head like a paltry serving of grey candy-floss. The tattered T-shirt he wore had a faded picture of the Beatles on the front of it. Somehow he had not been injured, and now he was giving his statement to one of the traffic police.

'You were speeding and he ran a red; it happens. Maybe he shouldn't be driving at his age, but whatever. I was talking about the Range Rover driver.'

The Range Rover that had been following Daniel had – naturally – fled the scene. Both men hoped that they could either track it on street cameras or find the dumped vehicle and be able to search it for evidence. Charlie had already called in a request for CCTV footage and a team to watch it. There was a squad of patrol cars out looking for the vehicle, but nothing had been called in yet.

The ambulance driver appeared from around the open rear door and gave them a weary smile. Charlie suspected he had been on the clock since much earlier than the two of them.

'Detective, I need to get on to the next job, if you're sure you're okay.' He nodded at Daniel's stitches, his gaze dropping to the splashes of blood soaked into Daniel's pale blue shirt.

'I'm fine, thank you,' Daniel responded, hopping off the back of the ambulance. Charlie prepared to grab him but his balance was good.

'Okay, but make sure you get that looked at if it doesn't heal. The stitches should be enough, but please take care. Any sign of dizziness or headaches, go to hospital.'

'Don't worry, I'll make him,' Charlie said. 'I'm his official chauffeur now, after all. He has to go where I take him.'

'I do have Uber, you know.' Daniel frowned.

They headed down the street to Charlie's car. He had driven to the Old Kent area the minute he had heard the crash over the phone. Now, with the road cleared and Daniel's car towed, everything had gone back to normal.

'Now that you've finished scaring the shit out of me, can we finally go to the crime scene?' Charlie asked as he unlocked his car and they got in. Daniel nodded. Charlie let out a long, quiet sigh of relief. For a short time he had thought that he had lost his partner for good, and it had terrified him. It wasn't the only thought that was causing him problems, though. He suspected that Daniel's theory was right. He didn't believe for a second that the car chase was linked to the serial killers they were hunting for, and it didn't sound like road rage – or random. Someone had wanted to hurt Daniel, or at least to scare him. If it was the same person who had cut out Jenny's heart and left it on Daniel's porch, who knew what else they were capable of? A car chase didn't seem like the end of it, especially since Daniel had escaped relatively unscathed.

Charlie tried to hide his unease as he started the car and pulled out into the chaotic London traffic.

It was a circus already, and their arrival only made things worse. Before Charlie had stopped the car they were surrounded by journalists and photographers. No doubt they had been called by people wanting a payout or their fifteen minutes of fame. The flashes were like strobe lights, and did nothing to help Daniel's headache.

'Bloody car chase delayed us,' Charlie said as he cut the engine.

'I know, right? How inconvenient. If someone hadn't rudely tried to kill me just now we could have beaten these guys to it.' Daniel groaned as he prepared himself for the explosion of noise he knew would come when he opened his car door.

'And now there's going to be photos of me looking like this in the papers too.' He groaned again as he looked down at the browning blood stains on his shirt.

'Mate, if you having a cut and some blood on you is a

headline then there's something even worse wrong with the world than serial killers. Ready?'

'It's not like we have much choice,' Daniel said. He took a deep breath, pulled the door catch and climbed out of the car. The noise was overwhelming: it was completely different from the first crime scene, where only Kelly Malone had picked up the scent. In under a fortnight the whole country had gone mad about this case, but in London it had reached the next level of rabid craziness.

Someone shoved into Daniel. He turned to scowl at the young man thrusting a microphone in his face. Charlie swooped around the bonnet of the car and together they pressed through the crowd to the police cordon. They were greeted at the front door of the house by Stephanie Mitchum, who was no more welcoming than the throng of journalists.

'Any success this time, Steph?' Charlie asked as they stepped into the hallway. Daniel contained a smirk as her face screwed up at the shortening of her name.

'Not yet, Detective Palmer,' she snapped, obviously unimpressed at Charlie. 'We've only been here for half an hour. This way.' She turned and led them towards a beige door with a gold letter 'A' nailed to it, her ponytail bobbing. Daniel saw that the door marked with a 'B' to his right was also open.

'Upstairs?' he asked.

'A bit of a mess, but nothing like down here.'

Daniel knew he would not get any more warning than that, and prepared himself as best he could. Stephanie pushed open the door and walked into the flat. Daniel could smell the tang of copper in the air, recognised it all too well. He walked behind Charlie along the small hallway, past a sitting room, towards what he assumed must be the kitchen at the back of the house. When Charlie reached the doorway he stopped and turned around, clapping his hand to his mouth.

'Fuck me.' He coughed, his eyes communicating his horror all too clearly. He stepped aside so Daniel could walk into the kitchen. What he saw trumped anything else the killers had left them so far. He stood still, stunned. He tried not to gag as his gaze panned over the scene in front of him.

One body lay on the table in the centre of the room. The dead man was on his back, his limbs dangling over the edges. His feet and hands had already turned darker, filling with the blood that no longer circulated around his body. His stomach had been cut open and was a large, ragged hole. It looked as if his organs had been removed, but the space they had previously occupied was not empty. Instead of intestines, stomach and whatever else Daniel assumed should have been there were hands, severed fingers, toes, a foot, and other pieces of ragged flesh that Daniel could not make out without getting closer to the body. Where they had come from was obvious. On the floor beneath the table was the second victim. He had been mutilated beyond easy recognition.

A plume of vomit arose in Daniel's throat as his brain finished processing what he was looking at, and he spun to retch into the nearby sink.

'Shit,' he sputtered as he realised he had just contaminated the scene.

'Don't worry, I'll make sure someone makes a note,' Stephanie said, unexpected compassion in her voice.

Daniel nodded. Straightening up, he dared to look back at the room. The two investigators cataloguing everything looked equally pale, which made him feel slightly less self-conscious.

'This is... I don't even know what this is,' Charlie said as he joined them in the kitchen, looking everywhere but at the bodies.

'It's almost... over the top,' Stephanie said.

'Yeah. It's the worst one yet. It's so...' Charlie trailed off.

'They're mocking us,' Daniel stated, his throat hoarse from the acidic bile. The others nodded their agreement. 'They feel they can keep getting away with this because we don't know who they are.'

'We think we know who one of them is,' Charlie reminded him.

'Fat lot of good it's done us, though. We haven't actually been able to find Calvin Cavendish. We couldn't stop him and his crazy partner from doing this. We're failing.' Daniel let out a frustrated sigh before leaving the kitchen to go and check the upstairs flat belonging to the victims.

'So you called this in?' Charlie asked the woman sitting in front of him. A police officer he didn't know sat next to her. Charlie had read her initial statement just minutes before entering her house, which was opposite the latest victims' house, but he was keen to speak to Alison Lott himself.

Alison Lott frowned at him, as though suspicious of his intentions, and he found himself wishing that Daniel had not stayed at the crime scene. His partner was better at questioning witnesses; he didn't seem to feel as awkward or uncomfortable as Charlie did.

'I called because I saw a man go around the side of their house. It was the middle of the night. Knew it was dodgy.' Alison tucked a grey curl behind her ear and pulled at her flowery top. She seemed nervous, although Charlie figured that was due to his and the silent officer's presence. No one liked having the police in their home.

'And what were you doing up in the middle of the night, Miss Lott?'

Alison pulled a face, as though taking offence, but Charlie

raised an eyebrow in response. It was, after all, a pertinent question.

'If you must know, I don't sleep well. At my age the body has so many pains, and I often can't sleep. I came downstairs to get some water and realised I'd left the curtains open. I went to close them and that's when I saw him.'

'And this man – he sneaked round the side of the house? How did you know he didn't live there? Or wasn't visiting?'

'Don't be dense, dear,' Alison said with a glare.

Charlie blushed.

'For one thing, it must have been past two. Who visits at that hour and sneaks around the side of the house? At any rate, I know who lives there. That young chubby woman and the loud gays. This person was none of them.'

Charlie fought hard not to roll his eyes at Alison's description of the neighbours. He wanted to get out of there. The officer, still quiet as a mouse next to her, also looked less jovial.

'And you said he looked late twenties or early thirties, white with dark hair, correct? Was he wearing a mask?'

Alison shook her head. 'No mask. And it was dark but yes, I'm pretty certain he was white.'

That could be Calvin Cavendish – potentially, at least. Charlie made a mental note to have someone show Alison Lott a picture of the man. Maybe she could confirm it officially.

'Did you see anyone else? Was there just one man?'

'I didn't see anyone else. I went to the phone to call you lot. Had a look out again but I couldn't see anything else, so I took some painkillers for my back and went back to bed.'

'Anything else you remember?'

Alison Lott hadn't told him anything useful apart from that a man roughly fitting Cavendish's description had been at the scene.

Without a word she stood, edged around the sofa and disappeared into a room at the back of the house that looked like a dining room. Charlie looked at the officer.

'No idea,' the man muttered, twisting to look over his shoulder as though the truth would reveal itself.

Charlie could hear Alison Lott shuffling what sounded like papers. Perhaps she was looking for something.

'Miss Lott?'

There was more rummaging, then suddenly Alison walked back into the living room. She was brandishing a torn white piece of paper. 'I totally forgot about this. Didn't think it was relevant, but perhaps it is.' She passed the scrap of paper to Charlie. It seemed to be a shopping list.

He frowned, which evidently Alison saw.

'Other side, Detective.' She sighed wearily.

Trying not to blush again, Charlie turned the scrap over. In neat blue ink was a number plate. He felt his heart leap.

'It's from a van – some gardening company. I wouldn't have noticed it, except it was outside their house a few times last week. Well, just down from it. I wrote it down because no one on this road gets their gardening done. Who would, at this time of year? Waste of money. But the van was gone this morning. If you ask me, it seems an odd coincidence that it was close to that house and had disappeared by this morning...'

Charlie's heart was pounding. 'I think you may be right.'

Standing with a rush of confidence, Charlie stuffed the piece of paper into his jacket pocket, thanked Alison Lott, and asked the officer to add the details of the van to his statement. In seconds he was back outside, darting across the road and around the crowd of journalists. He couldn't wait to tell Daniel that they had a way to track down Cavendish – and maybe even his accomplice.

CHAPTER TWENTY-SIX

After a few days of looking through the release details for various institutions across the country, Sergeant Amelia Harding and Junior Sergeant Ross Hayes were starting to feel like they had been locked away themselves. They had checked prisons, hospitals that allowed for extended stays, rehab centres, mental health centres, and had even looked into healthy living and yoga retreats – anywhere Calvin Cavendish or his accomplice could have been living that was separate from the outside world. Somewhere that would have kept them off social media, out of the news, basically off-grid.

Amelia had felt sick when she'd provided Graves and Palmer with an update. She hated to fail. They had thanked her for the time she and Hayes had spent researching, were disappointed but had not blamed her. That had not, however, appeased her in the slightest.

Amelia had set herself a challenge when she realised that she could show her skill, her expertise, by taking the junior sergeant under her wing and teaching him what she knew. It was one element of her personal development plan – something she needed to prove she was capable at to go for a promotion.

The research on this case had seemed like her golden ticket. Ross had even said he had learned a lot from her, such as the fact that police work involved a lot of research which didn't always pay off the way they wanted. That was the case now. They hadn't found anything pertinent to the case.

The office had felt stifling to her all day. Instead of buying lunch from the local Pret and working at her desk, for once Amelia had allowed herself to take a proper lunch break. It was a rarity. The weather was wet and bracing, but she wanted to be outside to blow away the cobwebs in her mind, to forget the days of wasted investigation time. On autopilot she walked past Westminster Abbey, dodging tourists taking photos of the impressive facade, and followed the Thames. When she reached Tate Britain, she stopped. Turning right, she headed up to the entrance to the gallery, then stepped inside.

She hadn't been to the museum in over a year, even though she loved the place. As she moved through the main lobby, something about the building spoke to her. It felt right that her mind had led her to such a beautiful place, quiet and majestic and filled with creativity and inspiration – the latter both things she felt sorely lacking. She felt certain it would inject some life into her.

The first few rooms were a little too busy for Amelia's liking. She wanted isolation, space to just be, to appreciate the art and distract her. A group of school kids were attempting to copy a landscape painting on large sketch pads while a gallery employee explained what was happening in the painting. The kids were behaving remarkably well, but Amelia didn't want to be around them. Again she let autopilot take over, walking past pieces she liked, ones she wasn't keen on, pausing every so often to take in colours or a composition that caught her eye.

As she reached the rear of the building, one painting drew her in. She had seen it before somewhere – in a documentary, perhaps, maybe even in the Tate itself – but had never paid it more than a passing interest. Moving closer, she leant forward to read the small plaque that listed the painting's name and artist.

Ophelia, by Sir John Everett Millais.

It was truly stunning. It portrayed the moment when Ophelia discovered that her father had been murdered by Hamlet, who was also her lover, and in a moment of madness Ophelia had fallen into a stream and drowned. Around the woman, who floated on her back in the water, were beautifully detailed flowers, meant to symbolise pain, innocence and forsaken love. Amelia stood back and let the painting flow over her, absorbing its beauty, its emotion. A thought jostled to the front of her brain.

She did it because of her father.

'Father...' she muttered. Something inside her knew instantly that it was important, some sort of revelation.

Amelia didn't believe in destiny, in spiritual awakenings. She had never looked for signs to guide her, never held any stock in mystical energies. Yet if someone had asked her at that moment, she might have been tempted to say she did. Even though she knew that she had made all her decisions, that this painting had simply got her brain thinking in a different way, she might have been inclined to say that something bigger was at play. That perhaps the cosmos had wanted her to be in that exact spot at that time.

'Father,' she said again, more definitely.

Then it hit her – the fully formed thought that had been residing somewhere hard to reach. Gasping, she broke her connection with the painting and turned and ran back towards the gallery entrance. She had to get back to the office immediately.

'All this time, and all we needed to know was that they drove a van?' Superintendent Peter Hobbs was grilling Daniel and Charlie when they reported back to him on Charlie's discovery. The comment seemed rather reductive to Daniel, but he resisted the urge to say as much.

'Technically, yes, but it's not quite that straightforward,' Daniel instead answered diplomatically.

'How so?' Hobbs said, his tone suggesting he was waiting for a good answer but not necessarily expecting one.

'We looked for the gardening company van that the neighbour of the latest victims mentioned, and found it on a few CCTV recordings. The thing is, the company doesn't exist and the number plate is a fake,' Daniel started.

'Not helpful,' Hobbs said.

'Not really, no,' Charlie agreed. 'But when we looked back over the footage we had from around the Altons' house, we spotted another van. Different company logo on the side, different number plate. But we enhanced and compared the footage... and found that the van had the same scratch in the paintwork on its front left wheel arch.'

'Okay, now we're getting somewhere.' Hobbs was more enthusiastic. Daniel felt that at long last they were winning him over, showing him that they weren't the idiot detectives Hobbs thought they were. Leaked stories to the press, leads going nowhere, a mounting body count. It had started to look bleak for the pair, and Hobbs had already told them he would take decisive action if necessary.

'So these bastards have been switching up the van details every time, helping to guarantee that no one would realise it was the same vehicle. Clever, I'll give them that. But so what? What do we do with this?'

'We checked footage from street cameras from the other murders and found the van again briefly near Daisy Kerswell's property. Patrick's team is trying to prove that it belongs to the suspects, and figure out where they're based, using CCTV footage to map routes the van has taken. He reckons if they can figure out which roads the van took to and from each scene, even with it only appearing on occasional video clips, they might be able to narrow down where these guys have been hiding out. Cavendish's flat gave us nothing; he was careful not to leave us any clues lying around.'

As Daniel finished explaining, he felt a sense of genuine achievement. They were really close now, he knew it. Importantly, it seemed that Hobbs knew it too.

'Brilliant. Graves, Palmer, this is it. Let's shut these evil shits down and finish this. Don't disappoint me.'

That had been the end of the conversation.

Since then they had been waiting for more intel from the crime scene team, from the coroner's office and, most importantly, from Patrick.

Daniel had not expected Amelia to call him. Sounding excited, she told him what she had discovered.

'You realise that's motive, right?' he said to her, delighted.

CHAPTER TWENTY-SEVEN

Something inside her was willing to admit that she might be crazy, but what was life without a few risks?

Kelly Malone wasn't entirely sure this was a risk worth taking, but she had talked herself into it. She had a plan, she would be careful, and therefore she would be fine. Totally fine.

She had figured out a few ways to protect herself. She had packed a hunting knife that she had bought from a small fishing supply shop, and a weak version of pepper spray – the only such legal product she had been able to find in the UK. It wouldn't stop an attacker dead, but could help out in a pinch. She had written everything she knew and where she was going on her laptop at home, leaving it charging and open in case she went missing and the police had to break her door down.

Kelly had even timed a tweet to go out revealing what had likely happened to her if she didn't survive. She had felt sick writing it, and made a note to cancel it when she returned home unharmed, but she had almost a thousand followers so if worst came to worst someone would spot it, she was sure.

She just needed photos, that was all. Maybe some video, if possible, but nothing else. She would wait until it was dark, park close to the building, somewhere well lit, and sneak in when she was certain he wasn't there. She'd take a few pictures or videos of the main suspect and then she'd be out of there. Easy.

Kelly knew that only half of her plan was about keeping her safe. The rest was about getting a story or releasing what she knew if she got killed, but she would be careful. And smart, obviously. She'd keep her wits about her. It would be simple. She had faith. Sort of.

She knew that, in reality, her investigation would go one of two ways. The first was that she would discover nothing. The abandoned building in Lewisham that she was convinced was the killer's base of operations would most likely be empty. She'd have timed her visit badly or he'd have moved on, careful not to stay in one place for too long. If that was the case, she might be able to find out some superficial bits of info for a story, but that wouldn't achieve what she wanted by a long way.

The second was that she was about to hit pay dirt. She would discover mounds of evidence – maybe even jars of body parts. After all, he had been taking pieces from some of the bodies. She would be able to command whatever price she wanted for shots like that. She could even start a bidding war. Brian would be desperate to keep her on too; he'd give her anything she wanted. Pay rise, promotion, maybe just a big fat cheque. And then she could leave for whichever news company she wanted and have a damn good chance at getting a major step up. She could easily see herself presenting on the BBC, delivering hard-hitting news into houses around the country every day.

Technically there was a third way. This involved the killer finding her and chopping her into pieces to send to the police just for fun, but she was choosing to ignore that one.

Earlier that day Kelly had driven to the old billiard building again. A recce of sorts. She had checked for possible entry and exit points and had found only two. One was the hidden gap in the fencing that she had seen Calvin Cavendish go through. The other was a small break in the chain-link fence that ran for a few metres at one side of the building. It had been poorly boarded up; when no one was looking, she had walked by and pushed the fence. The boards had moved slightly. That was another exit, should she need an alternative. And once she left the building, she could easily escape to her car.

Kelly scanned her flat to make sure everything was in place, checked her handbag for the knife, spray and her camera, and triple-checked that her phone had a full battery. It was already dark. By the time she got to Lewisham it would be gone eight.

'Right then, here I go,' she said with unconvincing bravado, pulling the door to her flat closed. As she made her way down the shared corridor to the front door she felt the air around her chilling. Goosebumps rose on her arms.

'Patrick, this is killing me!' Daniel groaned as he watched over his shoulder to check the status of the search. Onscreen a map of London was being run through a piece of software that Patrick informed him would narrow down where Cavendish and his partner could be. Flickering worms of blue were running up and down streets across the map, using the data that the tech team had gleaned from the hours of footage filmed around each murder scene.

At the head of each worm was a van icon. Daniel watched as the vans slowly worked their way closer to each other. One lurched forward and Daniel's eyes widened. Then it jumped backwards as though on rewind.

'What was that? Why did it go back on itself?' he asked Patrick. Steve Howard, who was the Head of Data, joined them, also watching over Patrick's shoulder. He was a tall, rotund man with a neat, but large, ginger beard. He put his hands on his hips, turning to Daniel.

'It's a sophisticated mapping algorithm. Basically, we put into it all the routes we know for sure that our suspects' van took, and from that it builds a picture of where the van likely went each time. It uses data from traffic jams, accidents, roadworks and such. What you saw was probably a result of it assuming the van would have gone a certain way, only to find that something had stopped it, meaning that route would have been impossible. Based on where the van seemed to be going, it will then suggest an alternative.' He leant forward to indicate the van, which was now moving forward again. 'See?'

'Okay, that makes sense. Question, though. How does it not lose the path pretty quickly, once the cameras lose the van? Surely it can only predict a few roads before it's just making it up?'

'Ah yes, my good sir, an insightful question,' Steve said, as though he was leading a game of *Dungeons and Dragons*, not running tech on a murder investigation. 'You are correct, to an extent. The system uses behavioural logic based on hundreds, if not thousands, of pieces of data we have about everyday drivers to apply patterns. For example, see how the vans on the map are all pretty much headed in a specific direction? Generally east or generally south?'

Daniel nodded, tapping his foot impatiently as he watched the van icons crawl across the digital city.

'Well, assuming that a driver will normally take the most direct route to a destination, the computer can choose options as to which roads the van might take.'

'What if the van is trying to lose someone? Deliberately take an unusual route? Also, what if it stops? The computer can't know that.'

'Well, it can tell based on the driving behaviour caught on camera if the route seems erratic, which in this case none have been. See the bold sections of line? Those are the roads we know for sure the van took. The routes in the algorithm assumed that people were going somewhere specific, not driving around aimlessly. As for the van stopping, no, it can't tell that, but what it can do is continue to map the most likely routes. Each van will end up with a few possible lines on the map and what we need to do is see where they cross over.'

'If they cross over,' Daniel said, not yet seeing any convergence on the map.

'Have some faith, Graves,' Patrick said, swivelling in his chair to smile at Daniel. 'I do. This system is good, I promise. And why would the van stop at totally different locations each time? It's most likely that Cavendish has one base of operations, no?'

'True – multiple hideouts goes against typical behaviour for serial killers. I can't just stand here waiting, though; it's driving me crazy. Call me as soon as you have something.'

'You have our word,' Steve said in a deep Gandalf-style voice.

Daniel smiled. 'Thank you.' He turned and headed for the lifts. Charlie and Amelia had been briefing Martia on what Amelia had discovered, and Daniel was keen to join them.

'Well, it certainly explains a lot,' Martia was saying as Daniel entered the glass meeting room. 'Many serial killers have strained or unusual relationships with their parents.' She stopped, clearly deep in thought, tapping her lip with one finger. Charlie was eyeing her up as though expecting more information.

'Your theory was correct then, I take it, Amelia? That Calvin Cavendish's father was linked to Mancini?' Daniel asked.

She nodded enthusiastically.

When he had spoken to Amelia on the phone earlier that day, she had told him she thought it was one of the killer's fathers who was the connection. She had surprised him at the mention of Carlos Mancini, given that the lead on the man had gone nowhere. He hadn't had time to speak with her and he had been asking for extra detail since then. He wanted her to join him and the team as soon as he was free.

'Okay, let's dig into all this, Amelia. First of all, why did you start down this route of investigation?' he asked.

'Because I didn't believe it was a coincidence that Mancini's name kept coming up. It was only when that reporter Detective Palmer knows said that Mancini had been spotted alive in Europe that we stopped going down that path. I know we had other eye-witness accounts too, but it bugged me, because we couldn't find any other connections between the victims.'

'I continued to look into it and it turns out that one of the latest victims, Aaron Hudson, had contracted for a recruitment company that dealt with Mancini's business, among others. I would have dismissed it – the recruiters dealt with a huge range of high-profile companies, but it seemed like far too much of a coincidence, since we had nothing else connecting the victims.'

'I get that you might question the photo the press published of Mancini. It was pretty low-quality, not exactly foolproof. Clearly we were too trusting there, so while we were looking for other leads, you kept digging into Mancini. Let's assume for now that the photo was *not* of him and that Carlos Mancini is still missing. Where did the father connection come from?' He took a seat, glancing at Charlie, who seemed equally interested.

'Well, I had a kind of art-inspired epiphany. I figured that any motive beyond senseless murder had to be something close to home, which made me think of family. And then I started wondering who we had in the picture who could be a family member, so I cross-referenced the people on our list that Mancini had wronged.'

'None were called Cavendish, so what about the name inconsistencies? Where did the link come from?'

'Well, I whittled the list down to all the people who had children. I thought maybe our killer's parent would be the same age as Mancini.'

'And then I got the tech team to pull all the information they could find on those people with a child around the same age as Cavendish – and voilà,' Charlie said, sliding a printout across the desk towards Daniel. He took the printout and examined it. It was a photo taken from a newspaper article dated just over a year ago. In the photo was Carlos Mancini, front and centre, with a few men who looked like colleagues. They were on a building site. At the edge of the photo was a man who looked extremely familiar.

'Wow. That's Cavendish. Nice find!'

'It is indeed. Or rather, that's Callum Rooney. His real name. Turns out his mother's maiden name was Cavendish. Seems he took that then changed his first name too, created an entirely new persona.'

Daniel studied the photo for a minute. Too many things were not adding up for him. 'Okay, so we couldn't find much on him because he changed his name, correct?' he asked.

Everyone nodded.

'But what we did find under Calvin Cavendish goes back to years before this photo was taken.'

'I think there may be some identity disassociation at play here,' Martia responded from across the table.

'Meaning?' Daniel asked.

'I believe that Callum Rooney had a reason to want to remove himself from his real identity as much as possible, to rid himself of a persona that perhaps he did not like. It's surprisingly common. Something could have happened in his life at an early age that made him reject the Rooney name and choose a new one.'

'Amelia, can you and Junior Sergeant Hayes look into that?' Daniel requested.

Amelia nodded.

'So Mancini and Callum Rooney's father–'

'Edmund,' Charlie interjected. 'Edmund Rooney.'

'Edmund, okay. So he and Mancini had a dispute over something, and that was enough to trigger Callum to act out?'

The room fell silent. In the quiet, Daniel thought back to the list of people they'd found who had issues with Carlos Mancini. One stood out.

'Didn't one of the lawsuits against Mancini have something to do with fatalities on a building site?' he asked.

Amelia's eyes widened. 'Yes – God!' Abruptly she spun around and ran out of the room. Daniel watched as she darted across the open-plan office. She was back within a minute, holding a laptop. Daniel, Charlie and Martia waited with bated breath as she tapped at the keypad.

'I've found the list I made. I can't believe I forgot this. Apparently men died on a project two years ago – no, almost three. It was ruled an accident, but as a result of the deaths the deal between Mancini and Rooney fell through and the project was cancelled. Perhaps it was Mancini who pulled out. The story was briefly in the news. No one was charged, but I guess it could have made Mancini nervous.'

'Which would have had quite an impact on Rooney's business, given the scope of projects Mancini normally deals with,' Daniel mused. It seemed to fit. He could see it in his mind, the mental picture building. If Edmund's business had been ruined or damaged, that could have had a ripple effect on his family and impacted Callum Rooney negatively. Had he lost his inheritance? Had that made him want revenge?

'It's a pretty extreme reaction, though, no?' Charlie asked, clearly thinking similar to Daniel. It was extreme, that was certain. They had to be missing something. There had to be more to it.

'Amelia, find out anything you can about the Rooney family and fill in Martia as you go. We need a full picture of Callum Rooney as fast as possible. You don't just start killing people willy-nilly. There's more to this, there has to be.'

'Sure thing.'

Martia raised a hand. 'This also doesn't explain the partner.'

'One at a time, Martia, one at a time,' Daniel answered, knowing she was right but desperate to start slotting in the puzzle pieces – and fast.

CHAPTER TWENTY-EIGHT

He was hungry – perhaps hungry enough to wish the men would come back, even if that did mean he'd be fed another body part. He felt sick; his stomach was surely eating its own lining. He was stiff from being tied up – the only exercise he got was the occasional guided trip to the bucket in the far corner of the room – and his limbs felt weaker than ever. He knew he had lost weight – a considerable amount, in fact. How long had it been? Two weeks? He wasn't sure any more. All he knew for certain was that they were only giving him enough food and water to keep him alive, no more.

Carlos Mancini was starting to wonder where his kidnappers were. No daylight came through the cracks in the boarded-up windows, only faint slivers of orange from a nearby streetlight. He suspected it was at least eight or nine, possibly later still. He hadn't seen either man since the morning of the day before. It wasn't the longest they had been away, but more than long enough.

He tried to swallow, but there was no moisture in his mouth. The men had replaced the old gag with a fresh one on their last visit. It had felt better for a while, hadn't rubbed against the insides of his lips as much, but it hadn't taken long for it to become just as uncomfortable as the old gag. Every so often he felt blood trickle from cuts on either side of his mouth. His brain mistook the droplets for life-giving water. The coppery taste made his stomach complain.

He had not long been awake, hence his guts growling at him. The painful need for sustenance, for liquid, was always worse after a sleep. He wasn't sure that 'sleep' was the right term, however. It was more that his body shut down every so often, as though trying to conserve energy. He would simply slip out of consciousness and wake, starving and disoriented, a few hours later.

From somewhere below him he heard a creak. His heart, and his stomach, lurched. Despite his thirst and hunger, he still dreaded the return of the sickos who had bound him up in this mildew-riddled hellhole. Sure, they had kept him alive so far, but they had also tortured him every time they paid him a visit. His body was covered in cuts, in festering scabs where they had taken turns in slicing thin pieces off him – enough to hurt badly without doing fatal harm. Even so, when he felt so incredibly hungry, so dehydrated that he thought he would turn into dust and blow away with a strong breeze, his body flooded with expectation at the thought of being fed and watered. He felt like his body was betraying him each time they came back, as though he should be stronger than that and resist eating human flesh to survive, that he should just let his body die to avoid giving these freaks what they were looking for.

The building was silent again. Perhaps the men hadn't returned after all. He felt a wave of disappointment.

And this is the part in the film where the intrepid journalist is hacked to pieces with a machete, Kelly Malone thought as she closed the battered old door behind her, the weathered hinges creaking with age. Seconds into her possibly suicidal mission, she had already announced her presence to anyone who happened to be in the building. It was going swimmingly.

She stayed stock-still, letting her eyes adjust to the darkness and her ears comb her surroundings for any sign that someone had noticed her arrival. With the door shut behind her, the sound of the evening traffic was a mere whisper. She tried to pick out any other noise but could hear nothing. A minute later, she figured she was probably safe. Her breath whooshed out, and the stiffness in her neck and shoulders dissipated marginally.

Please be alone, she thought, pulling out her phone and turning on the torch. The beam of stark white light came alive in front of her and she panicked, quickly turning it off again. It was brighter than she had expected. Again she waited, praying she didn't hear footsteps. Another minute passed and she was still alone. Unlocking her phone, she changed the settings so that it would not lock again and adjusted its brightness, using the phone screen to light her way instead of the harsh torch.

The building was in better condition than she had expected, though it was far from pristine. It was incredibly dusty, and the wallpaper was peeling off the walls. Elsewhere Kelly could see damp spots in the plaster, dark, sickly welts on the walls, some glistening. In one corner a small plant of some sort was attempting to grow, though she doubted it would ever thrive there. The large lobby in which she stood must once have been grand and bright, but the windows had long since been boarded up.

To her left and right the building opened up into derelict

spaces. Directly ahead of Kelly was a flight of wooden stairs. She thought they looked original, unlike the mouldy ceiling panels above. She held up her phone and turned around. Her heart stuttered when she saw the footprints in the dust and dirt. Multiple sets led towards the stairs and up, while a few more disappeared off to either side and into the shadows beyond the entrance. Unlocking her camera, Kelly took a few photos, the flash making her wince each time.

She was uncertain where to go. Clearly Calvin Cavendish had explored the building, but seemed to favour the upstairs. She knelt down to light up the prints further, and could make out a number of different sole patterns.

Oh God! What have I got myself into? she thought, swallowing. Should she turn back and get out of here? At home, in the safety of her flat, this had seemed like such a good idea. Well, not a good idea exactly, but certainly one that could launch her career into the stratosphere. Now, kneeling in the dank remains of a decrepit building in Lewisham, at night, on her own, the whole idea seeming downright foolish.

Standing up, Kelly turned her phone this way and that, trying to get a sense of the ground floor. She aimed the screen up the stairs too, but saw little more than a landing that led into pitch-black nothingness. Neither option was exactly enticing, though – given the footprints – she figured that upstairs she'd be more likely to find any evidence Cavendish had left.

A noise behind her sliced through the dusty quiet, interrupting her thoughts. A noise, close – perhaps right outside the big wooden door she had entered through.

Images from a shit slasher film she had seen with an ex flashed though her mind. In it the stupid person being chased had run upstairs to escape from the killer, so had no way of escaping. If she did that, she was trapped. She made a choice, running left and fumbling to turn off her phone. As the building was plunged into darkness, she heard the entrance door creak open. She spotted a door on her right and lurched at it, pulling it shut behind her as quickly and quietly as she could.

Daniel and Charlie were back to waiting, Red Bull and coffee in their hands, as the system Patrick and Steve were using to find Callum Rooney's base marched on. Daniel was beginning to feel like half of his job consisted of simply crossing his fingers and hoping.

It had taken Amelia and Ross just ten minutes to find their main suspect on a hospital release list, now they knew his alias. He had spent at least six months at a private psychiatric centre on the outskirts of Manchester. As far as their research told them, it was a small operation specialising in treating a range of psychotic, psychopathic and sociopathic disorders, though the website was rather vague. Still, it was officially licensed and they produced patient release reports, like other similar institutes. Many had refused to reveal patient details at first, until they were made aware that they could have treated a prolific serial killer. After that, for the most part, hospital staff had been co-operative; doctor–patient confidentiality being lessened due to the potential endangering of the public. A legal team had very carefully drafted non-disclosure agreements, then Amelia and Ross just had to sift through the reports until they found what they were looking for. Rooney had been admitted not long after the incident between his father and Mancini, and had left the facility a year and three months ago. They had not been able to track him since then. Everything aligned with Martia's profile of him.

Daniel felt better now he had some sort of motive. The

pieces were starting to slot together – at least, in regards to Callum Rooney. The man clearly had sociopathic tendencies, hence being in the mental health faculty. Martia had said it was likely that he'd experienced a life-changing event before that which had led to his changing his name, and this had probably been triggered in some way by the incident between his father Edmund and Carlos Mancini.

They still had to prove that Mancini wasn't in Europe, and they had to find him. Mancini had no living relatives to interview, and his assistant had last seen Mancini the night he disappeared. They found out that she had received two texts from Mancini's phone, explaining that he'd gone on an unplanned trip to detox, and she hadn't questioned them. They would, of course, try to trace the phone's whereabouts, but they had so many connections now they knew Rooney's real name that Daniel was certain their theory was correct and that the phone would still be in London.

He still had some unanswered questions, all of which felt enormous. Where was Rooney now? Who was his partner in crime? Was Rooney the less restrained of the two? Where was Carlos Mancini? And did the killers have more names on their kill list?

They were painfully close now, Daniel knew it. His bones hummed with anticipation. He longed to catch these brutal killers and end their reign of terror. He hoped that if they found Rooney, he'd be able to give them the answers they needed.

At that moment his phone rang. His heart leaped when he saw it was Patrick.

'Graves, it's Lewisham. They're in Lewisham!' Patrick practically yelled.

'This is it!' Daniel said down the phone but also to Charlie, who had sat up like a meerkat. 'Do you have an address?'

'We're narrowing it down now. I suggest you get a team ready.'

Daniel hung up and rushed for the lifts, Charlie hot on his heels.

CHAPTER TWENTY-NINE

Inching backwards in the darkness as though she could retreat further from whoever had just entered the old building, Kelly Malone stifled a scream when the floor vanished out from underneath her right foot. She waved her arms like a windmill to stop herself from falling backwards. The fingers of one hand traced over cold metal and she grabbed at it, steadying herself. It only took her brain a second to realise it was a handrail. The floor had vanished because she was at the top of a flight of stairs.

She let her heart slow down before pressing the home button on her phone. The stairwell lit up. The worn steps led down into a basement of some description. She doubted anything useful would come of going down there, and instead she stood on the spot, unsure what to do.

If she headed back out through the door she had hidden behind, she could probably sneak out of the building, if she was quick and kept quiet. That was sensible.

And in my bid for freedom I could run into a crazed murderer and get an axe to the face.

Her imagination painted horrific pictures in her mind and she shivered.

She could try going down into the basement and find another way out.

Or I could get trapped down there, then turn back, try to get out and get an axe to the face.

No, going down the stairs seemed pointless. The footprints she had seen indicated that she should go upstairs. Granted, there had been some dusty prints around the ground floor too, but her gut told her that the basement did not contain anything she wanted to see.

Of course, she could be brave and sneak up to the first floor. *Where I will most certainly get an axe to the face. Fuck.*

Standing in the spiderweb-riddled stairwell by the weak light of her phone, which had already drained to less than sixty per cent, Kelly found herself once again questioning her recent life choices.

She could wait. That was an option. She could just sit down on the top step and play Candy Crush for a while until the exit was clear. But then she might still be discovered and earn an axe to the face, plus it was cold, miserable and a pretty scary place to spend the next few hours. And she knew her phone battery wouldn't last that long, not if she played games.

Kelly checked the time. She had already been hiding for almost fifteen minutes. She had no real choice, if she was honest with herself. She should never have set foot in this place, and she should leave now while her face remained axe-free.

She put a hand out to the door handle. Her stomach churned at the mental image of someone standing on the other side waiting to kill her. Slowly she twisted the handle, her pulse racing. Cool air washed over her as she pushed the door open. There was now nothing in between her and potential death.

It occurred to Kelly that perhaps she should simply call the police and await their arrival. But what would she say? That she had broken into private property and got scared? For all she knew, the man she had followed could have been a building security guard, doing his rounds to make sure that nothing untoward was going down. Or a junkie, a vandal maybe. Her mind said that it had been Calvin Cavendish, suspected serial killer, but she had no proof. The police already hated journalists as a rule, and she certainly wasn't in the good books of anyone working on this case. If she called them out and caused a massive hoo-ha over nothing she'd do more damage than good – to the case and to her reputation.

No, she had to resolve her current situation herself, as nerve-racking as it was. She would only call the police if she had no choice.

She gave herself a moment to plan her route to the front door, then stepped out into the open, feeling horribly exposed. An attack could come from any angle.

Part of her wanted to leg it as fast as she could, but she knew that would be noisy and she had no idea where Cavendish might be. No. She needed to be more careful. She needed to be as silent and alert as possible.

Kelly began to inch along the wall, feeling tendrils of curled wallpaper tickling at her neck like the gentle touch of dead fingers. Her body shook in revulsion but she kept going. She had just reached the doorway that led back to the lobby and the main stairs when a scream of pure agony sliced through the silence.

She craned her neck upwards to the source of the sound, her blood running cold.

———

The siren was a blaring banshee even inside the car as Detectives Charlie Palmer and Daniel Graves raced down the Queen's Road well over the speed limit. As was often the case, Daniel gripped the passenger door handle tightly; Charlie drove as though he was trying to outrun the apocalypse. He was glad that it was almost ten, the roads quieter than they had been. The two squad cars in hot pursuit behind them did nothing to ease the tension in his body.

Something in his gut told him that this haunting, horrific case would be solved that day. They had one of the suspects, they had evidence that placed him at each crime scene, thanks to the van, and, best of all, they had the start of a motive. If they could find him and bring him in, Daniel knew they were golden. They would get a confession out of Callum Rooney and in turn he would give them his accomplice, whoever that was.

A mixture of adrenaline, nerves and excitement rippled over Daniel as they turned onto the A20, which would bring them to Lewisham. The squad cars were still behind him and he had ordered an armed response team, who were on route too. The bastard was not getting away. Maybe both men would be there. Two for one. That was the ideal scenario.

To their left Daniel spotted Lewisham shopping centre. The floral blue banner invited people to shop, browse and enjoy. It was just minutes from the abandoned building that Patrick Marsden and his team had located using the route tracking system. Traffic cameras had shown the van near it there. Daniel was glad it was late and that no happy shoppers were anywhere nearby. The fewer pedestrians around, the better. The last thing he wanted was a chase through crowds, should Rooney somehow get past them.

Charlie swore and honked his horn at a taxi that was parked awkwardly, awaiting a group of women on a night out who were busy taking selfies on the pavement.

'Sure, fucking park anywhere, I don't mind!' Charlie yelled as they drove past.

Daniel's skin hummed as Charlie suddenly slowed down. They went through an underpass and there it was – the boarded-up building they were looking for. Inside it, they hoped to find the killers who had terrorised the city.

They drove past, looking for a convenient place to park, the siren off. In his side mirror Daniel could see the other two cars stopping. The officers not driving jumped out into the middle of the road, getting ready to put up blocks, and the cars then pulled into positions that would stop traffic on the corner.

'The response team are here.' Charlie indicated the impressive black van parked a few vehicles down from them. 'You ready?'

Daniel simply nodded. Together they got out, the cold night biting at their faces.

Carlos Mancini spat out blood, feeling the gooey liquid dribbling down his chin. His mouth was in agony, the place where one of his front teeth had been just minutes before now a throbbing hole that sent shockwaves of pain through his skull.

'I don't know... where Clara Michaut... is,' he mumbled. 'Why does it... even matter any more?'

He just wanted it to be over. The fight within him had been doused entirely. He didn't care about surviving. His body could not keep going through this torture much longer and there was no end in sight – not while they still had people for him to eat bits of.

'Because, my dear Carlos,' Callum answered, leering over the bloodied pliers he held, 'that bitch was involved in all of this almost as much as you were, and more than any of the pathetic worker bees we've spoken to so far. To punish you even more and truly destroy your legacy, we're going to leak everything that you did and bring your beloved company to its knees – and she's going to help.'

Carlos thought the words 'spoken to' underplayed what his torturers had done. They truly were crazy, delusional in every way.

'She was the ringleader – she covered up those deaths on your building site. You tried to cut costs by using shitty materials and shitty equipment, and guess what? You cut too many. Those people died, and it was your fault. But what really gets me is that if you hadn't been doing a rush job, then the crane wouldn't have malfunctioned and my father wouldn't have been blamed. He was made the scapegoat. It was you who claimed his company hadn't done its due diligence and that he employed untrained workers. You fucking ruined him! You shut his business down and my family paid the price. But what a surprise – you got away with it because you're a rich motherfucker and you just threw money at everything to get out of trouble. Where the fuck did all the so-called evidence against my dad come from, hey? He did nothing wrong, yet suddenly he looked guilty of negligence and you were in the clear. He was lucky he didn't do time! He knew someone had done it – planted fake fucking paperwork, email trails and the like – but he didn't know who, and he didn't have the resources to do anything about it. He just let our world fall apart, took his anger out on me. I wasn't gonna let things slide, though. It took some investigating, but me and my pal Andrew here finally got some answers, got her name. She's the last piece of this puzzle, and we know she's going to spill a whole load of juicy details to save her skin.'

'Don't worry, though. We're saving you for last,' came

Andrew's voice from behind him. Carlos flinched as fingers brushed over his hair. His scalp prickled.

'Oh, come now, Carlos, you must have known we were going to kill you. Why do you think we told you our names?' Callum brushed the bloody end of the pliers down Carlos's throbbing cheek.

Carlos had always figured as much, but this was the first time he no longer cared. He was done.

'And because we're saving you for dessert, we really want to go and cut pieces out of Clara first. We can't find her, but you? I don't believe that you don't know where your former chief operating officer is now.'

Out of the corner of his eye, Carlos caught sight of Andrew. He had circled the edge of the dusty room to the two-metre-long wooden table off to one side. Andrew picked something up, something that glinted in the low light of the lamp they had installed.

'You can do what you want with that,' Carlos said, registering the weapon as a metal pipe of some sort. 'It won't suddenly make me... make me know where she is.' He swallowed a lumpy blob of blood, the taste somehow both revolting and pleasant.

'Let's try,' Andrew said with a shadowy grin. He pounced. The pipe connected hard with Carlos's left knee, shattering something. He screamed, his vision flickering as he tried to combat the pain.

'Anything?' Callum whispered, his hot breath ripe against Carlos's ear. As Carlos struggled not to pass out from the twin pain centres of his bruised jaw and broken knee, something caught his eye. Movement. And it wasn't Callum or Andrew. He tried to focus, to see what it was. Then it clicked. The door – it was the door. He could swear it was further open than it had been. He must have been staring, for Callum turned around to look in the same direction.

'What have you just seen?'

A hushed gasp came from behind the door.

Callum charged.

CHAPTER THIRTY

D aniel and Charlie watched anxiously as one of the armed response team members, a man named Mick, pulled back a large panel of rotten MDF. He was covered by his colleague, Jay, who aimed a semi-automatic at the space Mick was about to reveal. Behind the panelling Daniel could see a set of double doors. Mick stepped forward and pushed open the right-hand door slowly with a gloved hand. His colleague locked on to it with his gun in case they were rushed. With a squeal the door opened a crack.

Signalling to two more armed response officers, Jay stepped back, still aiming at the door. The two men moved past him, their Glock 17s and torches raised. As the door opened fully they quickly swept the immediate interior with light before darting through and into the darkness beyond.

Daniel's heart was pounding so hard, he felt like his ribs were rattling. He flicked a glance at Charlie and registered the beads of sweat on his forehead; his fringe was dark and matted. Daniel looked back to the door. The interior was hidden fully. Fear trembled over his skin despite the armed, combat-ready officers around him. It was as though the building were a forbidden place, full of monsters ready to pull him to pieces. It felt like the start of a horror film. He half-expected Pennywise the clown to pop his grinning face around the door, teeth bared and primed to attack.

'All clear,' one of the men called back to them, his voice low. Mick pushed open both doors and he and Jay followed the first two. Daniel heard Mick calling them Tommy and Evan.

Daniel felt a vibration in his pocket: a text.

It's not the time!

'Let's do this,' Charlie said, though his voice betrayed the nervousness that Daniel knew all too well. He nodded and they followed the armed response officers. The building swallowed them in one shadowy bite. It took Daniel's eyes a good few seconds to start adjusting. He could just make out a flight of stairs ahead and an open archway on his right. Then a high-pitched scream tore through their careful silence.

'I think we're in luck,' Charlie whispered.

All attempts at being quiet were thrown out of the window when Kelly Malone realised she had been spotted. Elation had run through her at the sight of Carlos Mancini, just about alive though extremely bloodied and bruised, but when she saw movement to the side of the room – a second man, who was also presumably a brutal murderer – her instincts took over. She screamed, the sound shrill and panicked, communicating pure horror.

RUN!

Pushing herself backwards off the door she had been peeking around, Kelly spun clumsily and set off at a stagger back down the hallway. Dust whipped up around her, a string of what she hoped was spider-less web went in her mouth, and she coughed and spluttered without slowing down. She could cope with dust and web; less so, a sharp metal object across the back of her head.

Even though she was wearing trainers, her feet struggled to find any grip. As she reached the corner to the top of the stairs, she skidded sideways. Her left hand scrabbled for purchase as she fell, and she hissed as splinters from the worn wooden flooring pierced deep into her fingertips.

The end of the hallway lit up and a man charged after her, his footsteps booming along the corridor. Within a heartbeat he was just metres away. Kelly screamed again, forcing herself up. She hit the top of the stairs at a sprint and charged down them two at a time, doing her best not to miss a step, but inside fearing she was about to plummet and break her neck.

She was halfway down when she realised that there wasn't just someone behind her; there was someone ahead of her too. She risked a glance up and saw the shadowy shapes of at least four more men, all in black, crouched in the lobby, guns raised. Not waiting to see who they were, she jumped the last three steps and darted right, heading to the basement that had previously seemed like such a bad idea.

Kelly screamed again as gunshots exploded behind her, illuminating her path through the shadows in flashes. She hit the door hard, didn't stop, let the darkness of the basement swallow her as she raced down the steps. She heard the low crack of something splintering at the same time as she felt the step under her foot give way. Then she fell.

'Kelly?' Charlie muttered, dumbfounded, as a familiar-looking woman charged down the stairs and shot off into the darkness, barely looking up. He stood where he was, stunned, so taken aback by her sudden appearance in the gloom of the old building that he was unable to react.

'Stop right there!' someone yelled. Charlie had only just seen the man who had been chasing Kelly when the lobby lit up with gunfire. It took him another few seconds to realise that Daniel was shouting at him.

'Charlie, follow him and Kelly. I'm going up!' Daniel ran up the stairs behind two of the armed response team.

'Detective!' Mick shouted at Charlie, gun in hand, signalling him to follow as they hustled after Kelly Malone and her pursuer. Charlie shook himself and took off after them.

Daniel climbed the stairs two at a time, following the pair of well-armed men as they sped up into the darkness. What had Kelly Malone been doing up there? Had that been one of the killers chasing her? Where was the other one? Daniel assumed the other suspect was either hiding or already trying to escape. He also expected to find a body, based on the screams they had heard.

He didn't have a gun as he tended to deem them unnecessary, a notion most other detectives agreed with. London was not a city where having a gun was often beneficial. Now, however, he wished he had put in a request for one.

Too late now.

At the top of the stairs the armed response guys slowed, taking a corner hunched down, Jay leading and Tommy keeping an eye on other possible angles of attack.

Around them, the building creaked against the wind outside. The momentary chaos of the lobby had faded; Daniel could no longer hear Charlie and the other men in pursuit of Kelly and her attacker. Was it Rooney? Had they gone down another floor? The building felt too quiet again, more menacing, as though it was hiding its own secrets as well as two killers.

Ahead of him, at the end of a long, dark corridor, light came from an open door – beyond which, Daniel presumed, something horrible lay. Along the left side of the hallway he could make out three other doors, all closed. He didn't have to tell the armed officers to check them. They had already paused outside the first one and in seconds, and together, had opened it, swept the room and deemed it clear. They shuffled to the next door, Daniel following but keeping a close eye on the open door at the end. The second suspect could appear from anywhere – if he was in the building. He was an unknown entity. They knew nothing about him, not even why he was involved in the murders. What Daniel was sure of, however, was that the man was psychotic and possibly psychopathic. He was lethal, and he wasn't going to go down easily.

Tommy kicked in the second door. Daniel jumped, expecting a response of gunfire or a figure charging them. Nothing happened.

'Clear,' Tommy grunted. They moved closer to the open door. The light that bled out from it touched them now. One more door to go. Daniel could feel his pulse quickening. He knew something was about to happen. He'd seen this film before.

Wait for the jump scare, wait for the jump scare.

His throat was dry as he swallowed, risking a glance behind him. The dusty hallway was empty, no shadowy men in black creeping up on him. He turned back to the officers as they checked behind door number three.

'It's clear.' The officers turned towards the last door, the open one, guns at the ready. Daniel followed, almost holding his breath. He looked into the third room as he passed it, saw an empty space with nowhere to hide.

After a slight hesitation, Jay pushed the end door fully open. Light washed over them. Tommy entered the room first. 'I've got someone here,' he called back. 'He's not in good shape. He'll need a medical team ASAP.'

Daniel already knew who the officer had found, but he needed to see for himself. His heart pounding, he followed, the room opening up around him, much less claustrophobic than the hallway had been. No more pleasant, however, not least due to the bloodied man tied to a chair in the middle of it. He looked like he'd been hit by a car.

'Mr Mancini?' Daniel asked as he approached the man, choking back vomit at the smell of old blood, other bodily fluids, and rotting flesh. The captive had angry wounds that were oozing pus. With eyes that looked barely able to focus, or even open properly, the man looked up, nodded gently. Daniel could sense his relief. There was a hopeful light in his eyes somewhere under the pain.

'I'm Detective Inspector Graves. You'll be safe now, okay? We'll make sure of it. But listen, how many men were here? We're in pursuit of one suspect already, but is there another?'

Carlos Mancini nodded again, though the gesture clearly pained him. 'Up,' he whispered, jerking his head towards the ceiling.

'What? Above us?' Daniel looked up. Square panelling spanned the ceiling. A few tiles were missing and his gaze flicked between them. Each square was an ominous black hole. He choked back a gasp when he spotted a grinning face staring back at him, perhaps three metres above. There was a flash, and a bang echoed around the room. Daniel felt something spray over his face. He opened his eyes. He just had enough time to see the chewed-up, ragged mess that had once been Carlos Mancini's face before the second shot came.

CHAPTER THIRTY-ONE

K elly groaned as she pushed herself up off the cold floor, feeling dirt and grit under her fingertips. Miraculously, she didn't think anything was broken, but she could feel what she assumed was blood on her right cheek and she had smacked her hip pretty hard on the way down the stairs.

'Fucking shithole building,' she muttered as she stood up, wincing when pain reverberated through her body. She had obviously bumped more than just her hip. Numerous body parts were complaining.

A commotion from the top of the stairs lit a fire of panic under her as her brain stopped focusing on her injuries and remembered why she had them in the first place.

'Shit, shit, shit,' she hissed, moving away from the stairs, her right hand following the wall. She had only gone a few steps when her foot kicked something, the metallic clang scaring her even more than she already was. It was no use; the basement was too dark. She would be found in a heartbeat, and her pursuer was surely mere seconds behind her.

Kelly pulled her phone out of her pocket and unlocked it, quickly swiping up to access her torch. The screen was cracked, but she would worry about that later. She retrieved the knife from her backpack, comforted by its reassuring weight in her grasp, even if she was terrified at the thought of using it. She looked around and saw that she was in a narrow corridor. It was an old rusty bucket she had kicked. Pipes ran along the ceiling, with chewed wires poking out of a long-abandoned fuse box. The corridor went left and right at the foot of the stairs. She had started right, and decided it would have to do. Neither option seemed great, and she didn't have the luxury of time to make a considered decision.

Although a painful limp impeded her speed, Kelly nonetheless started to run. She could hear footfalls on the stairs, worryingly close. She had no choice but to leg it.

Not daring to look behind her, Kelly moved as quickly as she could down the hallway, acutely aware that the swinging cone of light from her phone would immediately give away her position. She couldn't turn it off, though; she'd be blind without it. The hallway made a turn and she darted round it, correcting her balance as she went before speeding up again. Her footsteps echoed around her like shouting voices.

Here she is – we found her! Come get her!

She was making far too much noise. She knew she had to hide. Spotting a door on her right, a rippled glass square set into it, Kelly ran over to it, only to discover it was locked and wouldn't budge. She could hear movement not far behind her.

Running as fast as she could, she came to a fork. To the right was another door, closed. To the left, more corridor. Evidently it snaked around the breadth of the main building. Her pulse racing, not sure what to do, instinct took over and she found her hand on the door handle without even consciously making the decision. It turned, and her heart soared as she fell into the room beyond. The knife dropped from her hand and clattered away into the darkness.

'Fuck!' She pushed the door shut behind her, looked for a lock but found none.

Holding her phone up, she realised it was a storage room; not that it stored much any more. Metal shelving units created four aisles. A few rotten boxes had been left behind. A dead rat lay unceremoniously on the floor near her feet, its body as rotted as the mildewed boxes. That was pretty much it. There wasn't much in the way of hiding places. She couldn't see the knife either, and assumed it had skidded under one of the shelving units.

So much for that. Kelly hurried along the closest shelving unit, aiming for the far corner where perhaps the shelves would block the view from the door, where at least she'd have a chance of running past someone if they entered and came down one of the aisles. When she reached the corner she crouched and turned off her phone light, still feeling horribly vulnerable. She thought about getting the pepper spray from her backpack, but what was the point if she couldn't see anything?

She knew it wouldn't take much to find her. Her pursuer would either need to not have a torch or completely miss the room. Behind her, she felt more pipes running along at skirting level, cold to the touch and rough, like old dead skin. One of them rattled in place. That gave Kelly an idea. She put her phone down, turned around and gripped the pipe, then pulled as hard as she could. It wobbled but remained fixed. Shifting her weight, she put her toes against the bottom of the wall and pulled once more, gritting her teeth through the pain her hip sent through her in waves. With a screech that scared her half to death, the old metal cracked and a foot-long piece of pipe snapped off. Kelly fell backwards, banging her elbow but feeling better for having the makeshift weapon. She couldn't believe she had lost the knife; how pathetic she was in a crisis.

Hunkering down again, she pulled out her phone. She

didn't want to make a call; it was too loud, too risky, but she could send a text. The phone screen came alive, still unlocked, when she heard the door to the storage room click open. Quickly she pressed a button on the side of the phone to make it go dark, shoved it into her pocket and held the pipe with both hands. All she could hear was her panicked breathing. She took one hand off the weapon to cover her mouth, desperately trying to stay calm.

She couldn't see anything. The room was pitch black. She could hear tentative movement, the soft scrape of shoes on the dirty concrete floor. It was the most terrifying thing Kelly had ever experienced, and she could feel tears trickling down her face as she fought not to scream.

Her fingers hurting from gripping the pipe, Kelly held her breath, listening. She couldn't hear anything, couldn't figure out where the man was, or even if he was still in the room. Slowly she let out her breath, her lungs burning, then sucked a breath in, too quickly.

'I hear you,' came a singsong voice – close, too close, maybe just metres away. Her heart threatened to stop.

Move, move! her mind screamed at her.

One of the shelving units shook violently, and she jumped. It gave her a chance, though, and she took it. Pipe in her right hand, left hand on the brickwork for support, she took a quick step back towards the door. The room was so quiet that all she could hear were her breathing, her movements. She paused again, holding her breath.

'Marco,' the man said suddenly, making her jump. She couldn't place him exactly, but thought he was across the room from her. She had to move, but didn't dare to go at anything faster than a slow shuffle. She couldn't risk him realising where she was, though surely he couldn't see her either. Her pulse racing, Kelly took another step forward, then another, still following the crumbling bricks with her fingers.

'Maaarrrrcoooo,' her pursuer drawled, toying with her. He'd moved again; his voice echoed off the bare walls. She couldn't tell where he was. Still close, though. She thought for a second that she could see the outline of the door to the room, but perhaps her eyes were playing tricks on her.

Another step. Her right foot scuffed against a stone and Kelly rocked sideways. Panicked, she thrust out her hand, which collided with the cold metal frame of a shelving unit. There was a loud rattle. She stifled a gasp and froze. Even over the blood pounding in her ears, she thought she heard a whisper of movement behind her. Then silence. She waited a second. Another. No sounds other than hers.

Where is he?!

Kelly was desperately trying to think of a plan when she realised that she could make out the lines of the bricks to her left. She held one hand in front of her, could just about see her fingers in front of her. Light – there was light coming from somewhere.

It must be the door!

Carefully, quietly, Kelly twisted around so she was facing the weak source of light that she could see through the empty shelving. Just inches from her, on the other side of the shelves, eyes glinted back at her.

'Polo,' the man whispered, his mouth slicing open in a grin. As Kelly screamed he lunged forward, thrusting his arms through the metal unit at her. She fell backwards, her hands scraping across the floor. She felt something small and sharp bite into one palm. The floor felt wet, and she gagged the pain down. Not pausing, she ran along the side of the room in an awkward half-crouch, dodging the hands that darted out to grab her.

'No, you don't!' the man yelled. There was a thud and grunt, and the shelving unit toppled, slamming against the wall above her head. Her route to the strip of light that signalled the door was suddenly blocked. She screamed again when her attacker clambered on top of the tilting shelves. A hand grabbed her hair and then he was pulling her. Kelly screamed, scratching at his cold flesh as he tried to drag her through the metal frame, flailing the pipe in a desperate bid to connect with him.

Light bloomed over them. Kelly winced, as much from the sudden brightness as the sheer agony of the attack. She felt the grip on her hair loosen. Then there was a heavy thud and the man let go of her. She fell onto the edge of a shelf and moaned in pain.

'God, Kelly, are you okay? Thank Christ I found you!'

'Charlie?' she mumbled weakly, exhausted, using her last reserves of energy to climb out of the fallen shelving and past her unconscious attacker. She tripped and Charlie stooped to grab her.

'She okay?' came the voice of a man behind Charlie, invisible in the dark.

'I think so. Right?'

Kelly gave a weak nod against Charlie's chest, more thankful for his embrace now than she had ever been when they had been together. She felt safe, and it felt good – wonderful, in fact. She tried to push away her nagging injuries to savour the moment, even for a second.

'And the suspect?'

'He's out cold.'

Charlie swung his torch down, and Kelly finally had a good look at the man. A trickle of blood shone on the back of his head, echoed by the blood covering the end of Charlie's baton.

'Well, that's one down,' the invisible officer said. The nerves in his voice made Kelly shiver.

CHAPTER THIRTY-TWO

The armed response men let rip at the ceiling with their semi-automatics and the room exploded with gunfire. Daniel desperately looked for cover from the killer's gun, then lunged under the table. Chunks of ceiling tile and dust rained down from above like snow as bullets tore through everything they touched. The sound was deafening. Daniel kept his hands over his ears, again furious at himself for not having a gun.

The flashes from the semis ceased and the room was plunged into silence. Dust floated gently down. Daniel found it intensely unnerving. Both the armed response men were looking up at the ceiling, their guns at the ready.

Avoiding looking at Carlos Mancini's bloodied head, Daniel peered out from under the table at the ceiling.

'No blood,' he whispered, his voice carrying in the silence. He had hoped, macabre as it was, that the killer's dead body would have fallen from the ceiling and landed with a thud on the floorboards, torn to shreds by bullets.

'He can't have gone far,' Jay whispered back, scanning the ceiling. Daniel looked around the room. For the first time he saw the ladder leaning against the wall, almost hidden in the shadowy corner, leading up to another missing ceiling panel.

'I don't know. He could be anywhere,' Daniel hissed. The crawl space above could span most of the building. The shooter had to find a way back down, but the question was, where? He could drop into any of the rooms on this floor.

'We need to spread out,' Tommy said, crouch-walking towards the door. He paused, unclipping a Glock 17 from his holster. He held it out. Daniel scooted across the floor, his shoulders hunched, half-expecting a bullet to the back. None came, and he took the gun, relishing its weight in his hand.

'Thanks. But let's not separate too much. We need to stay close so we have the advantage.'

The officers nodded, and they all made their way to the door. Before leaving the room Daniel grabbed the ladder and carefully laid it flat on the floor. At least if the psycho was planning on coming down in there, trying to get behind them, he would have to drop and they would hear him land. *Here we go again*, he thought as they crept back out into the dark hallway, the open doors on their right ominous, potentially lethal once more.

The silence was overwhelming. Daniel could not hear any noises beneath him. Was Charlie still pursuing Rooney? Where was Kelly? The officers in front of him stepped with care, their rubber-soled shoes silent on the floorboards.

They took turns sweeping the rooms again, this time looking at the ceilings as well as checking at floor level, their torches chewing away the darkness in strips. The tension in the air was palpable. Daniel could feel a trail of sweat starting between his shoulders, more droplets around his hairline, despite the cold of the building.

When they reached the end of the corridor, the man was nowhere to be found. At the top of the stairs another corridor, one they hadn't unexplored, led into darkness, only pierced by the occasional shafts of light coming through cracks in the window boards. Daniel's tension grew. They had no idea what to expect if they headed that way. Jay aimed his torch down the hall.

'We need to eliminate it as an option,' he whispered, turning back to Daniel, who nodded. He didn't want to head down there, knowing they could be taken by surprise, but they couldn't ignore it. He didn't even want to consider the prospect of the second killer getting away because they hadn't been thorough enough.

'Lead the way,' he answered, his grip on the Glock tightening.

As he followed the men, Daniel found himself constantly glancing upwards. Mancini's killer could come from anywhere, could be anywhere. His muscles were tight to the point of pain, in expectation of an attack.

Their footfalls echoed softly as they walked. They found a closed door, its once white paint now a dank grey, rotting wood visible where flakes of paint had fallen away. Slowly Jay twisted the handle and pushed open the door. Daniel held his breath. Beyond was almost pitch black. As they moved slowly into the room, Daniel felt they were making a mistake. It felt wrong, he just knew it.

The torches swished left and right, revealing peeling walls, an old wooden chair on its side, one leg broken. Cupboards – storage built into the left side of the large room. Some of the doors were missing, some were closed. Daniel wondered if any were big enough to hide someone.

A soft cry came from deep within the dark.

'Did you hear that?' Jay asked, his voice a thin gasp. Jay and Tommy aimed their torches at the source of the noise, lighting up a counter, rotten like the rest of the building. It was an old bar, though no bottles or glasses remained.

'Is someone there?' Daniel asked, raising his gun, trying to sound authoritative. No one answered. The stillness of the room was a heavy blanket pressing down on Daniel's chest. He watched as two hands appeared from behind the bar counter. Daniel's stomach lurched until he registered the lack of a gun.

'Okay, don't shoot. I'm standing up.' The voice sounded rough, like a heavy smoker. The man stood up. When his life-worn face appeared, Daniel sighed – a mixture of disappointment and relief. The man looked homeless. He had evidently broken into the building seeking shelter for the winter months.

'Sir, you need to leave the building. This is private property and you're interfering with a live police investigation,' Tommy said.

The homeless man tutted, but nonetheless he shuffled out from behind the counter. His clothes were thick but dirty, full of holes. Daniel felt guilty that they had to kick him out into the night, and wondered if perhaps he could help the man more after the hunt was over. They couldn't just let him wander off into the building, though. It would be easy for them to mistake him for Rooney or his partner again.

'Okay, we're going to escort you out. It's not safe for you to be here,' Daniel said, beckoning to the man to join him.

'Oh sure, like it's better out there. Let me freeze to death,' the vagrant griped.

'Do you want to be shot?' Jay snapped.

'Fuck, no!'

'Okay, let's go,' Daniel said.

'All four of us?' Tommy asked, sounding irritated. Daniel heard his irritation, but what else could they do? He wasn't about to leave this homeless man to his own devices in a dark, decrepit building housing two serial killers.

'Leaving him behind then, are ya?' the old man croaked.

'Who?' Daniel asked a second before his brain caught up. 'Get down!' he shouted, just as the darkness in front of him lit up with gunfire. He dropped to the floor, felt a bullet whistle close above him. He rolled sideways, jumping up into a crouch, then levelling his gun. Behind him both officers fired their semi-automatics: bursts of fire lit up the room for split seconds. Daniel saw the killer dart off to the right, no more than a black blur of motion.

'Behind you!' the homeless man yelled. Daniel spun to look behind him, but saw nothing. A scream of agony ripped through the darkness and one of the torch beams whipped upwards, the circle of light scrabbling over the ceiling as if it was alive. Daniel twisted in the direction of the cries, saw two shadows wrestling. Jay's torch beam fell onto the faces of the struggling men and Daniel saw the knife glint as the killer stabbed Tommy. Vivid red spurted from his neck. The killer yanked the knife free, then stabbed him again, the blade tearing viciously through fabric, skin and muscle, blood spraying out into the darkness. Daniel tried to find a shot, his gun wavering in front of him, but he could barely see where he was aiming.

Tommy's gun fell to the floor with a thud. Daniel pulled the trigger. In the flash of light he saw the killer's face, crazed and splashed with blood, grinning like a Cheshire cat, before the darkness came back, even thicker than before. Knowing that the killer would know where he was, Daniel dodged to his right, almost losing his balance as his shoe caught the edge of a warped board that stuck up from the floor. Jay was frantically scanning the room, and backing up to a wall. The homeless man cowered in a corner, the torchlight settling on him for a second before running over the cupboards.

One looked odd... What could–

'Go back!' Daniel screamed, willing Jay to pan back to the cupboard door that had stood out from the others. The circle of illumination jumped back, darting across the cupboard fronts, just in time for Daniel to see the bloodied man burst out of the cupboard and charge at him. Jay fired immediately, hitting the man in the shoulder but not stopping him. He roared. Daniel aimed and fired just before his attacker lunged, knocking Daniel down, pinning him to the floor. Hands grabbed at Daniel, nails scratched at his throat, prying fingers looked for a soft spot to dig into. Daniel squeezed the trigger, again, again, emptying the clip into the body on top of him, screaming as he felt hot breath and spittle on his face, feeling the bullets explode against his chest, burning the back of his hand. The man stopped, his limbs dropping like lead as the life drained out of him. Daniel could barely breathe, had just enough energy to push the dead body off him. He heard the Glock clunk onto the floorboards.

Daniel lay in the dark, exhausted, barely squinting when the torchlight fell on him and Jay asked if he was okay. His voice sounded like that of a ghost, floating somewhere just out of sight.

CHAPTER THIRTY-THREE

A crowd had gathered outside the old building; the cold night not enough to deter journalists and passers-by from investigating. Cordoned-off roads and a job lot of flashing police lights, as well as ambulances and an armed response van, had no chance of avoiding being noticed in a busy area of London, despite the late hour.

'Okay, I think I get it,' Kelly Malone said to Charlie, limping despite Charlie's arm around her waist, supporting her. 'This is... intense. It's making me feel really uncomfortable, all these people shouting at us.'

As soon as they were spotted, every journalist surged forward, vying for a money shot that would go on their front page the next day.

'It's about time,' Charlie answered with a wan smile. Daniel noticed his smile, wondered what it meant for his colleague and the woman who had caused him so much heartache. It wasn't the moment to comment, however. He pulled out his phone, saw he had a few missed calls, then his phone rang again. It was Amelia.

'Oh, thank God you're okay. Did you get them both?'

'We did. Rooney is in custody now, the other one is dead.'

'That's why I was calling. We found out who he is. A guy named Andrew Hogan – he was at the same clinic Rooney had been treated at. According to one of the therapists there, they had bonded because they'd both been abused as children. Callum had sociopathic tendencies – he had eventually told a counsellor there that he had been beaten regularly by his father, especially after he'd lost the family business. Andrew was psychopathic, a very dangerous and troubled young man, who had been sexually abused by his uncle and had been used as a punching bag for many of the adults around him when he was a kid. They had a similar pattern of violence over the years. Callum would lash out regularly and get involved in frequent fights – and Andrew, well, he had been caught torturing and killing a cat. Both were very angry, blaming everyone around them for their problems, and of course Andrew liked causing people pain anyway. Horrible, really.'

'So that's how he fits in. They must have talked during their time there, come up with a plan to get back at the world, to get revenge on Mancini for tearing Rooney's family apart.'

'Exactly. Martia said Rooney most likely changed his name due to physical or mental abuse by his father. Edmund Rooney had been reported once or twice to the police but was never charged, and Callum had never pressed charges, but evidently when Mancini effectively ruined Rooney senior's life, Callum had suffered the brunt of his father's anger and decided to make Mancini pay for it.'

'Thanks, Amelia. Good job.'

'No problem. Really happy you're okay, Graves. Speak to you tomorrow?'

'Sure.' When he ended the call he registered his other notifications.

'Shit,' he mumbled. Seven messages, three missed calls and a voicemail. They were all from Rachel, who was still at his house.

A paramedic came running up to them, immediately heading for Kelly and leading her to the closest ambulance.

'Such a relief she's okay. I'm even more glad this is over,' Charlie said as he watched Kelly climb up into the ambulance, the pain on her face evident. 'You going to get your hand seen to?' he asked, looking at the raw, burnt skin on the back of Daniel's fingers.

'Sure, in a minute. I just need to make a call,' Daniel answered absently. He had barely registered what Charlie had said. He tapped his screen to call Rachel and ducked back into the old building, away from the chaos outside. Inside was busy too, with teams of crime scene investigators, officers and medics buzzing about, but at least it was quieter. Free-standing spotlights lit up the rickety old place, making it feel safer, though no less dilapidated, but Daniel paid no attention as he waited for the call to connect.

'Thank God,' Rachel said, her voice full of relief.

'Sorry, been wrapped up in the case, are you okay? What's going on?' Daniel asked.

'The case – is it over? Did you catch them?'

'I'll fill you in later. Why so many calls and messages? What's happened?'

'It's Amanda...' Rachel started. Daniel's stomach lurched. What was Rachel about to tell him? Worry, anger and resentment flooded through him. That was all he needed after the night he'd had – his sister ready to stir up more headaches.

'Oh God, what has she done?' He sagged against the nearest door frame. It creaked from his weight, though Daniel could have believed it was actually his own bones sighing from all his recent exertion.

'Well, she's here. At your flat. I think you need to get back here. She... has some pretty important stuff you need to know.' Rachel's voice sounded tight. Daniel knew instantly that she wasn't exaggerating, that it was important. Amanda turning up out of the blue was unusual enough, but Daniel had heard that tone in Rachel's voice before. Whatever Amanda had told Rachel was not just the same old.

'Okay, I can be home in maybe an hour.' He hung up, dropped the phone back into his pocket. 'Fuck!' he yelled, kicking the wall in frustration. Dust billowed out. A nearby forensic examiner looked up from her clipboard at him, one eyebrow raised.

'I'm fine, honestly.' He gave her a fake smile. She took the hint and without a word left through the doorway out to the foyer. Daniel stood still for a moment, composing himself, steadying his breathing. Then he headed back to the entrance to find Charlie, hoping his colleague wouldn't mind driving him home. Statements, paperwork, interviews – they all needed to be done, but Daniel decided he would wait until after he'd dealt with Amanda.

***

'Good luck,' Charlie called from the driver's window as Daniel hurried across the road and up the steps to his flat. He heard the car driving off as he went to unlock the door. The door opened, and Rachel stood in front of him. He could see Amanda behind her, a glass of what looked like whisky in her hand.

'Hey, buddy,' Rachel said, stepping back to let him in. She gave him an apologetic smile, which Daniel did not return.

'Hi, Amanda. Fancy seeing you here,' he said, taking off his jacket, moving into the open-plan living space.

'Hi,' she responded, her voice timid, as though she was expecting to be yelled at. Daniel could already feel anger stoking up inside him, but he would wait to see why she was here.

Amanda offered him the bottle of Jack Daniels. He grabbed a glass from a cupboard and poured himself two fingers. He took a breath, then a sip, more of a gulp, avoiding his sister's eye. Why was she here? What had happened?

His throat burning, Daniel leant back against the kitchen counter and looked directly at his sister. 'Okay, let's cut to the chase because I'm exhausted. Why are you here? It has to be important for you to drive down here and be waiting for me.'

'It is,' Amanda answered, her face pained.

'Okay, let's hear it.'

'Okay. Remember on the phone the other day, I asked you to look into this guy, the one I'm seeing–'

'And I haven't yet. I've been busy and it's only been three days. What on earth is going on that you couldn't wait?'

'Let me explain, I'll get there,' Amanda said. 'When I didn't hear from you, I hired someone. I found him online. And the thing is... he found something.'

'What?' Daniel took another swig of whisky, tired and eager for Amanda to get to the point.

'Daniel, let her speak,' Rachel snapped. He looked at her, wide-eyed, and she frowned at him.

'Okay, sorry.'

'This guy I hired, he did some digging. He didn't find anything at first. Nothing dodgy at all. But then he found a photo and... well, you need to see it.' Amanda picked up her phone from the coffee table where she had left her handbag. Daniel waited with a mixture of anticipation and irritation as she unlocked it and searched for the picture. She passed it to him and he took it hesitantly. He glanced at her, then down at the photo.

'Is this a joke?' he stammered. He put the whisky down. 'Can you explain this to me? Why do you have a picture of Jenny Cartwright in your phone?'

As he waited for an answer, images of Jenny shot through his mind: her smile, her energy, her heart in a box. He swallowed Jack Daniels-flavoured bile.

'I thought I recognised her from the news – you know, when she... after your other case. So I double-checked on Facebook, found her memorial page. She... she's... that's him on the right. He knew her – I don't know how...' Amanda trailed off.

'It gets worse, Dan,' Rachel said, looking uneasy. 'Tell him, Amanda.'

'The man I hired, the investigator, I got him to follow Greg – that's his name. And he found that he's been coming to London. He's been staying in a cheap bed and breakfast four roads from here. Regularly. I think... Dan, I think he might be after you.'

Amanda's words lingered in the air.

'I'm scared, Daniel. I haven't confronted him, haven't told him what I found out. I didn't know what else to do apart from come here. I think he must have known I was your sister.'

'He's trying to get close to you. It's a clever move,' Rachel said.

'If you're right, he's already started to carry out his plan. If it was him who broke into my flat, who ran me off the road...'

'I'm so sorry, Dan!' Amanda bawled, her face wrinkling into a mess of tears. He looked at her for a second, seeing her in a new light all of a sudden: as someone who needed him, needed love and protection. Her fledging trust in men had been shattered completely with the information she had discovered about Greg. She needed her big brother more than ever. And for the first time in a long time, he knew he needed her too. He crossed the kitchen and pulled Amanda into a hug. As she sobbed against his shoulder, he felt a tear rolling down his own cheek, and a worm of terror writhing in his gut.

Daniel let Callum Rooney talk. Rooney was all too happy to. It was a common trait shared by sociopaths. They loved to hear the sound of their own voice, and clearly wanted others to hear it too.

'They were all culpable,' Callum said, trying to gesture but failing, due to the cuffs and chain attaching him to the metal table he and Daniel sat at. 'Sure, none of them killed those people on the site and none of them made my dad a fucking nutjob, but they all knew, I guarantee it. They knew what a fucking slimy, underhand piece of shit Carlos Mancini was, but all they cared about was lining their pockets. Jesus, I mean, did you see the size of that fucking house that woman bought?'

Daniel glanced over Callum's shoulder at the one-way glass, knowing that Charlie was on the other side, probably frowning at Rooney's complete lack of empathy or guilt for his victims.

'Do you think that justifies your actions? And those of your partner, Andrew Hogan?'

'Hey, Andy was a fucking whacko, let's get that clear right now. What he did to some of those bodies made my stomach turn. But yeah, as far as I'm concerned, Mancini destroyed my family. If it wasn't for him, my dad's business wouldn't have gone under and he wouldn't have spent his life beating the living shit out of whoever he could find.'

'Your dad had a history of anger issues and various

accusations of domestic abuse against him over the years. None of that is on Carlos Mancini,' Daniel said.

Callum slammed his hands down on the table. Daniel hid a flinch at the sudden motion. Callum's face had changed in an instant. He had been fairly calm, but now his rage was clear again.

'That man killed people and blamed it on my dad. He ruined him! Ruined me! Even my mum... she wouldn't have had to put up with that shit if it wasn't for Mancini. But he got away with everything, didn't he? Just kept getting richer while my life spiralled down the fucking drain! No way was I letting him get away with it. But you can't just waltz up to the mega-rich and powerful and get an apology and be done. How does that help anyone?'

Daniel knew Callum wasn't looking for an answer. He shrugged to signal for Callum to continue.

'He needed to pay – properly pay. I wanted him to know what it's like to have someone strip your life away from underneath you, to see people around you get hurt. It was the only way. It actually wasn't hard kidnapping him, you know? He pulled into the underground garage at his swanky pad and we grabbed him, stuck him in the back of Andy's van before the gate even fully opened. I parked his car in the closest spot and ran back out, hopped in the van and we were gone. Wasn't a fucking camera anywhere. Guess money can't always buy you sense, eh?'

'So that's how you took him.'

'Piece of piss, honestly. But even tied up and smacked around, the bastard wouldn't confess, can you believe that? Wouldn't even give me a tiny fucking apology. That's when I realised I could make him pay – by taking down his business. Destroying his reputation. And I wanted to show him that all those people that me and Andy had to kill – their blood was on his hands.'

'And the body parts... whose idea was that? What did you do with them?'

Callum laughed, a deep belly laugh that came from nowhere. The sound chilled Daniel. He had, of course, known there was something very wrong with Callum Rooney, but that laugh was edged with evil. His eyes glinted with it too. He felt no guilt, no remorse, no anxiety. Just unbridled glee at the mention of cutting out organs from his victims.

'Oh man, you'll love this. We fucking fed them to Mancini!' Callum bellowed again, kicking his legs under the table. He went to wipe a tear of laughter from his eye, forgetting he was restrained, and instead tilted his head to wipe his cheek on his shoulder. It took him almost a minute to recover. Daniel waited but, in truth, he was done. Callum had confessed to everything. He would receive multiple life sentences, and that would be the end of him. Daniel was about to stand when Callum spoke again.

'Shame about Andy killing Mancini, isn't it? That's right, isn't it? I heard an officer mention it. I really wanted to do him myself. I wanted to take his face by the chin, look deep into his eyes, see him realise that he was responsible for all of this. God, that would have made me happy. And then I would have ripped his throat out with my bare hands and let his blood wash over my skin. It would have felt so bloody good.' Callum's eyes widened at the accidental pun and he burst out laughing again.

Daniel was done. He stood, left the room, and instructed the two officers outside to take Callum Rooney back to his cell. The trial was being fast-tracked; Callum would be serving life in maximum security within days. Daniel would have to supply evidence, testify, that sort of thing, but it was over. As Rooney disappeared around the corner at the end of the corridor, Daniel felt a weight lift off his shoulders.

'I don't have the words,' Charlie said, suddenly next to Daniel, having left the viewing room.

'Me either. I've never met anyone quite like that. I can't help wondering how many others like him are wandering around the country, ready to strike.'

Charlie patted Daniel on the shoulder. 'One less, thanks to us. Two less, in fact! Double the celebration!'

Daniel smiled. It was true. Another monumental case was under his belt, and it felt good. In fact, it felt incredible. They had found and stopped the killers, and knew that they had saved one life, maybe two. Clara Michaut, Carlos Mancini's long-time business partner and the next name on the hit list, was safe and sound, as was her wife. Daniel knew, if it hadn't been for their hard work, that the Michauts could have been found dead any day. He felt proud. Michaut was coming in for an interview the next day, as a formality more than anything else. Daniel didn't think she'd be able to tell them anything they didn't already know, but the fact that she was still alive and could talk to them, thanks to him and Charlie, was quite something.

'So, drinks after work? What do you say?' Charlie said, clicking his fingers at Daniel. 'Wow, you spaced out there for a second, huh?'

'Shit, sorry. Yes to drinks. Drinks are needed!'

'Oh, and don't worry. Kelly won't be joining us. She's at home, licking her wounds.' Charlie pulled a face.

'She get fired?'

'Suspended by the paper, pending an investigation. Also, she'll likely be fined, maybe charged, even. She broke a few laws, after all. Mainly, though, she's pissed off because she's lost access to all press conferences here. Zero access. Hobbs was pretty insistent about that. She's allowed to write one last piece on the case for her boss – an eye-witness account, kind of thing, cos clearly he's as desperate for headlines as she is, but after that... I dunno.'

Daniel wanted to say that she deserved every shitty thing she got, but he bit his tongue. Instead he asked another question, one that had been on his mind since the previous night.

'So... are you two... getting back together?'

Charlie looked away.

'Shit, you are, aren't you? Dammit, Charlie, are you a glutton for punishment?'

Charlie raised his hands at Daniel. 'Look, I don't know. Honest answer. We're not back together, but... who knows? We have some stuff to chat through, unpack.'

Daniel frowned. 'Hmm, not gonna lie, I don't like it, but keep me updated. And you know I'm here for you if you need me. Anyway, now that Rooney's out of the way. I have other fish to fry.'

'Oh shit, yes. Amanda. That guy who knew Jenny.'

Daniel looked both ways down the corridor, glad they were alone. 'Yeah. Honestly, I'm pretty freaked out. Who is this guy? Like, did he seriously start dating my sister just to get to me? And if he did, was it him who broke into my house? Tried to run me off the road? And...' He found he couldn't say it, and he shivered when Charlie finished the thought for him.

'And maybe killed Jenny, left that box...'

'Yeah.' Daniel sighed.

Charlie's phone buzzed and he quickly checked the message. 'Shit, Dan – sorry, I have to run. But let's chat this evening. Figure it out over a few pints. Text Rachel as well, and Amanda if she's still in town. We'll crack it, Danny, we will. Look at us – we just brought down two serial killers!' Charlie gave an encouraging grin, then spun around and headed off down the corridor, leaving Daniel alone.

The station felt weirdly silent, deserted. Somehow it was fitting, though: no matter how many people were around, trying to help him find this guy, whoever he was, Daniel was the target. What had started months ago was not over – and it was all going to come back to Daniel, one way or another.

THE END

A NOTE FROM THE PUBLISHER

Thank you for reading this book. If you enjoyed it please do consider leaving a review on Amazon to help others find it too.

We hate typos. All of our books have been rigorously edited and proofread, but sometimes mistakes do slip through. If you have spotted a typo, please do let us know and we can get it amended within hours.

info@bloodhoundbooks.com

Printed in Great Britain
by Amazon